WE'RE FOR SMOKE

WE'RE FOR SMOKE

OUTLAWS AND OUTLIERS OF PANTHER CITY

A NOVEL

Mark A. Nobles

TCU Press

FORT WORTH, TEXAS

Library of Congress Cataloging-in-Publication Data

Names: Nobles, Mark A., 1960- author.
Title: We're for smoke : outlaws and outliers of Panther City / Mark A. Nobles.
Description: Fort Worth, Texas : TCU Press, [2021] | Summary: "From Hell's Half Acre to
    Quality Grove, We're for Smoke tells the wild and woolly story of turn-of-the-century Fort
    Worth, a cow town on the cusp of becoming a modern industrial city. Told through a series
    of fictionalized characters drawn from actual newspaper accounts detailing their tangles with
    the law, ranging from high and low society, black and white, male and female, perpetrator and
    victim, We're for Smoke reveals a society scrabbling to emerge from the chaotic growing pains
    of the frontier West. The book reproduces actual turn-of-the-century newspaper accounts of
    gunfights, jailbreaks, attempted lynchings, and riots. Readers and fans of The Son by Philipp
    Meyer, Boardwalk Empire by Nelson Johnson, and Larry McMurtry's Horseman Pass By would
    enjoy We're for Smoke"— Provided by publisher.
Identifiers: LCCN 2021021356 | ISBN 9780875657868 (paperback) | ISBN 9780875657981
    (ebook)
Subjects: LCSH: Frontier and pioneer life—Texas—Fort Worth. | Outlaws—Texas—Fort Worth—
    Biography. | Women outlaws—Texas—Fort Worth—Biography. | Fort Worth (Tex.)—Social
    conditions—20th century. | LCGFT: Biographies.
Classification: LCC F394.F7 N63 2021 | DDC 976.4/5315063—dc23
LC record available at https://lccn.loc.gov/2021021356

TCU Box 298300
Fort Worth, Texas 76129
To order books: 1.800.826.8911

Design by Preston Thomas

DEDICATION

This book is dedicated to the historians and archivists who did the painstaking research and collected, protected, and catalogued the material used to write this book. Without their prior work and love of local history, my work as a fiction writer would not be possible.

EDITOR'S NOTE: The actual newspaper accounts in this book were reprinted verbatim, without any editorial corrections of spelling, grammar, or punctuation. As a result, spelling of some names in the text will vary from spellings employed by the early twentieth-century journalists who reported on these events.

CONTENTS

ACKNOWLEDGMENTS

Not to beat a dead horse, but this book simply would not be possible without the decades of work done prior by the many historians whose books I own and treasure. Being petrified to leave anyone out, I will refrain from naming names. It is safe to say if you have written a nonfiction book about Fort Worth or somehow mentioned Fort Worth, I have read it and acknowledge your influence. Fort Worth and Tarrant County are also blessed with many wonderful archives including but not limited to the Fort Worth Public Library; Tarrant County College Archive; a branch of the National Archives; the Tarrant County Archives; the Tarrant County Black Historical and Genealogical Society; and others I'm sure I am forgetting.

Of course I also wish to acknowledge my family and friends for their encouragement and support. It isn't easy putting up with someone who is liable to shout out some random piece of information about the history of a used car lot on Jacksboro Highway or a vacant lot on Lancaster. If you are in the car with me and we drive past the Water Gardens you are likely to get bored out of your mind for twenty minutes with random tidbits about Hell's Half Acre. Extra acknowledgment to my two daughters Elliott and Eleanor Nobles who have been subjected to this madness since infancy.

1904-1913

THE WOMAN OF NO MAN'S LAND

1904
Hell's Half Acre

Thin, worn out, and withered, Jed slouched along the gulley. His weary footsteps lit by a yellow moon, three days past full and just risen above the tree line. Jed was a beaten man of twenty-nine years. His shoes tattered and soleless, his clothes more patch than whole cloth.

One hundred yards past a slow bend in the gully Jed met his wife, Anne, sitting in the dirt and rocks. She looked at him with her hollow eyes and knew the girl was gone.

Without prospects, itinerant, and slowly starving, the small family of three had come to Fort Worth looking for work and shelter. After three days wandering the streets, alleys, and slums of the bustling town on the Trinity and being turned away at every saloon, livery, slaughterhouse, and mercantile, Jed had decided they could no longer keep the girl in tow.

Anne slipped away and headed towards the rail yard, and Jed took the girl into the busiest and roughest part of town, a few square blocks on the south side known locally as Hell's Half Acre, and abandoned her. He simply told her to wait in an alley and walked away. His mind screamed with guilt but was easily shouted down by the gnawing hunger in his belly.

Anne rose from the rocks in the gully and accepted the loss without grief. Grief required energy, and she needed what little she could muster for the journey down to Waco.

The two thin shadows of Jed and Anne climbed the gully and crossed the barren field towards the Lancaster rail yard.

Anne knew that if work were not found in Waco, Jed would catch the next train alone.

✳ ✳ ✳

Bessie was not her given name. Her given name was soon forgotten on the dusty back streets of Fort Worth. Young about-to-be-Bessie did not fall into prostitution so much as reality in the Acre kicked her into it as a sole means of survival.

Bewildered and alone, the young girl was shortly set upon by the denizens of the flop and whore houses of the Acre. Resources were scarce, food was scant, and life was cheap in the Acre, and another mouth was seen by most as unwanted competition.

She was saved from a back-alley rape and knifing by an enterprising bawd named Effie, who saw the foundling as an easy, steady source of income. At twenty-six Effie was an over-the-hill prostitute scraping together pennies and table scraps from cowboys and day laborers too broke to afford younger whores with less wear. For fourteen months Effie rented Bessie to any man with money, drugs, or alcohol.

Confinement or restraint was unnecessary. Bessie did not run, partly because she was too weak and abused to gather the energy but mainly because Effie's hell was better than the certain death she would meet alone on the streets, and she knew it.

One morning Bessie found Effie cold, clammy, blue-tinged, and already in rigor mortis from a morphine overdose. Bessie herself became rigid with confusion and fear. When the man came to collect the rent from Effie, he found Bessie standing silent, slowly rending her clothes and methodically eating the shreds. The landlord was afflicted with Jake leg from drinking too much Jamaican Ginger, a cheap snake oil "medicine" that was cheaper than the worst rotgut whiskey doled out in the Acre. Jake, as it was called, would get you high as hell, but imbibing too much would permanently paralyze your legs and hands. The man clumsily but roughly pushed Bessie out of the shack and into the alley.

After rifling through the one-room shack, pocketing a few pennies and Effie's remaining morphine, the man lurched out of the room to fetch the police.

A new whore from Amarillo, only one day in town, had moved in before Effie went feet first out the door. No one noticed Bessie during the brief bustle as Effie was removed.

She was still standing in the dank alley when a Jake fiend stumbled upon her and clumsily attempted to raise her skirt. Life slipped back into Bessie's eyes, and she deftly cold cocked the man and drifted out of the alley.

An odd, slowly smoldering ember burned in Bessie's eyes. She would never again be sold or pushed around by others.

1912
Battercake Flats

Bessie had fled the Acre for Battercake Flats and had been on her own since the day Effie died.

"Bessie Williams" first came into the public record in 1905 when the young girl was arrested for theft of person and required to identify herself in court. Bessie and Williams were simply the first two names that came to mind to the frightened twelve-year-old girl. No name or age verification was asked for or given. No one asked after Bessie's parents. She was given no representation. She was merely booked, charged, fined, and unable to pay the fine, Bessie was jailed. The twelve-year-old sat in the Women's Ward of the Fort Worth jail and fumed and fidgeted. It was the first and almost the last time Bessie sat near motionless in jail.

Bessie Williams was about to become famous as the most prolific woman jail breaker in Texas, maybe even the entire country.

Now nineteen, as best anyone knew, Bessie was a veteran of the streets and an expert pickpocket, hustler, and prostitute when marks were scarce.

✳ ✳ ✳

Annie Morris stood at the bars to the cell staring at the thick metal door at the end of the hall. She absentmindedly tapped her foot in rhythm with the thud and scrape of metal on brick coming from behind her. At eighteen years Annie was tall and bigger and as muscled as most men. Her rust-colored, short-cropped hair hung on her head as loose as sewing thread. Determined not to live the life society planned for her, Annie turned her back on marriage or domestic servitude and turned her life to thievery and larceny. Annie was jailed for highway robbery. While attempting to rob a man outside a bar on Throckmorton, she beat and blackened the man's eye. The friends of the man thought it funny a woman had bested him in a fistfight and had called the police. The police were little amused to be called out for a trifling bar fight and had insisted on booking Annie and taking everyone's statement. Every minute or so Annie would swivel her head around to look at the small woman behind her, then turn back to watch the door and listen for the clattering of the turnkey on the other side.

Bessie was hunched over by the exterior wall, methodically swinging a small hunk of metal repeatedly and rhythmically into the solid brick wall, persistently knocking chunks of brick and mortar to the floor. Every fiber of her soul intent on her task, Bessie swung and dug, swung and dug, blow after unceasing blow. The work was monotonous and slow but not as hard as it could have been. While the wall was solid brick and mortar, the brick was brittle and the mortar more chalk than solid. Several years ago the good citizens of Fort Worth had desperately wanted a new, stout jail but were unwilling to pay top dollar for top materials, so the bricks were cheap and the mortar watered down.

After one last swing the shards of brick did not fly back into Bessie's eyes but out into the darkness. A cool fall breeze blew in over Bessie's hand and onto her face. After a solid hour of attacking the wall, she had broken through to freedom. She bent down further to peek through. Her lips pursed tightly together. It wouldn't be too long before the hole would be wide enough for her to slip through.

In the cell directly across from Annie and Bessie sat Granny Mullins, clutching the moth-chewed, lice-filled blanket placed on each bed in the jail. Granny rocked back and forth and sang a gentle lullaby to Annie.

I left my darling lying here,
a lying here, a lying here,
I left my darling lying here,
To go and gather blackberries.

I've found the wee brown otter's track,
the otter's track, the otter's track
I've found the wee brown otter's track
But ne'er a trace o' my baby, O!

I found the track of the swan on the lake
the swan on the lack, the swan on the lack
I found the track of the swan on the lake,
But not the track of baby, O!

I found the track of the yellow fawn, the yellow fawn
I found the track of the yellow fawn,
But could not trace my baby, O!

I found the trail of the mountain mist,
the mountain mist, the mountain mist
I found the trail of the mountain mist,
But ne'er a trace of baby, O!

After sweeping the brick dust and chunks with her hands into a pile under Annie's bunk and replacing the broken metal drain cover she had used as her digging tool in the floor, Bessie and Annie laid down silently in their beds. It was quarter to midnight, and the women waited for Deputy Sheriff McCain to make his hourly rounds. Bessie and her bunk hid the hole.

Granny Mullins sat in her cell directly across from Bessie and Annie, her eyes darting from the thick metal door to Annie lying on her bunk. Annie, her eyes locked with Granny Mullins, silently smiled. Fear crossed Granny's eyes. She darted one last furtive look at the jailhouse door, then looked back to Annie. Fearful of further punishment from the sheriff if she did not report the escape attempt, Granny quickly calculated that Annie could mete out much greater punishment for giving it away. Annie stared cold and pitiless. Granny Mullins slowly closed her eyes and feigned sleep, humming a Baptist hymn for comfort.

Ten minutes later Deputy Sheriff McCain walked through the creaking metal door and performed his headcount. Eighteen minutes later Annie and Bessie had tied their bed linens together, crawled through the aperture, and slithered down their makeshift rope to freedom. Safely on the ground the women quickly picked up the largest of the few pieces of brick scattered on the jailhouse lawn and ran northwest, away from the jailhouse into the darkness, ditching the brick shards halfway down the alley.

Sticking to the shadows, the pair made their way down Franklin Street toward the home, generously described, of Mamie Joyce. When the ramshackle house came into sight Annie broke into a fast trot, Bessie close behind, her eyes darting side to side. Annie led them around the side and burst through the back door.

Mamie bolted straight in her cot, fully dressed and exclaimed, "Mercy, please!"

Annie retorted, "It is me, Mamie."

Mamie leaped from bed and the two women embraced and kissed.

"You were not to be let out for two more days but Lordy be, you are here."

"In the flesh," said Annie. The two shook each other, then Mamie turned to gaze at Bessie, standing almost invisible in the corner, but close to the dying stove.

"Who is your new companion?" asked Mamie.

"This is Bessie. She is the one what dug us out of the calaboose."

Mamie released Annie from her embrace and eyed Bessie. "Pleased to meet you, I'm sure." Mamie looked Bessie up and down. "You must be a might more powerful than you look to dig through a rock wall."

"It is brick and not strong brick at all. I've busted out of the calaboose a few times. It is not as hard as it would seem . . . I do not like it there." A fair amount of the wildness had left Bessie's eyes, but she was clearly not comfortable being only a few blocks away from the jailhouse.

Mamie eyed Bessie. Mamie was a middle-aged bawd who ran prostitutes and pickpockets in the Acre. She was always on the lookout for new talent to siphon off the spoils of their labor. "Your clothes are where you left them." She pointed to a bureau against the far wall. Annie immediately began to strip her jailhouse dress and walked toward the bureau.

"Thank you, Jesus," shouted Annie. By the time she reached the bureau Annie was naked as a jaybird. She opened the top drawer and rifled through, pulling out and putting on a ragged calico shirt, well-worn and patched overalls, and a too-short tie. Lastly, she donned a beat-up, sweat-stained hat and turned to face Bessie and Mamie.

Face tilted towards the floor and fidgeting with her dress, Bessie said, "We should leave. The coppers will be all over us in no time."

"Bessie is right. We need to put more distance between us and the law," said Annie.

"I know a place. On White Settlement. You can get money and food," said Mamie. "My son, Homer, hangs out there often."

"What do you say, Bessie? Easy marks and scratch. Sounds like the place."

"I know of that place," said Bessie.

Mamie turned to Annie, grabbed, hugged, and kissed her one more time. "I'll send word when things have cooled down. You know where to go. Hang tight there until then."

Annie nodded and with that, the two fugitives slipped out the back door as quickly as they entered. Mamie followed them out and immediately returned with an armload of kindling to throw into the small stove.

* * *

The flophouse on White Settlement was a well-known location for vagrants, low-level sporting men, and addicts to find a game of dice or to get high and pass out and perhaps not wake up dead. Robert Vann, Charlie McDaniels, and Homer Joyce knelt close to the stove throwing dice against the wall. Vann was on a winning streak and one more winning toss away from being accused of cheating and beaten to an unrecognizable pulp by the other two men. Virgil Miner sat quietly rocking in the corner, burned out of his mind on cocaine. Bessie walked in the front door without knocking. Suddenly, she was a different person, talkative and outgoing.

"Hello gents, Bessie is back."

"Hello, Bessie," said Vann, looking up from the dice game. "I thought you were in the slammer."

"Ain't no man or cracker box can keep me unless I want to be kept, sugar. You know that."

"That I do, Bessie. That I do." Vann then turned his attention back to the game. McDaniels and Joyce eyed Annie suspiciously. The two men did not know what to make of her.

Bessie and Annie walked to the middle of the room with Annie quietly surveying the surroundings and sizing up the men. Homer did not recognize her as one of Mamie's girls. He did not recognize her as a girl at all.

Vann tossed the dice off the floor and wall and again, miraculously made his number. McDaniels and Joyce cursed as Vann laughed and picked the few coins off the floor.

"Those dice are weighted," screamed Joyce.

"Aye!" concurred Vann.

"Wait a minute, boys," objected Vann. The other two gamblers rose from their knees and eyed Vann, who nervously and quickly pocketed the dice.

Bessie stepped between the three men. "Wait a minute, boys. Simmer down. I think all four of us can get along just fine." Bessie turned to McDaniels and placed her hand on his chest.

"I done lost my wages, Bessie. You are scratching the wrong post," said McDaniels, never changing or taking his glare from Vann.

Bessie turned her attention to Vann. "Come on Bobby. Pay for all three of ya. Show there ain't no hard feelings."

Vann looked from Bessie to McDaniels and Joyce, weighing his options and odds of a beating. The dice were crooked, and Bessie seemed to be the out he needed. There was, however, the matter of the stranger in the room.

"Who is your friend, Bessie? I never laid eyes on him before."

"Pay no never mind." The three men eyed Annie and did not seem willing to ignore her presence. Annie shifted uneasily from one foot to the other, well aware of her fate if discovered to be a woman. Her eyes pleaded with Bessie to leave.

"Join in or git gone," Bessie ordered.

Annie replied, "They will come lookin' soon. You should not stay long or you will be back from where you just came, Bessie."

Turning her attention back to Vann, Bessie rejoined, "No bother. I leave there when it pleases me."

Without a further word Annie slipped out the way she slipped in. The three men laughed and surrounded Bessie.

Virgil Miner, now passed out on the floor, was breathing, slow and labored.

❋ ❋ ❋

November 11-1912
Fort Worth Star-Telegram

2 Girls Tunnel Through County Jail Wall and Effect Escape
Annie Morris and Bessie Williams Effect Second Jail
Delivery in Two Days.

Annie Morris and Bessie Williams, white girls, tunneled out of
the county jail Sunday night. They make three prisoners to escape
within thirty hours. Tom Tate was the other.

The two dug their way through the west wall near the front
of the building. All tools were carried away or concealed. One
woman was recaptured at noon.

Their absence was reported to the jailers at 1:15 a.m. by Mrs.
T.J. Mullins, known as granny an aged woman held on an insanity
charge.

Investigation disclosed an aperture nearly two feet square just
under a window. An improvised rope of blankets tied to the foot
of an iron bedstead enabled the women to reach the ground fifteen
feet below without difficulty.

Bessie Williams was captured by Deputy Sheriffs Alderman,
Musick and Fitch and Deputy Constable Turner about 10 o'clock
Monday in a house at White Settlement. Five men found at the
house were arrested for vagrancy.

Annie Morris accompanied the Williams woman to the house
at White Settlement, but left, and the officers were hot on her
track at noon. She with the Williams woman went, after escaping,
to the house of Mamie Joyce on Franklin street, and there she put
on male attire, as follows: A pair of old blue overalls, a work shirt,
a tie and slouch hat. She is an exceedingly large woman and the
men arrested said that she looked much like a man.

It is believed the girls began their attempts to escape Sunday
morning and after discovering that they would have little difficulty
in working their way through the soft brick, postponed further
work until after dark Sunday night. Their only tool, as far as jail
attaches could discover was the circular iron covering to a drain in
the floor of the women's ward. A fragment of this had been broken
off, forming a sharp edge that proved effective.

Crack Helps Workers.

Just at the point where the hole was made a narrow crack on the outside of the building extends downward for several feet. This crack and the soft condition of the plaster between the bricks rendered the prisoners' task comparatively easy. The wall is approximately two feet thick and is covered on the inside by a thin coating of plaster.

So quietly did they work that Mrs. Mullins, according to her statement to the jailers, knew nothing of their plans until she awoke at 1 a.m. and found them missing. Deputy Sheriff Fitch, who had just returned from an all day hunt for Tom Tate, the Smith county murderer, who escaped Saturday night from the condemned cell, entered a room adjoining the women's ward to retire. Hearing his voice, Mrs. Mullins shouted information of the escape.

Fitch notified Night Guard Day and Deputy Sheriff McCain and hurried into the ward. A pile of brick and plaster was found by the hole partially concealed by a bed. The prisoners, fearing to attract attention, had refrained carefully from dropping any portion of the debris outside of the building.

An alarm was sent at once to the police station and officers throughout the city by means of the new Gamewell fire and police alarm.

The girls, though they had but a slight handicap in point of time over the posse of deputy sheriffs who set out after them, made good use of their opportunity.

In Jail at Midnight.

According to Deputy Sheriff McCain, the women were in their ward when he made his rounds at 12 o'clock, it is believed that they had already completed the aperture at the time and made their way to liberty a few minutes later. Jailer John Moore was not present to direct the search for them. He left the city early Sunday evening for Austin.

Annie Moore was held on a charge of highway robbery. The charge against Bessie Williams is theft from person. Both are under 20 years of age.

The clock on the wall read a few minutes past midnight when Deputy Sheriff Fitch walked into the office. He was tired and dusty from a six-hour search for an escaped prisoner. Sheriff Rea and Police Chief Montgomery were madder than wet hornets that Tom Tate had seemingly strolled out of jail and vanished the day before. Tate had recently been convicted of murder in Tyler and had been sent to Fort Worth because a sizable mob had formed outside the Smith County jail hell bent on lynching the rogue. It was not a clean mark for Panther City's finest that the man half of East Texas wanted swinging from a tree had apparently sawed his way through the jailhouse bars as if they were soft putty, slid down sixty feet of fire hose, and made his way to freedom while his jailers were watching a passing parade.

Shortly after the alarm was sounded the entire force and a sizable, newly deputized, civilian posse had been quickly mustered and was scouring the river bottoms and shanties without rest or relief.

Fitch had become a Deputy Sheriff a scant fifteen months before and had worked his way into the relatively safe and easy position of assistant jailer through a friend-of-a-friend connection with jailer John Moore. Rancor was high in Tyler over the episode, and Judge Simpson, fearing a lynch mob might beat the state to its punishment, ordered Tate removed to Fort Worth.

Sheriff Rea did not like inefficiency in his police force and had been hell on wheels since receiving the news of Tate's escape. A fair portion of Rea's wrath had fallen on Fitch, but Fitch was more worried that Jailer Moore would relieve him of his duties at the jail and he would wind up walking a beat in Battercake Flats or the Acre. Two beats where a lone policeman had about the same chance of keeping the peace as a fireman had dousing a three-alarm fire with a shot glass full of gasoline.

Fitch was lost in his thoughts when wailing from the women's cell-block pricked up his ears. Granny Mullins was making a row. Fitch sighed, then rose to find the matter.

He cursed when he opened the creaking metal door to the women's cellblock. Granny Mullins was balled up on her bunk wailing away, and there was a hole in the wall of the empty cell.

Now, two more escapes, making three in less than thirty hours. Even though it wasn't Fitch's fault the jail was as solid as a sieve, someone was losing their job over this and he was the low man on the pole.

Fitch stood motionless, a solid litany of curse words running through his head. Granny Mullins continued her serenade.

Steal away, steal away, steal away to Jesus!
Steal away, steal away home,
I ain't got long to stay here.
My Lord, He calls me,
He calls me by the thunder;
The trumpet sounds within my soul,
I ain't got long to stay here.
Steal away, steal away, steal away to Jesus!
Steal away, steal away home,
Green trees are bending,
Poor sinners stand a-trembling;
The trumpet sounds within my soul,
I ain't got long to stay here.
Steal away, steal away, steal away to Jesus!
Steal away, steal away home,
My Lord, He calls me,
He calls me by the lightning;
The trumpet sounds within my soul,
I ain't got long to stay here.

Fitch had argued like hell to go back out and search for Morris and Williams. Being in charge of the jail while Moore was down in Austin, he reckoned the only way he could dodge a demotion was to be a part of the capture and hope the wrath passed him and fell on Night Guard Day or Deputy Sheriff McCain, both of whom had been at the jail while the escape was perpetrated.

Chief Huddleston pulled Deputy Sheriffs Alderman and Musick and Deputy Constable Turner away from the search for Tate and sent them out with Fitch to scour "No Man's Land" and Battercake Flats for the two women.

While the larger hunt for Tate continued to prove fruitless, the five lawmen found Bessie by midmorning. A soiled dove had tipped the men to Mamie's relationship with Annie, and when confronted and threatened with jail, Mamie had pointed them to the flophouse on White Settlement quicker than pigs after a pumpkin. McDaniels and Joyce put up a bit of a scuffle, but Bessie and Vann surrendered without protest. Poor Virgil Miner barely knew who or where he was, let alone what was happening to him.

Annie Morris remained at large. Whereabouts unknown.

11-13-1912
Fort Worth Star-Telegram

4 Men Fined $360 On Vagrancy Charge
Quartet Arrested With Escaped Woman Prisoner
Get Heavy Sentences.

The escape early Monday morning from the county jail of Bessie Williams and Annie Morris found an echo Wednesday in Justice Peden's court, when four men captured with Bessie Williams received fines aggregating $360. They were charged with vagrancy.

Robert Vann, who pleaded not guilty, was fined $200 and costs by the court, and Virgil Miner, the youngest of the quartet, $10 and costs after he had entered a plea of guilty. Charles McDaniels and Homer Joyce demanded jury trials. They were found guilty and fined $100 and costs and $50 and costs, respectively.

11-13-1912
Fort Worth Star-Telegram

Grand Jury Says New Jail Needed
Report Follows Three Sensational Escapes Within Week.
Site Change is Favored
Removal to Another Location Would Open Way to River
Bluff Improvement.

The investigation of the county jail by the grand jury of the Sixty-seventh district court, following the recent jail deliveries, resulted in a recommendation by that body to the commissioners court Wednesday for the building of a new county jail.

There has been considerable discussion for years concerning the removal of the jail and the building of a modern structure at some other location. The sensational escape of Tom Tate, the Smith County convicted murderer and of two women, Annie Morris and Bessie Williams, has accentuated the need for the new structure.

Report of Grand Jury.

The report of the Grand jury with reference to the jail follows:

"We have visited the county jail since the recent escape of several prisoners, and have made examination of same, and we all concur in a hearty recommendation to the county commissioners that immediate steps be taken for arrangements necessary for the building of a new and modern jail. We all feel that the jail in its present condition is certainly inadequate, as evidenced by the easy manner in which one of the recent escapes therefrom was made."

Talks with the county commissioners revealed the fact that they are not much in favor of the new jail. None, however, was strongly opposed to the idea. "If people want a new jail, they can have one," said one of the commissioners.

A change in location would open the way to improvement of the river bluff and approach to the new viaduct to the north side.

Bessie walked onto the colored women's ward like she owned it. In only a slightly hushed voice she declared, "I am about to git gone. Who here is with me?"

Earlier the colored women had heard Bessie was an inmate across the way. They had gotten word to her she could have all their food if Bessie would take them with her when she escaped. Growing up as she had and living the life she lived, Bessie never turned down food when offered.

Ora Ross was awake but unsure who had walked onto the ward, so had remained perfectly still in her bunk. Hearing Bessie she hit the floor.

"We's all goin', Bessie. Open on up."

Bessie walked to the cell door and stood. She held a twisted tin spoon in her left hand. "I'll open when I see it."

By now all seven Negro women had stirred from their slumber. Five were standing by Ora; a sixth was still sitting on her bunk side. "Eula, git here," Ora commanded. A small, timid woman near the back of the group came forward holding a rolled up sheet. "Thas all the hardtack we's given for the las' day 'n' half."

"No salt pork?" asked Bessie suspiciously. "I got salt pork."

"They don' give nigger women salt pork. You'in know that."

"That ain't right. Just another reason we all should take our leave."

And with that Bessie thrust the blunt end of the spoon into the lock and it clicked open in a switch. Six of the seven negro women filed passed Bessie. The seventh stayed put.

"Ora," said Bessie as she stood in the open cell looking at the women on the bunk. Ora turned and looked at the woman.

"Virgie! Come on, now," Ora half-yelled.

"I ain't. I leave here my husband gone beat me for missin' his supper last three days I be gone. I ain't goin'."

"She start screaming and we do not all get down the rope," said Bessie, never taking her eyes off Virgie.

"You ain't gone scream now, is ya Virgie?"

"No," said Virgie and with that she lay back down in her bunk and pretended to sleep.

"Fine with me," said Bessie, "because I am dropping first." She walked out of the colored women's ward grabbing her hardtack as she left.

A few moments later the tied bed linens fluttered out the second story window and one by one the seven women skittered down and disappeared into the darkness. Bessie headed west; the six other women all ran east.

— 1913 —

4-1-1913
Fort Worth Star-Telegram

Tires of Breaking out of County Jail
Bessie Williams of Spoon and Curling Iron Fame
Returns to Jail

Bessie Williams, famed as a jail breaker, who escaped from the county jail on one occasion with a spoon and on the other occasion with a curling iron, returned to jail Tuesday morning, because she failed to appear in justice court on a charge of disturbing the peace.

She promised Jailer Moore that she would be good this time and not try to break out.

"I might try some other stunt," she said, "but breaking out of jail is getting sort of tiresome. I want to do something new."

1910-1912

SOMEBODY OUT
THERE NEEDS KILLING

1910

February 10, 1901
Dallas Morning News

Shooting at Lancaster
Richard Wentworth Wounded Four Times
City Marshal Surrenders

Special to The News
Lancaster, Tex., Feb. 9

Richard Wentworth was shot four times tonight and may die, though the wounds are not necessarily fatal. One of the bullets entered his neck and another his lip and two lodged in the abdomen. The shooting occurred on the public square. City Marshal Kid Yates has surrendered to the Constable.

Lancaster, Texas

Flora Yates jumped like a broom-whipped dog when her husband, Kid Yates, unexpectedly burst through the front door of their home in midafternoon. Kid was half-drunk, exhausted from being up the best part of two days, and mad as hell.

"I cannot live in a town that has no respect for the law or honor-bound white men," he shouted.

Upon regaining her wits and balance, Flora hurried to the cupboard where Kid kept his pipe and tobacco and snatched them up. She scuttled to Kid's rocking chair by the fireplace, but he blustered by and went to the back porch where he kept his beer in the wintertime.

"That drunkard Wentworth threatened to kill me." Kid suddenly stopped and wheeled, facing Flora. "So, I ask you, woman. What is a man to do but kill him first?" Thrusting his hands out, palms up, he looked at Flora seeking confirmation.

"That's natural, Kid. He had it coming."

"Damn right, he had it coming." Forgetting the beer, Kid headed to his rocking chair. "They're gonna try and railroad me, Flora. I know it." He dropped into the chair and put a white-knuckle grip on the arm rests, his body tense and coiled. Flora stood next to Kid holding ready his pipe and tobacco. There was a knock at the door, sending Flora almost out of her skin. Kid did not seem to notice.

Flora hurriedly scuttled to the door and opened it. Lancaster's Marshal Benet stood, hat in hand, in the doorway. "How do, Mrs. Yates."

Kid rose from his rocking chair and turned to the door. "Come to fire me, Benet, or just haul me out and string me up?"

The marshal grinned and rotated the brim of his hat with his hands. "Now, Kid. You know I ain't here for neither." He turned his head to address Flora. "May I come in, ma'am?"

Flora looked to Yates; he nodded, and then she stepped aside to make way for the marshal to enter the Yates home. The marshal strode in. He was tall and slender with rough-as-hide, deeply tanned skin, even in the winter.

"I just left the mayor and council, Kid. As you might imagine they are all in a tizzy."

"Cowards and dandies every one of 'em." Kid turned and spit into the brass cuspidor by his chair. "Not enough between 'em all to make even half a real man."

"That may be true enough, Kid, but you gunned down an unarmed man in broad daylight in the middle of town." The marshal paused to let that sink in but understood that to Kid, it made not one whit. "That ain't exactly keeping the peace, which as night marshal, is what you are sworn to do." The marshal paused again. "You have to see that, Kid."

Kid strode two steps towards the marshal, his teeth clenched. "The ass threatened my life. I had a right. You, the mayor, and the goddamn council ought to be able to see that." Kid bowed up, frightening Flora even more.

The marshal paid no heed to the approaching Kid Yates. "Times and attitudes are changing, Kid. The law must change with 'em."

The two men stared at each other a brief second until it was silently decided Kid would calm down.

"Doc says it is just a matter of hours before Dick Wentworth passes. No great loss to Lancaster or anyone in it, but we can't have stories slipping over to Dallas of Lancaster lawmen killing citizens less than a hunnered paces from city hall." Marshal Benet looked Kid straight in the eyes. "The council and mayor are up in arms hollering that it just ain't good for business and growth, and business and growth pay my salary, Kid."

"I guess it don't pay mine no more, though, do it."

"No, Kid, it does not." The marshal's eyes never wavered from Kid's. "That is why I came. I will have your badge, if you please; then, in a week or so the grand jury will no bill you. Then, it would be best if you and your family move on."

Flora's heart was beating like a rabbit chased by a coyote. She stared at Kid, waiting for him to explode. She knew he would either fly into a rage at the marshal or take it out on her after he left. Neither was a preferable option in her mind.

"You are a good lawman, Kid. Truly. But, like I said, times are changing. You can't mete out justice from the end of your club or the muzzle of your barrel anymore. Wentworth was not much of a man, but it is on the backs of men like him that this town will grow and line the pockets of the mayor and council with coin. If Lancaster gets branded as a town that shoots men in the street for being drunk and stupid, well, then the drunk and stupid will flock to other towns."

Marshal Benet turned to Flora. He looked at her with a worry, knowing what Kid would likely do after he left. After a moment, he turned back to Kid.

"Why don't you come with me back to town and I will buy you a drink. It is the least I can do."

"I do not need your sympathy or drink, Marshal," Kid replied. "Thank you kindly." He added sarcastically.

"Sorry to cause a tussle, Mrs. Yates." The marshal tipped his hat. "My best to your daughters." He turned his gaze back to Kid. "The mayor wanted me to tell you to be cleared out two days after the grand jury no bills you."

The marshal turned and vacated the Yates home. Flora stood frozen to the floor. The February chill filled the house, easily beating back the warmth of the fire in the hearth.

Kid Yates went out the back door, picked up his beer, and walked alone to the nearest saloon.

Hogan's Alley, Fort Worth

Jimmy Orr sat in the saloon with his back to the door and drunkenly slurred his argument to the oil field roughneck sitting across from him. Not a particularly wise thing to do, but eighteen-year-old boys are rarely, if ever, best described as wise. Johnny's father was fairly well-to-do and well-respected, so most people referred to Jimmy as a "comely lad" and stayed away from referring to his intellect out of deference to his father.

"By God, I could do the work and do it a fine bit better than you," said Jimmy. "I'll be out in the oil fields come spring. Mark my words."

Calmly, the roughneck replied, "And you will be missing a hand or arm in sight of a week. Or worse, you'll get a real man injured because of your Tom foolishness."

As the roughneck was speaking, D. B. Ray, Jimmy's friend and neighbor, walked in the back door after a brief visitation with a soiled dove in the alley. Seeing D. B. enter gave Jimmy some confidence, and he jumped from his chair.

"I'm as tough as any man in here," exclaimed Jimmy. "You want to take it outside with me?"

The roughneck turned his eyes to the barkeep and then slowly returned his gaze to Jimmy. The barkeep, not wanting to mop up blood again tonight, ordered Jimmy to leave his establishment. Jimmy flew into a rage.

"Come on, Jimmy, we are done here, let's go home. Dawn will break early and we both have to be at work," said D. B.

D. B. bear-hugged Jimmy and back danced him out the door and into the street. Jimmy was too drunk to care who he fought. Out the door and onto the sidewalk Jimmy continued to flail blindly at D. B. A few patrons of the saloon followed the two young men out on to Main Street to watch what they hoped would turn from a scuffle into a beating.

The crowd got a lot more than they had hoped.

Kid Yates was a bad man, not to be trifled with. Spend much time at all around him and you quickly learned to choose your words carefully, for it was unclear what offhand remark would offend or set him in a rage. He was indiscriminate with his anger, and his fury was swift. Yates could do more damage with one punch than most men could do in a three-minute beating. A hulking man of over six feet, Yates had all the physical tools needed to bludgeon a man senseless with his bare hands.

James Kidwell Yates was born March 22, 1872, in White County, Tennessee. His father Sam was killed in a feud when Kid was eight, and his mother packed up him and his three brothers and hit the well-worn "Texas Trail" to avoid further family bloodshed. They ran out of supplies and gumption in Lancaster, a small town due north of Dallas. Mom put the four boys to work, and the family eked out a pitiable living.

Kid inherited his father's foul temper and habit of settling disputes with quick and often deadly violence. Reaching adulthood in Lancaster, Yates took a job as night marshal and had barely pinned on the tin when he shot and killed his first man. The man, Dick Wentworth, was a drunkard and had publicly threatened Yates, known by all in the small burg as an unwise thing to do. After killing the unarmed Wentworth, Yates calmly walked to the police station and turned himself in. In Texas and throughout the South, publicly threatening to kill a man was an unwise and dangerous thing to do unless you actually meant to carry it through. While technically still murder, killing a man who had threatened you was adequate defense, even if he was unarmed and unwarned, and so Yates was no billed.

Yates met and married Flora Brogdon in Lancaster, and two daughters were born in short order. His temperament and reputation were well worn in Lancaster, so Yates moved his small family to Fort Worth in 1903. His reputation as a nasty man with a bad attitude followed.

Yates kicked around Fort Worth for a few years working as a day laborer, mill worker, and meat packer before returning to police work of a sort as a special officer with the Pullman Company. He was indicted for murder once again after he point blank shot a black porter three times in the chest. Yates was found innocent at trial even though two officers testified against him. There were, however, no eyewitnesses to the crime, and the porter was black. An all-white male jury really did not see much of a crime in killing a back-talking black man. Yates was summarily let go by the Pullman Company but quickly caught on with the Fort Worth Police Department.

Tragedy of a different sort struck Yates in the fall of 1908 when his wife, Flora, succumbed to consumption and passed at only thirty years of age. Yates had never been a kind or caring man, but Flora had somewhat of a calming influence on him, and he had patience and love for his daughters. However, the pressures of being a single parent took their toll, and Yates knew only one way to blow off steam.

Twelve-year-old Bessie Yates held the deathbed vigil for her mother as she slowly let go her life. Death by consumption is slow, messy, and interspersed with violent coughing fits. Covered in sputum and speckled with blood, Flora Yates passed as the sun rose one Tuesday morning. Bessie's first feeling as her mother turned blue and cold was of fear and depression, as she was now alone in raising herself and younger sister Selma.

Shortly before joining the Fort Worth Police Department Kid Yates killed yet another man, brutally splitting his head open with an iron pipe. Again, however, he walked away a free man. With no eyewitnesses a jury could not convict.

Yates did not walk his beat in the Acre so much as prowl it. His intent was not to keep the peace or make friends and alliances in the neighborhood but more to stamp out trouble quickly and harshly. Doors closed, windows were shuttered, and sidewalks emptied when he walked the streets and alleys at night.

As he walked up Main Street and saw the crowd gathered to watch Orr and D. B. scuffling in the street, his eyes widened. He broke into a slow trot and began to shout for the crowd to part. When the bystanders saw it was Yates bellowing they dispersed quickly.

"Break it up you bastards!" Yates yelled.

"It is over, Jimmy!" squeaked D. B.

Jimmy looked at Yates slowly rumbling up the hill and quickly calculated he could easily outrun the copper. Yates was carrying his club in his right hand.

It never occurred to Jimmy the policeman might pull his revolver and shoot.

If Jimmy had been from the Acre, he would have known that Yates was coiled violence waiting to be sprung, but Jimmy had grown up in the better, north side neighborhoods, where this would have been a non-event. But not in the Acre and not with Kid Yates handling the situation.

Jimmy lit out. As he ran Yates moved his club to his left hand, pulled his revolver with his right, took aim, and fired. Jimmy dropped like a sack of turnips. Shot in the back. The bullet pierced his left lung.

"What the holy hell," said a wide-eyed D. B.

By now Yates pulled even with D. B. on his way to check Jimmy, and as he passed Yates clocked him in the temple with his club, barely looking at the boy. D. B. was out before his head hit the dirt.

Jimmy lay facedown on Main Street, his body convulsing in an attempt to draw enough breath to keep him alive with only one lung. Blood gurgled in his throat with each labored exhale. Yates turned from Jimmy back to D. B. Then looked around for someone to help with the two disabled boys.

The street was deserted.

"Well, shit," Yates muttered. He holstered his pistol, drew his whistle from the breast pocket of his coat, and heartily blew three short bursts. Any officer within hearing distance would recognize this as a policeman's call for assistance.

September 4, 1910
Fort Worth Star-Telegram

Orr, Running, Is Shot By Policeman
Fort Worth Patrolman Uses a Bullet to Stop Fugitive Fighter
Yates Is Held for Trial
Wound of Victim May Be Fatal—Officer Makes Statement

Jimmy, son of R.H. Orr, president of the Fort Worth Garbage Company, and an employee of the Wells Fargo Express Company, was shot by Patrolman J.K. Yates late Saturday night when he refused to obey the officer's command to halt after having been put under arrest. Orr and a companion, whose name is not known, were fighting on the sidewalk in front of the "Sweeney Chili Parlor" on Main and Eleventh streets when they were separated by

Yates and put under arrest. Orr broke from the policeman's hold and started to run across the street. When he refused to stop the officer shot, the bullet entering the back and passing through the right lung and out above the right nipple. Orr ran about twenty steps before falling.

According to the statement made by Yates, he shot to the right of Orr and would not have hit him had he not stumbled as the gun was fired, causing the bullet to take effect in the back instead of passing to the right of the man.

An automobile party which was passing carried Yates and the wounded man to a drug store at Second and Main streets, where they thought they would find a physician. When they arrived at Second and Main streets, however, they found the drug store closed and carried Orr to the Scott hotel, at Fourth and Main streets. An ambulance was called, but did not arrive for some time. The injured man, who had been living in the lobby of the hotel, was then carried to the Medical hospital, where a hasty examination showed the bullet had passed through the right lung. Soon after the examination, a slight hemorrhage occurred. It was impossible to learn late Saturday night whether Orr would have a chance to recover.

Yates was placed under arrest soon after the shooting. His examining trial probably will be held Sunday. Yates made this statement at the police station after the affair: "I was walking down Main street when I saw a large crowd of men in front of the Sweeney Chili Parlor on Eleventh street. When I investigated I found that there were two men fighting. After separating them, I told them to come to the station with me. Orr ran. When I ordered him to halt and he did not, I shot, but shot to the right of him. Just as I shot, he stumbled and the bullet hit him instead of passing to the right."

"We can't have policemen gunning down our sons on the street!" shouted Mayor W. D. Davis.

"You mean we can't have policemen gunning down the sons of prominent and influential businessmen in the street," said Judge Simmons. "There are boys and young women gunned down most every night in the Acre, and I haven't heard the din of self-righteousness about that."

The mayor and judge had been discussing the arraignment of policeman J. K. Yates for over a quarter hour. They were not discussing whether Yates should be indicted so much as the veracity and/or forgone conclusion of his trial.

"With no credible witnesses, it would be a waste of money and time to bring the man to trial," Judge Simmons said, more to himself than the mayor.

"The man is a menace. He has killed three times. Once in Lancaster and two more in Fort Worth," said Mayor Davis.

"Just one here," said Simmons. "Orr is not dead yet."

"Well tell me how many has he beaten while on patrol? Hell, for that matter, how many has he possibly killed? You yourself just said they pull bodies out of the Acre every day . . . Even the other officers tread lightly around him. If something is not done now, mark my words, Yates will become an embarrassment to us all."

"Commissioner Mulkey likes him. Feels a kind of kinship," said Judge Simmons. "I think Yates reminds Mulkey of the old days, when sheriffs and marshals made the law off the cuff and enforced it with the butt end or the muzzle of their six shooters."

The mayor sank back in his chair and muttered random obscenities to no one in particular. Mayor Davis was not accustomed to push-back on his wishes. "He will be suspended until found guilty," said the mayor, tapping his desk for emphasis. "Then we can be rid of him for good. We can no longer have the police department wiping the streets of Fort Worth with the blood of its citizens."

Judge Simmons wrinkled his brow at the forgone verdict. A proud man himself, he did not much hanker to be told how to run his court.

"Do you think it prudent to convict a Fort Worth lawman for gunning down a citizen on the street? The people of the Acre and No Man's Land already have a deep dislike and distrust of the patrolmen. We may be doubling down on the hardship of the police to maintain order. Mulkey will not be pleased."

Davis pounded on his desk three times with his tightly clenched fist, shouting "suspended" at the top of his lungs to emphasize each blow.

September 15, 1910
Fort Worth Star-Telegram

Patrolman, Who Shot Boy, Indicted
Bill Charging Aggravated Assault Returned
by the Grand Jury

Patrolman J.K. Yates, who shot Jimmy Orr on Main Street five weeks ago, was indicted for aggravated assault by the Sixty-seventh district grand jury Friday.

Young Orr was engaged in a fistfight with another man when Patrolman Yates reached the scene. Orr ran when he saw the officer and when he refused to stop, Yates fired.

Yates claimed that he fired to frighten Orr and aimed to the right, but stumbled as he pulled the trigger. The bullet penetrated the young man's right lung, and for a time it was thought he would die. Orr has recovered and has been dismissed from the hospital.

In his charge to the grand jury, Judge Simmons instructed them that an officer had no more right to use his gun than a citizen, unless he was using necessary force to defend himself from attack, or trying to stop a dangerous criminal.

December 3, 1910
Fort Worth Star-Telegram

Yates Acquitted Of Shooting Youth
Former Patrolman Freed of Aggravated Assault Charge –
Gun's Discharge Accidental

A county court jury Saturday morning acquitted former Patrolman J.K. Yates of the charge of aggravated assault in connection with the shooting of Jimmy Orr September 24. The jury was out thirty minutes before the verdict was returned.

Patrolman Yates came upon young Orr and a companion fighting on Main street. The fighters separated when the officer approached and Orr took to his heels. The officer called for him to stop, and when he refused, fired his pistol. Patrolman Yates said he did not fire to hit the boy, but stumbled as he pulled the trigger, and the bullet struck the young man in the shoulder. Yates was indicted by the Sixty-seventh district court grand jury for aggravated assault.

Mayor Davis paced in his office while Chief June Polk, Assistant Chief Parsley, and Judge Simmons sat quietly in chairs facing the mayor's desk.

"The man is rabid just as sure as church on Sunday!" The mayor was red-faced and livid. "I have him suspended, and you," the mayor turned and glared at Polk, "you immediately certify him as a damn special policemen and put him right back on the street." Mayor Davis paused for affect, glaring at Polk and daring him to rebut.

"Yates is a good officer. I believe and stand by that fact. He also is a widower with two daughters to feed and shelter. I made him a special policeman and posted him in a quiet hotel. There have been no incidents." June Polk replied to Davis in a voice as calm as grandma in prayer.

Mayor Davis was not swayed. "There will be blood on the streets in a month if Yates is put back on the streets." Davis sat in his chair and glared at the men across his clean, dark oak desk. "Mark my words gentlemen. Mark my words, you will have that blood on your heads."

December 30, 1910
Fort Worth Star Telegram

Officers Ask Yates' Return To Force
Ex-Policeman Charged With Shooting Youth, and Acquitted, May Be Reappointed as Cop.

Practically every member of the police department, including Chief Polk and Assistant Chief Parsley have signed a petition which will be presented to Police Commissioner Mulkey asking for the reappointment of J.K. Yates, the patrolman suspended for shooting young James Orr.

Orr, who is only 20 years of age, was engaged in a fight with another young man on Main street, when Yates attempted to place the two under arrest. Orr fled and Yates fired, the bullet striking the young man in the shoulder. Yates said that he fired to frighten the fugitive, but tripped as he pulled the trigger, causing the barrel of his pistol to point at Orr instead of upward. Yates was suspended from the department. He was indicted for aggravated assault, and acquitted in the county court by a jury.

Orr recovered. The petition recites the fact that Yates was acquitted by a jury in the county court and asks for his reinstatement. The petition asserts that while Yates was in the department he was a good officer.

1911

Bessie Yates had grown into a smart, beautiful fifteen-year-old girl straining the bit to become a woman. Life with Papa Yates since Flora's passing was tense and dangerous. While Yates was gone most of the time, out working or drinking, when he was home his temper was swift and violent. He would never intentionally inflict permanent injury on his daughters, but his rage was chaotic and his strength immense. He could have snapped Bessie's neck as easily as a boiled chicken bone.

Bessie was old enough to find respectable work and leave the Yates home, but there was no way she could leave her sister with their father. There was also no way for her to earn enough to feed and shelter herself and her sister without turning to the bawdy houses of the Acre and that she would not, could not, do. Not only did she not have the stomach for the work, she knew Yates would hunt her down and kill both girls rather than sustain the shame of a daughter in prostitution.

A year ago, Claude Styers had moved into the quiet Southside neighborhood a few blocks away from the Yates house. As an insurance clerk in Wichita Falls, he had struggled to make ends meet for himself and his small family and had come to Fort Worth in hopes of securing a better-paying position. He intended to send for his family once he had found a good job, but this was proving difficult in Fort Worth. Often, he was the only man in the neighborhood during the daytime, and the housewives felt sorry for him and sometimes chatted with him from their porches as he came and went in his search for work.

Bessie and her sister Selma often stayed with neighbor Jenny Smith while Yates was on duty. The girls helped with housework and ran quick errands for Mrs. Smith. One day Bessie took over a small dinner Mrs. Smith had cooked for Styers of fried chicken, collard greens, and corn on the cob. She had been instructed to leave the dinner on the table and return to the Smith house. When Bessie entered the small house, she was surprised to find Mr. Styers reading the morning edition of the *Fort Worth Press* in the living room. The two chatted for twenty minutes, and Styers gave Bessie a dime to repay Mrs. Smith for her kindness.

From that day on Styers made it a point to run into Bessie from time to time, and the two had developed a relationship that was most inappropriate between a married man and young girl. For Bessie, Styers was an escape from her brute of a father. For Styers, well, who can say why a grown, married man develops an attraction towards a teen-aged girl?

Eventually, Styers did find employment, but not in Fort Worth. He moved to Dallas for a fairly good-paying job with room for advancement. He kept in touch with Bessie. He did not immediately send for his wife and children waiting back in Wichita Falls.

❊ ❊ ❊

Selma Yates silently shook her head. She tried to hide the fear in her belly but knew it showed in her eyes. Bessie reached across the corner of the dining table and took her hand.

"It will be fine, Selma," said Bessie. "I'll be back before Papa gets home. Long before."

"But Papa does not need to know. He just has to suspect something is amiss and . . ." Selma's voice trailed off. Her eyes moved from Bessie's reassuring face to the twice folded dollar bill on the table between them.

"Claude loves me. He said he will take us both away from here. It is our chance to get away. Have a life. But I need to go to Dallas and make all the plans. I am doing this for you . . . I am doing this for us."

Selma continued to fidget in her chair. She fought them back but could not stop the tears welling up in her eyes.

"I just know something bad is going to happen."

March 27, 1911
Fort Worth Star-Telegram

Ft. Worth Officer Kills Dallas Man; 13 Shots Fired
Claude Styers Fatally Wounded in His Office.
No Explanation
Policeman J.K. Yates Surrenders Without Statement
of Cause of Act Two Pistols Are Used
Three Bullets Take Effect. Shots Fired
From Two Automatics.

Patrolman J.K. Yates of Fort Worth shot and instantly killed Claude Styers, an accountant of Dallas, in Styers private office, Main Street, in Dallas, Monday afternoon at 1:30.

Yates secured Desk Sergeant Newby over long distance phone at 2 o'clock and said: "I have just killed Claude Styers. I left Fort

Worth on the Interurban car at 12 o'clock and went directly to his office when I stepped from the car. I emptied both magazines, and believe, that every bullet went in his body."

Asks Chief to Come to Him.

Yates was at the sheriff's office at Dallas when he phoned. When Sergt. Newby questioned him regarding his act, he evaded the subject but admitted that family trouble was the cause. Yates requested that Chief Polk come to Dallas as soon as possible, saying that he would "fix everything all right with him." Chief Polk probably will go to Dallas today.

Little information regarding the shooting could be gained here. According to an Associated Press dispatch from Dallas. Styers was alone in his office, so far as is known, when Yates entered.

He was found in a crumpled heap, sitting in his office chair, with twelve to sixteen wounds on his body, some of them made by the same bullet dodging in and out of the flesh in more than one place. He was unconscious when found.

Styers was a cost accountant and had his private office in a two story brick building near the corner of Main and Murphy streets.

Yates has not been a regular patrolman on the police force since his investigation following the shooting of young Jimmy Orr on Main street last fall. After his reinstatement, his regular place had been filled and he was placed on the force as an extra policeman.

He was at the police station Sunday night, but did not work because there was no room. He gave no intimation of his contemplated act to anyone, not even his closest friends on the force. He had not appeared at the police station Monday.

Yates a Widower

The patrolman had been a widower for several years. He has two daughters. 10 and 14 years old, respectively. When he talked to Sergeant Newby soon after the shooting, he asked that someone take care of his children and furnished him with a telephone number.

Yates told Sergeant Newby that he first met Styers two weeks ago and that he had seen him several times since then, but did not say whether it was in Fort Worth or Dallas.

> A case charging Yates with murder was recently dismissed in one
> of the district courts. Yates killed a negro eight years ago. The negro
> was resisting arrest, and threatened the officer with a hammer.

Mary Gaines had finished her morning housework before ten o'clock. She was filled with uncontrollable nervous energy. Early that morning she had determined to tell her neighbor about Styers and his daughter. She busied herself on the front porch until she saw Yates turn the corner and walk by, weary from a night walking his beat but still straight as a rod.

"Mr. Yates," she called. "Might I have a minute with you?"

Yates did not alter or slow his gait and replied, "Can it be put off, Mrs. Gaines? I am a might tuckered this morning."

"Well, I suppose," Mary Gaines nervously replied. "But it does concern Bessie."

Yates halted dead in his tracks. He turned his gaze to the Gaines porch. He stopped only two feet from the gate. "Has she offended in any way?"

"Oh my, heavens no. Bessie is a sweet, mindful girl. No trouble 'tall."

"Then what is the matter?" Yates was short in his reply.

Mary stepped off the porch and approached the fence. As she walked she hesitantly reached in her apron and removed a letter. She tugged and turned the letter in her hands as she approached Yates. Finally, standing across the fence from Yates, she looked down at the envelope as if deciding one more time if she were doing the right thing.

"This came in the post yesterday." Mary handed the letter to Yates. "Remember Claude Styers? He lived in the neighborhood only a short time before moving to Dallas a while back."

"I met him a time or two. Kind of a dandy as I recall. Did not have much call or inclination to speak to him much."

Yates took the letter from Mary and read the envelope. It was addressed to Dearest Bessie with a return address for Claude Styers. Yates ripped open the letter and began to read the contents.

His face flushed crimson. At this time the neighbor across the street, Mrs. Edwina True, rounded into her front yard from the back of her house. Seeing Yates and Mrs. Gaines she called a cheery "hello."

Mrs. True's salutation startled Mary but fell on deaf ears to Yates, who continued to be caught up in the contents of the missive from Styers to his daughter. Mrs. True crossed the street and approached her neighbors.

"Good morning Mary, Mr. Yates. How are you both?"

"Have there been other letters from Styers to my Bessie? This letter mentions another letter posted less than a week ago." Yates glared in fury at Mary.

"Not to my knowledge, Mr. Yates. God's honest truth. If there had been another letter, Bessie must have took it before I knew."

"Styers?" said Edwina. "Claude Styers?"

"Yes, Wina, it seems he has been writing to Officer Yates's little Bessie."

"Oh, of that I am not surprised," said Edwina. "That man is up to no good, I say. Why, not a week before he left I saw him follow Bessie into Jenny Smith's house while all the Smiths were off to Wednesday church. I said to myself, 'Now don't that seem queer?'"

Yates turned to Edwina and bore his eyes into hers. "You saw this and did not think to tell me? Or even to tell Boney, so he could have told me?"

"Why, well," Edwina stuttered and stumbled like a three-year-old caught in the honey pot. "Bessie and Selma are such good girls and even though you work so hard, Mr. Yates, you keep on top of those girls. You are a good, strict, God-fearing father. You know me, I keep to my own business and thought you would have known."

Mary did know Edwina True and her husband Boney. She also knew if Edwina could not talk about other people's business, she likely could not talk at all.

Yates thrust the letter and envelope into his coat pocket, wheeled, and began to walk back toward downtown.

"Where are you headed, Officer Yates?"

"The interurban to Dallas."

As Yates rounded the corner out of sight, Edwina True walked back to her house with a somewhat satisfied look on her face.

Mary Gaines stood in her yard several seconds staring in the direction Yates had walked. There was a grave look on her face.

March 28, 1911
Dallas Morning News

Find Lifeless Body Huddled Over Chair
Claude Styers Killed and Officer J.K. Yates Gives Up.
Remains Riddled with Bullets – Man in Jail Came Over
from Fort Worth

Riddled with bullets, the lifeless body of Claude Styers was found huddled over a chair at 1:30 o'clock yesterday afternoon in his office on the second floor of the Blaylock Building on Main street, just above Poydras street. The sound of a fusillade of pistol shots attracted men from the Burk clothing store downstairs and from other offices in the building, these men being among the first to reach the body.

J.K. Yates, a policeman of Fort Worth and formerly Constable of Lancaster, left Styers' office immediately after the shooting with two automatic pistols in his hands and went direct to the office of Sheriff Brandenburg, where he laid the two pistols on a desk and surrendered.

Styers body was found in a kneeling position with the head bowed over into a chair in the southwest corner of his small office overlooking Main street. A pool of blood from numerous wounds had formed in the seat of the chair and blood dripped on the floor below. C.E. Hodes, who was one of the first to reach the office, said that Styers was dead when he entered. On the floor of the office were found thirteen empty shells.

Eleven Wounds in Body.

In Styers' body there were eleven wounds, the majority of them appearing to have entered from the right side and somewhat from the rear. There were six wounds about the back of the neck, one through the right side of the body, entering the back and coming out near the nipple; one low down on the left side of the body, entering the back and coming out in front; one through the left arm, one through the right arm and one through the left leg. The flesh around one wound beneath the right ear was powder burned and the hair was singed. One bullet that entered the back of the neck lodged just beneath the skin in the front of the throat.

Two bullet holes showed in the seat of the chair, another bullet pierced the window sash, one struck the door frame and another against the wall. The chair over which the body was huddled was in the corner farthest from the outside entrance of the office and against a door leading into other offices in the building.

Met Man on Stairs.

C.E. Hodes who went to Styers' office said: "I heard a number of shots and rushed up the steps. On the steps I met a man with two pistols in his hand. He was shoving these into his pockets. He didn't say anything to me and I didn't speak to him. He was running down the steps as I came up. When I got in the office Styers' body was huddled over a chair and he was dead."

A stenographer in an office across the hall from Styers' office said she heard a number of shots, but that she was too frightened to count them.

James Coleman, 804 Alexandria street, a night worker at the Central Ice Company, said: "I was coming down the street when I heard a number of shots fired upstairs. I ran up to Styers' office. As I got a part of the way up the steps some one ran against me coming down. I don't know who he was. Styers was dead when I got in the room."

Styers occupied office No. 201 in the Blaylock Building and on the door besides his name were the words: "Cost systems." He was apparently about 35 years old. The records of Aldredge & Knight, agents in charge of the building, show that Styers rented this office Dec. 30. He had been in the rental office a number of times, but had never spoken of himself or his business. Judge Patton, who has an office on the same floor and near Styers' office said: "Styers moved into his office about three months ago, but I do not know anything about him. He was a quiet sort of man, I believe."

Contents of Pockets.

In Styers' pockets were found a watch, a pipe, a knife, $1.50 in silver and several cards. A pencil in the upper left-hand pocket had been snapped in two about the middle, presumably from Styers falling forward in the chair.

Officers Harrison, Emicke, Phillips, Hauk and Mayes answered the call and all viewed the remains.

Styers body was taken in charge by Welland & McCreary, undertakers.

Says Stranger Came to Door.

W.R. Simmons, an attorney, the only eyewitness to the affair said: "I was sitting in Mr. Styers' office, talking to him. A stranger came to the door. He stopped in the doorway and drawing a revolver began firing. The bullets came fast and I was frightened. I got out of the room as quickly as possible and ran down the hall and into another office."

Mrs. Lydia Styers, the wife of the deceased, was located last night in Wichita Falls. Through her communication was established with the father of the deceased, George F. Styers, at Memphis Tenn., and a sister at Edgewater, Ill. Funeral arrangement will be announced when the desires of the relatives are made known.

Bessie and Selma huddled in their room, believing their father would soon return. They sat separate, bolt upright on their beds. Each, in their own way listening, dreading the sound of their father's footsteps climbing the front porch into the house. Bessie was practically catatonic, her lifeless eyes staring into the ether. Selma was dangling on the brink of hysteria.

✳ ✳ ✳

In the courthouse, two miles and a stone's throw away from the Yates house, a small group of men sat contemplating Yates and their future.

"I shudder to think what I would have done if in his place," said Mayor Davis.

"I don't shudder at all," said Assistant Chief Parsley. "Styers had a killin' coming to him . . . or worse."

"Or worse?" said Commissioner Mulkey. "From what I have been told by a Dallas Detective, it could not have been much worse."

"You, sir, have not seen what Kid can do with his bare hands." Parsley shook his head and continued, "Styers could indeed have met a worse fate."

"Indeed," said Mayor Davis in agreement.

Mayor Davis had been staring out the window. He turned and faced the men. "But the question remains of what to do. As a city, what is our reaction?" Mayor Davis looked from one man to the next, carefully gauging their countenances.

"I see no question as to what part we play," said W. M. Rea. "We stand firm and tall behind our officer." A shallow chorus of "aye" came from the other men in the room.

"We have already passed the hat in the Policeman's Benevolent Society and raised a sum to help take care of the daughters while he deals with this matter," said Parsley.

"He will surely be no billed or found innocent," said Mulkey. "For, 'Of a truth, God will not do wickedly, and the Almighty will not pervert justice.'"

Parsley added, "I hold the word of the good book firm and dear but . . . We are talking Dallas courtrooms, nothing is assured."

"I can assure you Yates will go to trial. A no bill is out of the question. It was too much a stunningly violent assault. The public will demand he be tried," said Rea.

"One can never be assured of righteous justice coming from a Dallas jury," said Parsley.

"True enough," said Mulkey.

"And what about his defense?" asked Parsley. "Surly there are good, God-fearing lawyers that will come to Kid's aid."

"He needs a Dallas lawyer. Someone impeccable and known to their courts and citizens," said Rea. "As such, I have inquired with Judge Nelms about his availability to act as counsel for the defense. He is amicable to the idea. He has experience in murder cases, a winning record, and is well-known and respected in all of Dallas County."

"I know the judge. He would be a good man and see to it this case was tried on good Christian values," said Mayor Davis.

"To my knowledge, he has never defended a white man for murder that has been convicted," said Parsley.

"While I fear for Yates and his daughters and agree we must aid in his well-being and defense, we also cannot have Fort Worth painted as a lawless, violent town still in the grip of frontier, vigilante justice," said Mayor Davis. "A lot of money flows from Dallas to Fort Worth."

"Iron sharpens iron, and one man sharpens another," Parsley said. Several of the men bowed their heads and punctuated the verse with a solemn "amen."

"The mayor's point is well-taken and I feel I must bring up the fact that this is not the first time Yates has called the integrity of the force and the city into question," said Rea. "And we all know why he was driven to Fort Worth and out of Lancaster. While he may be justified in this instance, it cannot be denied he has a quick and bloody temper."

"Surly you are not suggesting fault in defending his daughter's honor, Rea," said Parsley.

"No. But I wonder how many times justifiable homicide can find one man."

The men sat in silence as all contemplated Rea's question. Some men looked deeper in their conscience than others.

Eventually Mayor Davis broke the quiet. "We will support Yates with time and money, but every time any city official speaks for public consumption we will let it be known that while Fort Worth is not a city that condones violence on its streets, we will support our police and a father in his quest for justice."

March 29, 1911
Fort Worth Star-Telegram

———————————

Styers Shooting Discussed at Trial
Hearing of Policeman Yates on Murder Charge
Begins at Dallas Daughter Will Attend
Mayor and Other Fort Worth Officials Leave
Also to Be Present.

———————————

Special to the Star-Telegram

The examining trial of J.K. Yates, the Fort Worth policeman who shot and killed Claude Styers, a cost accountant, Monday afternoon, is being held before Justice Work this afternoon.

W.R. Simmons, a young lawyer who was in Styers office when Policeman Yates entered, told of the beginning of the shooting. He said Yates entered and after saying "How do you do, Mr. Styers?" began shooting.

Styers rose from his chair hastily, he said, when he saw Yates. After the shooting began Lawyer Simmons immediately left the office.

Daughters Go to Hearing

Bessie Yates, the 15-year-old daughter of Patrolman J.K. Yates, who killed Claude Styers in Dallas Monday, was accompanied to Dallas by Assistant Chief of Police Parsley Wednesday afternoon at 12:30 o'clock to testify at her father's examining trial. Mayor Davis and other city officials attended the meeting.

Letters received by this child from Styers were believed to have led to the killing. The girl had known Styers when he lived in Fort Worth and turned over to her father correspondence received from him after he had gone to Dallas.

Mrs. Remus G. Smith, 1306 Elizabeth street, explained to a Star-Telegram reporter Wednesday that Styers had walked home with the little Yates girl two weeks ago from the Smith house, and did so at her request.

"He knew her," said Mrs. Smith, "just as a child in the neighborhood. When Patrolman Yates was on night duty at the police station, the little girls would come to our house and to other houses and stay until late at night. My two boys were accustomed to walking home with them and turning on the lights in the house so the children wouldn't be frightened, but on the night two weeks ago the boys had a childish quarrel about who should walk home with the girls, and I asked Mr. Styers to accompany them home. Mr. Styers lived for a while only a couple of doors from the Yates home and knew Bessie as any other child in the neighborhood. There were no social gatherings at our house and I never knew Mr. Styers to accompany Bessie home but the one time I requested him to. Mr. Styers and his wife were friends of my son and daughter-in-law and when Mr. Styers' sister moved to Chicago we held a sort of neighborhood farewell party for them, but Bessie Yates wasn't there, unless it was that she was around the house playing with some of the smaller children. Mr. Styers was a good man and highly thought of by everyone in our part of the city."

The Fort Worth Police Benevolent Association will give financial aid for defense of Yates, according to a member of the association.

"This does not mean," he said, "that the association indorses his act, but we feel it a duty to a brother member to aid him. Every member of the association is sore at heart because of the lamentable tragedy. The little Yates girls will be cared for well. Many friends of the officer have offered to take the girls into their homes and at present they are provided for as well as possible. The policeman will not want for aid from his brother members of the association."

Judge W. W. Nelms walked down the hall of the Dallas city jail as if he were leading a royal procession. Not only was his suit impeccably pressed and clean, it was as if dust, dirt, and grime were invisibly repelled and forbidden by a higher power to alight on his garments. No one the judge passed in the hall hailed or acknowledged him. This was not out of rudeness but out of respect.

Yates was pacing about the small rectangular holding room when Judge Nelms burst in.

"Mr. Yates, I am Judge W. W. Nelms and I have been engaged by your brothers in the badge to defend your good name and secure your freedom." Yates began to speak, but Nelms paid no heed and continued. "I believe, Mr. Yates, you were in the right to have shot the base-born libertine even if the angels of heaven had been guarding him and verily, should do so a thousand times over in defense of your sacred home and family bond, and we shall stand in defiance of all the penal statutes of the world if need be for there are some things in which a man must fix his own standards and this is just such an instance!"

Yates stood silently and watched Nelms as he stalked to and fro, waving and gesturing as if to a great gathering.

"In your defense I will aid the judge and jury to a thorough understanding to the comprehensive greatness and designs of the Creator in arming his children with divine authority to slay the destroyer of family ties.

"You, sir, may be surprised when I tell you that strategy, both to prevent and to punish with death the crimes of the libertine, comes to us with divine sanction, and was often practiced by those who are conspicuous in the lineage of the Savior."

Judge Nelms dropped his tone to a solemn baritone. "Society itself is on trial here, at a critical period when virtue and morality are on a fearful downward trend, without any apparent protest against the advance of the social revolution which threatens so much of the sanctity of the home and the state itself. We are yet fighting the battle of civilization! Your struggles today, Mr. Yates, may be the struggles of tomorrow for every man on that jury. We shall make them understand.

"Your case, Mr. Yates, is governed by the higher law and your actions ought make you worthy to have your name carved in letters of gold on the columns of the Pantheon. You have ascended the rugged heights of Sinai and on its flaming summit, shaken hands with God!"

Judge Nelms ended his sermon with eyes and arms stretched towards the heavens.

Kid Yates stood slack-jawed in the holding room, not quite sure what had just transpired but feeling much more secure in his future and freedom.

March 29, 1911
Dallas Morning News

J.K. Yates Hearing Is Today
Man Charged with Killing Claude Styers to Be Brought Before Justice Work.

J.K. Yates, charged by affidavit with killing Claude Styers Monday afternoon by shooting him with a pistol, will be given a preliminary hearing before Justice of the Peace T.A. Work at 9 o'clock this morning.

Yates received several callers at the county jail yesterday, and appeared to be in good spirits. Neither he nor his attorneys have as yet made any statements as to what defense he will present to the charge.

The preliminary hearing will not likely consume much time as there seems to be so far as known only one eyewitness to the shooting.

March 30, 1911
Fort Worth Star-Telegram

Yates Released On $1,000 Bond at Hearing in Dallas
Mayor Davis and Defendant's Brother Are Signers.
"I'd Do It Again"
Policeman on Stand Said He Went to Dallas Intending to Kill Styers.
Letters to Girl Cause Pictures of Seventeen Women Found in Victim's Desk Shown in Court

Patrolman J.K. Yates of Fort Worth, who shot to death Claude Styers, a Dallas accountant, Monday, was released under $1,000 bond following the preliminary trial before Justice T.A. Work here today. Mayor Davis of Fort Worth, T.J. Yates of Fort Worth, a brother of the defendant, and A.B. Floyd, a Dallas county farmer, are the signers.

When Justice Work announced his decision to allow bond, Mayor Davis rushed up to him and gave him a hearty slap on the back and Justice Work threatened to fine the Fort Worth executive for contempt of court. The mayor then apologized. Just before the decision was announced, Yates paced the floor and sobbed. He appeared deeply affected throughout the progress of the hearing and seemed relieved when the decision was announced.

"Yates would not have been a white man if he had not shot Styers," said Judge W.W. Nelms, Yates leading counsel, in the closing speech for the defense. "No white man with red blood in his veins will convict him for his act."

Assistant County Attorney Wilson cited the rage of Yates when he received the first letter written by Stylers to his 15-year-old daughter and declared that he deliberated over the killing two weeks, for he delayed his trip to Dallas on account of business during the Fat Stock Show in Fort Worth.

Yates Tells of Letters.

Yates told the story of the events that led up to the killing of Styers. The first of the two letters received by Bessie Yates from Styers was March 17, when he found the letter in the mailbox on the front porch of his house, 1024 Elizabeth Street, Fort Worth. His daughter had not seen the letter. Yates said that the letter invited the girl to come to Styers office at Dallas and inclosed (sic) a $1 bill for Interurban carfare. He was enraged then, he says, but delayed action. A few days later a letter inquiring why the first had not been answered was received. This letter, Bessie Yates turned over to her father. He says he would have gone to Dallas then, but was busy at the Fat Stock Show and delayed his trip.

Told by a neighbor.

On the morning of the killing, he said, a Mrs. Gaines told him that someone should have told him about Styers. Then Mrs. Boney True, a neighbor, told him the same thing. Mrs. True came across the street to where Yates was standing in front of his house.

"What is the trouble," she asked.

"I am feeling bad," he answered.

"Is it about that man in Dallas?"

"Yes."

"Well, someone should have told you about him," she said and then told him that she had heard indirectly that a neighbor had seen Styers fondling the little Yates girl in a neighbor's house.

"That was told me about 10:30 in the morning." Yates testified. "I caught the 12 o'clock car for Dallas and on the way over I told a man named Hines that I was going to kill a man. I knew Styers office address, having seen it in the letters and went directly there from the car.

"When I walked into Styers office, I asked if he were Styers. He answered, 'Yes, by God, that's my name.' and reached his hand to his desk. His hand was concealed. I raised my gun and fired. I killed him and would do it again. I don't know how many times I fired."

Yates also asserted that after he met Styers in the latter's office Styers placed his hand on the desk in such a manner as to indicate that he was preparing to get a weapon.

Yates admitted that he borrowed money to pay his way to Dallas to kill Styers. "I'm a poor man," he declared to the court.

As evidence for the defense, a large cardboard with the pictures of seventeen women pasted on it was introduced. This cardboard was found hanging on the wall in Styers office. Most of the pictures were of young girls. Only two of them were of mature women.

Mrs. Claude Styers was one of the witnesses at the hearing Wednesday afternoon. She was called to the stand to identify one of the letters said to have been written by her husband and identified the handwriting. She said she could not be sure about the writing on another letter.

The funeral of Styers was held on Thursday morning from the undertaking rooms of Welland & McCreary.

1912

Bessie Yates scrubbed Mrs. Gaines's kitchen floor on her hands and knees, naked as the day she was born. Mrs. Gaines sat in a straight-backed chair, arms crossed, eyes glaring at Bessie. Selma stood in a corner, a quiet, disconcerted observer.

"If it is your plan to go whoring around, you need to get used to doing dirty work on your hands and knees," said Mrs. Gaines. Selma, uncomfortable with the entire ordeal, turned her eyes to the window.

"Look at your whore sister!" shouted Mrs. Gaines. "You need to get an eyeful of your future because you will surely follow in her wicked ways! God forbid, God forbid." Selma turned her gaze back towards her sister but stared at the floor just in front of Bessie.

Mrs. True walked in the back door carrying a basket of groceries.

"Lordy me, what is happening here?" she declared.

"The Lord's work, Edwina, the good Lord's work," replied Mary Gaines. Mrs. True looked at the naked girl on the floor, then over to Mrs. Gaines, her brow furrowed.

"If little Bessie here wants to go whoring around, she needs a taste of shame and hard work. This is as close as I'll let whoring into this God-fearing house."

"Amen," muttered Mrs. True as she knowingly nodded her head in understanding.

She placed the groceries on the table. "True enough, Mary, true enough. It breaks my heart, seeing that poor girl travel down the road of sin, but her path was likely set and writ in stone the day her sainted mother passed." Mrs. Gaines and Mrs. True shook their heads in unison. "I have your cabbage in here somewhere," said Mrs. True as she placed other vegetables on the table and rummaged for the cabbage Mrs. Gaines had asked her to buy.

"Thank you, Edwina. What is my debt?"

"No debt at all, Mary, I still owe you for borrowing that spool of thread last week." Bessie paused in her labor to catch her breath and rest her arms.

"There is no rest for the wicked, Bessie Yates, you continue until I say no more," said Mrs. Gaines.

"I can't help but feel a little guilty," said Mrs. True. "Is there anything more we could have done for these two to save these wayward girls from the bawdy house?"

"A good Christian example from two good Christian families should have been enough," said Mrs. Gaines. "They simply did not have God in their hearts to start."

Bessie continued to scrub the floor, her arms shaking from fatigue and knees bright red from the lye soap and bare floor. A tear fell from Selma's eye but she dare not move her hand to wipe it away.

Mrs. Gaines and Mrs. True shook their heads and tisked tisked the plight and sinful futures of the two girls.

March 3, 1912
Fort Worth Star-Telegram

Cop Faces Murder Trial On Monday
J.K. Yates, Who Slew Dallas Man Over Letters to Daughter, Expects Acquittal.
Self Defense Is Plea
Contents of Two Revolvers Emptied into Body of Claude Styers in Dallas

---

J.K. Yates, the Fort Worth police officer who shot and killed Claude Styers, a Dallas accountant, early Monday afternoon, March 27, 1911, will be placed on trial for murder Monday in the Second district court at Dallas.

Confident of his acquittal, Yates left the city Saturday afternoon for Dallas. Brother officers with whom he conversed at police headquarters before his departure expressed optimistic convictions concerning the outcome of the trial and shook hands warmly with him as he bade them farewell.

Expects Acquittal

"I have no fear of the outcome," said Yates to his friends. "I believe my action was fully justified."

The shooting of Styers followed the discovery, on March 17, of letters in the post box at Yates' home, 1024 Elizabeth Street, written by Styers to the officer's fourteen year old daughter, Bessie. At the preliminary hearing, held the Thursday following the killing, Yates testified that the missive contained an invitation for the girl to come to Styers office at Dallas and a $1 bill for her car fare.

A few days later, a second letter inquiring why the girl had not accepted the invitation was received by his daughter, Yates testified, and the girl gave it to her father.

Neighbors Tell Father

On the morning of the killing, it developed a Mrs. Gaines told him that someone should have told him about Styers. A neighbor, Mrs. Boney True, told him the same thing and said that she had heard indirectly that Styers had been seen fondling the little Yates girl in a neighbor's house.

"That was told me about 10:30 o'clock," Yates testified. "I caught the 12 o'clock car over to Dallas and went directly to Styer's office. I knew his address, having seen it on the letters.

When I walked into Styers' office, I asked him if he were Styers. He answered, 'Yes, by God, that's my name,' and reaching his hand to his desk. His hand was concealed. I raised my gun and fired. I killed him, and would do it again."

Bond Signed by Mayor

Following his preliminary trial before Justice Work at Dallas, Yates was released under bond of $1,000 signed by his brother, T.J. Yates of Fort Worth, and A.B. Floyd, a Dallas farmer, and Mayor Davis of Fort Worth.

So delighted was the Fort Worth mayor when Yates' bond was allowed that he rushed up to the defendant and slapped him on the back, narrowly escaping a fine from the courts. Yates was much affected and sobbed as his friends gathered around him.

In a telephone message to Desk Sergeant Newby after the shooting, Yates said that he had emptied the contents of the two revolvers into Styers' body. The corpse was found to be pierced by a dozen bullets. The officer is a widower and has a daughter ten years of age beside the daughter, Bessie.

At the time of the killing, Yates had just been reinstated as
a member of the Fort Worth police department following the
investigation into the shooting on Main street a year ago last fall of
Jimmie Orr, a young white boy.

Yates remained on the police force after Styers death, serving
for some time as an extra officer. On Nov. 20, he was assigned to a
regular beat and has held the position continuously since.

Bessie and Selma lay in their bed but neither slept. Their father sat alone
at the kitchen table, drinking sip after sip from a bottle of whiskey. There
were no human sounds in the clear night air. A horse-drawn wagon
clacked and squeaked down the street and crickets and toads played cat
and mouse in the yards.

Bessie dreamed of ways to kill Mary Gaines. She had already considered and pictured more than a dozen and was currently picturing a particularly slow and painful death utilizing a bull whip and straight razors.
Her heart beat slowly.

Selma lay stiff as a three-day corpse and breathed slowly. Her eyes
open and glassy, her mind blank and black as pitch.

Kid Yates's mind whirred in a whiskey fog. While the town stood
firmly behind him in support, especially the mayor and city council, it
seemed no one was willing to support him with companionship or personal friendship. He walked his beat alone, some not bothering with any
pretense to cross the street to avoid his path. He had not spoken to a soul
in four days excepting Mrs. Gaines, and Mrs. Gaines was like as not to
bore the knots out of a fence post.

The trial would start in a few days. Yates had practiced his testimony
hundreds of times exactly the way Judge Nelms had instructed. In his
heart he felt justified and burned with the sword of the Lord. In his mind
he saw Styers slump back in his chair and relived the moment life left
his watery eyes. The sight of Styers expired lit a fire in Yates's belly hotter
than the cheap whiskey.

March 5, 1912
Dallas Morning News

Testimony Is Begun In J.K. Yates Case
State Closes After Introducing Two Witnesses
Man Charged with Killing of Claude Styers Begins
in Judge Miller's Court

With the introduction of the testimony of two witnesses the State yesterday afternoon rested its case against J.K. Yates, on trial in Criminal District Court No. 2 charged with killing Claude Styers on March 27, 1910. The witnesses were Dr. L.H. Painter and W.R. Simmons. Dr. Painter described the wounds in the body of the deceased and said that the death was caused from the wounds. W.R. Simmons, the only eyewitness to the killing, told of the events in connection with the shooting. The defense will begin the introduction of testimony this morning and the case will probably go to the jury by noon Wednesday.

Both sides announced ready for trial when the case was called and the selection of the jury was at once begun. The special venire was exhausted by noon. The court ordered forty talesmen for 2 o'clock in the afternoon and by a few minutes after 3 o'clock the last juror had been chosen. The jury is composed of R.M. Phelps, H.L. Terry, T.W. Terry, J.C. McEntee, R.E. Hignell, J.H. Deberly, J.Z. Phillips, Will Lusk, J.M. Pidgway, J.L. Bsahsear, T.M. Halbert and C.H. Starks.

Yates is represented by Lively, Nelms & Adams. Assistant County Attorney Currie McCutcheon has charge of the prosecution.

Police Commissioner C. E. "Ed" Parsley sat across from Officer Mike Middleton at a table in Tinker's Diner near the Fort Worth courthouse. Parsley seemed distracted and uninterested in his dinner.

"Did you get a plate full of gristle, Ed?" asked Middleton.

"Naw, the dinner is fine; I just have not possessed much of an appetite lately. Too much thinking I reckon."

"What is your mind chewing on that is keeping your teeth from chewing your food?" said Middleton.

"Yates will walk, Mike. That is a cast iron guarantee. He will be standing in front of my desk, shy of two weeks, looking for duty and . . . " Parsley paused and fiddled with his potatoes.

"I do not understand the cause for concern, Ed. He will be standing in your office a free and unburdened man. Found innocent in a court of law and righteous in the eyes of God."

"How many men has he killed, Mike? Three? Four? That we know of?" Parsley stared at his potatoes and gravy, slowly twirling his fork.

"Two white men and a nigger, so depends on how you want to count them."

"There is the rub, I reckon. I count three souls took unnatural and sent to their maker by a man who counts himself judge, jury, and executioner," said Parsley.

"The courts have all said otherwise, Ed. Seems to me you are the one passing judgment on Kid."

"Maybe so, Mike," said Parsley as he looked up and stared straight into Middleton's eyes. "Maybe so . . . But in less than a fortnight Kid Yates will come into my office and I will assign him a beat, and I swear blind, Mike, when I send him out there, I know I'm killing someone sure as I did the deed myself, and I'm not sure how I feel about that."

"You do not know that, Ed." Middleton's eyes clouded as he came to understand what was bothering his friend. "Yates is hard, that is true enough, but each killing was justified in the eyes of the law and most Christian folk would say in the eyes of God Almighty himself."

"Trouble does not follow one man that long and that hard unless he carries it around with him, at least some. You know that, Mike." Parsley cut a piece of steak and stabbed it with his fork. "I'll ask you . . . What would you do? Have him swinging a stick in the Gold Coast where when he loses his temper he is likely to shoot the drunk son of a banker or merchant and I'll catch hell fire, or do I put him walking the Acre or Bohnunk Alley where he will just beat some poor nigger or drunkard to death for not much cause?"

There was a long pause in the conversation.

"I do not think it is my job to place value on a man's life." Parsley shoved the hunk of meat in his mouth and chewed without joy. The rest of Middleton's meal went cold.

March 6, 1912
Fort Worth Star-Telegram

Yates Acquitted of Killing Dallas Man
Jury Trying Fort Worth Policeman Takes Only 21 Minutes to Reach Verdict.

After a deliberation of but twenty-one minutes, a jury in criminal district court No. 2 in Dallas, Tuesday afternoon, acquitted J.K. Yates, a Fort Worth policeman, of a charge of murder, growing out of the shooting of Claude Styers, a Dallas accountant, last March.

Yates' plea was self-defense. His attorneys also cited the unwritten law in connection with Styers' attentions to the defendant's 15-year-old daughter, Bessie.

On the stand, the police officer testified that at the time of the killing he believed that Styers already had accomplished the ruin of his daughter. With tears in his eyes, he told of intercepting letters written by Styers to the girl, and said that when he was apprised that there had been misconduct in the neighborhood of his home on Styers part he borrowed a dollar from a friend and went at once to Dallas to find Styers. He said he shot the accountant in self-defense and because of his conduct.

The jury cordially shook hands with Yates after the return of the verdict.

The courtroom was crowded, among the spectators being Chief of Police Renfro, Captains Bills and Blanton, Desk Sergeant Charles Newby and a delegation of Fort Worth policemen. When the verdict was returned they surrounded Yates and congratulated him.

Yates has served actively as a police officer since the shooting of Styers. He is a widower and has a daughter younger than Bessie.

1913

TOM LEE

Tom Lee awoke with blood boiling. Most mornings Tom Lee awoke pissed at one thing or another, but today he aimed to do something about the anger. Today Tom Lee decided not to drink to forget the humiliation of being less than a man; today Tom Lee would drink to bolster the courage to be a man. A man of action.

Tom Lee spent six days a week, twelve to fourteen hours a day on his knees at the feet of Fort Worth's elite, shining and polishing boots and shoes at the Congress Barber Shop. Tom Lee was, according to the Congress's owner, S. I. Rodick, a "good nigger," which meant he did what he was told when he was told to do it, and acted happy about it all the time. There was, however, nothing about Tom Lee's life that made him happy or proud.

He spent most evenings in the Acre, drinking rotgut whiskey and gambling. He drank to numb the humiliation and he gambled because sometimes he won. A man needs to win every once in a while. Most times he lost, but the maybe one time in ten that Tom Lee won, it made him feel whole, even a little human.

Last night Tom Lee joined a craps game in an alley behind McGar's saloon. On this night Lee lost badly. He had been foolish to leave his brother's house with his entire bankroll, but he had, and within an hour it was gone. He had rolled dice with Pete Soles and Walter Moore. Lee had shot pool with Moore on a few occasions but had never laid eyes on Soles. Lee knew Moore never played straight in pool and hustled drunks and young men too inexperienced to know they were being taken. Lee offered that Moore and Soles had cheated him out of nearly a hundred dollars and he aimed to take it back in hide.

Tom Lee left the lean-to in back of his brother's house where he laid his head and crossed into his neighbor's yard. He knocked softly on the back door. Mrs. Heath walked over to the screen and the two exchanged pleasantries. Lee was polite and jovial; there was no hint of his real mood. Every black man that lived past the age of thirty knew how to laugh, joke, and act pleasant, no matter the true emotions roiling in the pit of their stomachs.

"I's going bird hunting, Mrs. Heath, or I would like to," Lee said. "Do you think Jim would mind me borrowing his shotgun? I'll gladly drop off two quail for dinner when I return it, if I'm lucky enough to shoot three or more."

"Of course, Tom," said Mrs. Heath. "I'm sure Jim won't mind a bit." She opened the screen door and Tom entered. A few minutes later he left out the front door with the twelve-gauge, double-barreled shotgun and turned towards town, his pockets, front and back, loaded with bird shot.

Tom Lee walked with a single purpose down the middle of East Eighth Street. He drew a few stares from the white men on the street as they looked uneasily at the black man carrying a shotgun. The few carriages and cars on the road gave him a fair berth. When he was dead center of McCampbell's Barbecue, he turned and eyed Pete Soles, who was standing at the street-side counter eating a plate of chicken, his back to the street.

Jack finally had a moment to step back from the grill and wipe the sweat from his face. The lunch rush was easing up, and he finally had a chance to step away from the grill's heat and collect his thoughts. Right now he was thinking he needed a long draw of water.

"Would you look at the no account pig sloppin' down on a plate of chicken," Lee said to Soles.

Soles looked around and saw Lee addressing him. "Unless you're carrying more money to lose shooting craps, take that shotgun, stick it up your ass, and walk back home," Soles responded with a smile across his lips.

From behind the counter Jack quickly sized up the situation. It was not good, he surmised. The man in the street toting the shotgun had a blank, cold stare, like he had already pulled the trigger and cared not of the consequences.

Tom Lee raised the shotgun chest high, cocked both barrels, and let fly with one. Pete Soles was still smiling when the bird shot hit him square in the chest, blowing through his right hand, which he had feebly raised for protection. Soles was knocked back against the counter, blood and stray bird shot splattered around him. He fell motionless to the ground.

Lee turned and did a one-eighty, surveying the street. Men women, children, and dogs scattered away in all directions. As he began to walk back down the street, a few men gathered the courage to confront Lee.

As he reloaded the spent barrel he shouted, "I shot one man and I'll kill anybody I don't like! All you niggers get back, I say!"

The men retreated to the sidewalk, and Tom Lee strode west down East Eighth, feeling ten feet tall. He was so excited and felt so in control he momentarily forgot where he was headed next. When he hit Calhoun he realized he was walking the wrong way, so he turned south and circled around the block to Jones.

Heading north on Jones, he left the street and climbed the sidewalk in front of McGar's saloon. Lee placed his thumb across both hammers to make sure both barrels were still cocked.

Stump was seated in his usual place by the door, holding court and spilling tales of his days as a porter on the Missouri rail line when Lee stepped over the threshold. The men seated facing Stump immediately hit the floor, dropping out of their chairs like they had been leveled by sledgehammers.

"Naw the women in Kansas City . . . " Stump never finished his sentence as Lee drew the shotgun to his shoulder.

"I've got you now!" Lee shouted. He squeezed off one barrel.

The bird shot hit Walter Moore square in the face. He had been shooting pool at the table closest to Stump and the door. He had been standing by the table, facing the door but watching his opponent line up a shot. Blood, bone, and brain flew in a splatter pattern against the wall, and his lifeless body dropped to the floor.

The twenty or so men in the pool hall scattered. Stump stayed motionless in his seat. He was close enough to Lee that he could smell the gunpowder. But Lee had accomplished what he had set out to do. Soles and Moore would not ever cheat another man out of his hard-earned pay. He backed out of McGar's saloon and swung around to face the street. A crowd of men had gathered to find the cause of the gunfire, but by the looks on their faces, they were sorry they had run to the sound. Summing up that they would not try to stop him, Tom Lee walked straight through the men and into the street. For the first time in a long time, he felt in control. He had taken action. He had imposed his will on the situation. He headed north on Jones, taking long, confident strides.

* * *

Back at McCampbell's barbecue, it seemed Lee had not been as successful as he assumed. Soles was torn up from the bird shot and unconscious, but alive. Jack had come to his aid and with the help of a few more men loaded him in an automobile and rushed him to John Peter Smith Hospital, the only hospital in Fort Worth that provided charity care.

* * *

Tom Lee continued his march down Jones Street, then turned east on Eighth. His confidence began to drain as he realized he no longer had a purpose or a plan. He panicked, plain and simple.

As soon as he turned on Eighth he confronted a boy on a bicycle. Harold Lee Murdock was seventeen, fresh-faced, and just setting out to discover his purpose and passions in life. When he looked up and saw Tom Lee holding the double-barreled shotgun, he back peddled the brakes and threw up his hands.

Tom Lee's brain was frizzing out. He saw Murdock and without a single thought, he raised the shotgun and let loose both barrels. Murdock was thrown from the bike. He was peppered in the torso and right arm. Everything stopped for a moment.

Tom Lee looked at the white boy bleeding in the street.

He continued walking. As he walked the shouts and screams from bystanders on the street faded, and the rage and alcohol haze drained down through the soles of his feet.

He had killed a white boy.

Tom Lee had never considered his fate from killing Soles and Moore. All he knew was they deserved killing. But now he had killed a white boy. Things had changed. The police would likely shoot on sight and ask questions later. If they didn't shoot him down in the street, they would surely hang him. Or worse, they would turn him over to vigilantes. They would hang him, and not so efficiently, or castrate him or simply beat him to pieces.

* * *

Officer John Ogletree heard the blast that felled Murdock from a block and a half away. It took him a few seconds to process what he had heard. The morning had been so uneventful he had been lulled into daydreams, and his mind had wandered far afoot.

He turned toward the sound and began to trot in its direction. He quickly calculated the location of the nearest call box, but it was three blocks over in the wrong direction. There was no time to call the station, and blowing his whistle for backup would be useless. He was the only policeman in the Acre that afternoon.

Ogletree lumbered up Grove from the south and spotted a black man with a shotgun as he reached the intersection of Grove and Eighth.

Ogletree had walked the Acre for quite some time and recognized Lee from several minor encounters, usually from breaking up some back-alley craps game or simply rousting him from a drunken stupor on the street.

"Stop right now, Tom Lee!" Ogletree shouted. When he saw the blank stare in Lee's eyes, he drew his side arm.

Ogletree never even saw recognition in Tom Lee's eyes. Lee simply leveled the shotgun at him and squeezed both barrels.

Ogletree was hit and dropped immediately. Still clutching his pistol, he rolled over and crawled to the sidewalk. Turning to face Lee he fired wildly in Lee's direction. Blood poured from his birdshot wounds. He did manage to pull himself into an upright position before passing out from loss of blood.

* * *

B. L. Pope stood in the doorway of the smoke shop on Eighth and could not believe what he had witnessed. A lazy afternoon had suddenly erupted in gunfire. He had been so lost in thought he didn't notice Lee or

Ogletree until the sound of the shotgun tore through his head.

He looked up in time to see the policeman drop, crawl, and return fire. The black man toting the shotgun was already walking away. Pope rushed to the fallen officer and retrieved his gun. While he reloaded the pistol, he thought it odd that the black man seemed to be walking in no hurry or sense of urgency. He reloaded and took two steps into the street and fired in the retreating man's direction. Pope was a pawnbroker and had only ever handled a pistol to examine its condition and worth. The shots flew wild and were as likely to hit a bystander as Lee.

Tom Lee continued walking, his mind a blind frenzy.

* * *

Bob Grimes heard the gunfire from inside his saloon, the Brewery Exchange Bar, on Eighth and Grove. He walked straight into Lee's path.

Lee spotted Grimes out of the corner of his eye, turned and fired. Lee was more than half a block from Grimes, and the saloonkeeper was only hit in the ankle. He quickly hobbled back inside the saloon.

* * *

An unexpected calm flowed through Lee. He no longer felt helpless, he no longer felt powerful, he felt resigned. Whenever Lee was overwhelmed with hopelessness his mind always went to the same place. His grandmother. As a child he would sit on his grandmother's back porch and play while she shelled peas or sewed in her chair.

Lee began to hum at first. Slowly the words began to form, and he sang one of his grandmother's songs.

> God's settin' happy on His throne
> De Angel dropped his wings en moan
> I'm tired uv yo' wicked ways
> I'm tired uv yo' wicked ways
> God's gittin' tired uv yo' wicked ways
>
> Go down, Angel, en bolt de do'
> Dat time whut's been shan't be no mo'
> I'm tired uv yo' wicked ways
> I'm tired uv yo' wicked ways
> God's gittin' tired uv yo' wicked ways

Walk en yo' room en fall on yo' knees
It's Lord, have mercy ef you please
God's worryin' wid yo' wicked ways
God's worryin' wid yo' wicked ways
God's gittin' worried wid yo' wicked ways

Silver shall tinkle en gold shall ruin
God is getting' worried wid yo' wicked coin'
God's worryin' wid yo' wicked ways
God's worryin' wid yo' wicked ways
God is gittin' worried wid yo' wicked ways

Go to church en weep en moan
Jes' well's ter plead as to stay at home
God's worryin' wid yo' wicked ways
God's worryin' wid yo' wicked ways
God is gittin' worried wid yo' wicked ways

Time, Time, Time is windin' up
Time, Time, Time is windin' up
Oh, destruction is dis lan', God's done moved His han'
En Time is windin' up

Oh, when I am er dyin'
I don't want nobody to moan
All I want yer to do fer me
Is jes' give dat bell a tone

Den I'll be crossin' over
I'll be crossin' over
Den I'll be crossin' over
Jesus gonna make up my dyin' bed

In life, Tom Lee had no control. Life had denied him his fundamental right of manhood. Death was coming. It had topped the horizon, but that was all right. In death, Tom Lee had a say. In death, Tom Lee had control.

✳ ✳ ✳

Anne Colton busied herself about the kitchen. The ingredients and implements for making and baking the cake for tonight's birthday celebration sat on the counter. Anne busily prepared the stew; the cake would have to wait until David returned with the flour. She was still slightly mad at herself for letting the pantry run low on such an everyday staple. She had hastily sent David out on the errand over an hour ago. Her anger was rising, as he should have already been back.

Anne's spine stiffened and the hairs on her arm stood up. She left the kitchen and slowly walked to the front door. She stared out the screen looking at the walk. The street was empty. Birds chirped and dogs barked, but Anne did not hear them. She reached out, opened the screen door, and stepped onto the porch.

She stood staring straight ahead into the yard and street, frozen with dread. After several moments she began to walk down the steps, just as a Chaparral motorcar pulled up and screeched to a halt. Two men, one a policeman, were in the car. The policeman stepped out of the car and approached Anne.

"Someone has already told you?" asked the policeman. Anne just kept walking to the automobile. "We came as quick as we could. He will be fine, I'm sure. It is a terrible thing."

The policeman helped Anne into the automobile and they sped away.

※ ※ ※

After Lee had disappeared down the street, Grimes reemerged from his saloon and went to Ogletree's aid. Pope was attempting to halt the rush of blood, but the birdshot had left multiple wounds. A man pulled up in his automobile and offered to take Ogletree to Saint John's. By now a crowd had gathered, and it took several men to carefully place Ogletree in the rear of the car.

"What in tarnation happened?" came a voice in the crowd.

"There is a nigger with a shotgun on a rampage," shouted Grimes.

There was an audible intake of breath from the crowd.

"I returned fire but he was too far away," continued Grimes.

"He headed that a way." Pope turned in the direction Lee had fled and pointed. "Toward the rail yards."

"Well, let's get the boy!" said another voice from the crowd.

"Aye!" came a collective shout. The crowd was quickly turning into a mob and was growing larger by the minute.

A more calm and subdued voice questioned, "Where are the police? Shouldn't we call for the police?" The voice was barely audible above the rumble of the mob.

"The police were here and he was gunned down in the street! Let's go get him!"

Another cry of "Aye!" went up along with raised fists and a few brandished pistols. The mob turned as one and headed off in pursuit of Tom Lee.

* * *

The call came in to the station and was answered by the duty officer at the desk. Lee had been loose on the streets for over thirty minutes. The officer jotted down a few notes, hung up the phone, and hurried into Chief O. R. Montgomery's office.

"There is a report of a negro armed with a shotgun shooting up the Acre," said the officer. "Two people have been shot down and taken to hospitals. He was last seen on Eighth."

Montgomery stared at the officer. "Shooting up the Acre."

"Yes, sir," said the officer. "More than one man shot, at least two different establishments. It is not exactly clear what is going on."

"Who is available? Never mind, I want every man available. Now!" The officer scrambled. Chief Montgomery grabbed his gun and holster and followed close behind. "Every man out front, load up!"

* * *

Tom Lee entered the rail yards and made straight for a thicket of trees. He had been on a spree for well over thirty minutes and amazingly, no one had made more than a slight attempt at stopping him. The mob was well behind him, but he could hear them.

The yard was empty as far as he could see. As he approached the thicket he turned and saw the mob now not fifty yards behind him. He disappeared into the high weeds and bull nettles.

* * *

"There he is!" shouted Grimes. The mob moved as one and quickly formed a semicircle around the thicket. It was dense with trees and brambles, and they could not make out Lee's position, but they were sure he was in there. The mob had tracked Lee with enthusiasm and gusto, but now that they had him cornered, their fervor faded. No one really wanted to barrel into the thicket after an armed man that had already proven a willingness to kill anything that moved.

However, no one really wanted to say they didn't want to dive in, either. There was a bit of hemming and hawing.

The two carloads of policemen pulled up to the edge of the yard, dismounted, and ran to the mob.

"What is going on?" demanded T. N. Blanton. Blanton was a former police captain. He spent much of his time at the station, reliving his days in uniform and helping out when needed. Even though he was no longer on the force, no one thought much about it when he had grabbed a gun out of the arms cabinet and loaded into one of the cars along with every other available officer at the station.

"He is holed up in there somewhere," offered Grimes. "It seemed a might foolish just to run in blind." Grimes seemed to wait for affirmation from Blanton. None was forthcoming.

"I saw him shoot John Ogletree down in the street with no warning or cause. He is mad and dangerous."

"Well, he ain't coming out of his own accord and offer us brisket, now is he?" Blanton did not wait for a reply. He moved to the head of the mob, turned, and motioned for the policemen to fan out.

"Come on, boys, let's go in after him!" he shouted, and then blindly charged the thicket.

The other policemen had by now gathered time enough to assess the situation, and their sentiments were more in line with the mob's. They charged into the thicket anyway.

* * *

Tom Lee had not been waiting on the mob and police to charge. There was a culvert running under the Fort Worth and Denver rail yards only a short distance from the thicket. He had been weighing his odds of making the run to the culvert without one of the mob on the periphery of the thicket shooting him down. He had about summoned the courage to make the run when Blanton charged. Now was his chance.

He broke from the brambles as the police and mob entered the tangle. He disappeared into the culvert just as Blanton and a few of the others emerged on the other side.

"Dammit, where did he go?" shouted Blanton.

The men, relieved not to have run straight in to the business end of a shotgun barrel, regained their bravado and cursed their luck at not having been the one to gun down their quarry.

An engineer on a slow-moving freight train spotted Tom Lee coming out the other side of the culvert. Spying the fleeing black man and police running frantically in circles, he blew his train whistle in an attempt to signal the posse.

Officer Garrison and a small group from the mob heard the whistle and ran towards the train. They spotted Lee in the mouth of the culvert, and Garrison squeezed off two rounds. At fifty yards or more his pistol was wildly inaccurate. Lee had two choices. He could run to another culvert not forty feet distant that would provide cover, or he could break for the river bottoms about five times the distance.

He headed to the culvert and disappeared into only temporary safety.

The second culvert was much smaller than the first. Tom Lee dropped to his hands and knees and crawled into the darkness. As he slopped through the mud and muck, the culvert seemed to close around him the farther he crawled. Tears running down his cheeks, Tom Lee began to whisper, "Walk en yo' room en fall on yo' knees, It's, Lord, have mercy ef you please, God's worryin' wid yo' wicked ways, God's worryin' wid yo' wicked ways, God's gittin' worried wid yo' wicked ways. Don't let them burn me Lord, don't let them burn me. Please, oh Lord, don't let them burn me."

His words turned to whimpers.

He turned sideways in the culvert. His back to the wall, Lee broke open the shotgun and looked at his final two shells in the barrels. Turning his head upwards he saw not the mold on the top of the culvert but the open sky of heaven.

All the men had regrouped and were slowly approaching the culvert. Even Blanton seemed to be wary of the prospect of crawling in single file and on hands and knees.

A shotgun blast echoed from the tunnel. The mob and police hunkered down; two men dropped to their bellies like they had been felled by an anvil. Everyone looked at one and other and then back into the darkness of the tunnel.

May 16, 1913
Dallas Morning News

Negro Kills Two; Wounds Four Others
Policeman John Ogletree One Of Tom Lee's Victims in
Wholesale Shooting Mob Plans Frustrated
Small Army of Officers Guard Black,
Who Is Also Injured by Own Bullets
Early Morning Situation

Special to the News

Fort Worth, Tex. May 16. – Bent upon having the Lee negro placed in its hands, the stubborn mob that has hung about the county jail for several hours was only slightly weakened this (Friday) morning at 12:40 o'clock, when the last street cars ran. Most of the spectators left prior to the midnight hour, but the mob participants are holding on becoming impatient, at 1:15 o'clock.

Regardless of the efforts of the county officials and the police to maintain order, several outbreaks late have resulted almost seriously. Policeman Boyd was struck on the forehead by a rock thrown from the crowd, and painfully hurt.

A Belknap street car was attacked by more than a hundred angered men, three negroes stoned and beaten and almost every window glass in the car shattered.

The mob has not been pacified by the statements that the Lee negro is not in the jail. A long steel rail was brought to the front of the jail shortly before 12 o'clock.

Militiamen under the command of Major Elliott took charge of the situation at the jail at 12:30 a.m. The militia was ordered out at the call for aid by Sheriff Rea.

Special to the News.

Fort Worth, Tex., May 15 – Two men were killed, one of them a policeman, and four others were seriously wounded when Tom Lee, a negro, ran amuck in the southwestern outskirts of the business section of Fort Worth this afternoon. Tonight a mob failed in its attempt to take Lee from the county jail.

The dead:

JOHN A. OGLETREE, policeman of 908 Missouri avenue.

WALTER MOORE, negro express wagon driver.

The wounded:

Lee Murdoch, white school boy of 17, residing at 811 Florence street, shot through the body; probably will recover.

David Colton, white boy of 18, residing at 308 Adams street, scalp wound, right arm punctured, wound on the body, condition serious.

Peter Soles, negro, shot in upper part of body.

Tom Lee, negro, lower part of face shot away.

Mob Plans Frustrated

When Lee was captured he was conveyed to the county jail, where a strong guard was stationed. At 9 o'clock tonight a mob of about 1,000 men and boys gathered at the jail and endeavored to obtain admittance. About twenty-five deputy Sheriffs and policemen were then on guard. They reported that the wounded negro had been removed.

The mob did not believe this and a committee was admitted to search the interior. It reported that Lee was not in the prison. This report did not stop the clamor. Half a dozen policemen and Deputy Sheriffs stood guard on the high steps leading to the entrance. The crowd pressed these closely and demanded the right to pass to the landing half a story above the street, where the front door is located. The officers pressed back those on the steps. One man called for another committee to search the jail and received twenty responses. The officers finally ordered the man to get down off the steps and he did so.

The men slipped around to the rear of the jail and began an attack on the door there with a battering ram consisting of a piece of heavy timber. They had pounded on the door about five minutes when Sheriff Rea, from within, ordered them to desist and threatened to open fire. This brought a defiant response. Then a pistol was discharged from inside the walls and part of the mob lost its enthusiasm.

Mob Renews Efforts

At 11 o'clock the mob in front of the county jail was augmented by 500 people from Ninth street, the scene of today's tragedy. The mob on Ninth street attacked the negro Masonic Hall corner on that street and Jones avenue, shattered window frames and did other damage.

The negro saloons in that locality were wrecked by having their front windows and other glassware broken. At the jail the mob attempted to force an entrance at 11 o'clock. The members of the attacking party resorted to throwing stones. Sheriff Rea was struck on the head by half a brickbat but was not seriously injured. Several window glasses were smashed. A rush was made to gain the main entrance where the policemen and Deputy Sheriffs were stationed outside the building, but it was discouraged by Chief Deputy Estes, who threw two men bodily off the high steps into the top of a tree and clubbed several others. He drew his revolver, but did not use it. A policeman leveled his six shooter at the crowd and said he would kill the next one who threw a brick. Sterling P. Clark, former Sheriff, attempted to make a speech to assure the gathering that the negro had been removed from the jail, but he was hooted down.

Lee Used Shotgun

Lee used a breech loading shotgun and his shells carried turkey shot, which are almost as large as buckshot. He seemed to have been well supplied with ammunition and frequently reloaded his weapon.

The trouble started at a lunch stand on Eighth street, between Calhoun and Jones street, where Soles was shot as he was eating a piece of barbeque meat. This was about 2 p.m.

After leaving the lunch stand, Lee entered a negro pool hall between Eighth and Ninth streets, on the east side of Jones street. Twenty negroes were congregated there, some seated at tables playing dominoes, some playing pool and others loafing.

Frank Cooper, known as Stump, was in a chair near the entrance. Lee leaned over him and raised his shotgun.

"Look out," said Lee, and he fired point blank at Moore, who was about eight feet from the muzzle of the gun. The charge of the gun struck Moore in the right side of the head. He collapsed and slid to the floor, sprawling there, and died in two minutes.

Reloading the empty chamber of his gun, Lee cocked both hammers and covering the crowd of excited blacks, backed out of the door.

General Stampede Follows

In the meantime a general stampede was in progress. The panicky negroes scattered in all directions and tore their way through screened windows and narrow doors.

Reaching the Jones street sidewalk Lee, clutching his cocked gun, hurried north to Eighth street and turned east to Grove. Policeman Ogletree, who had heard the shooting, was hastening to the spot from which the report emanated when he encountered Lee near the corner of Eighth and Grove streets.

Ogletree was near the middle of the street and the negro was on the sidewalk. Without pausing, pistol in hand, the policeman advanced toward the negro. Lee raised his gun and fired both barrels, the charges of turkey shot lodging in the policeman's body above his hips, making many wounds in his chest and abdomen.

As he fell, Ogletree fired four times at the negro, but the bullets went wild. The officer died on the way to the hospital.

After this encounter Lee turned northwest and fled at the top of his speed toward the railroad yards. B. L. Pope, who saw the policeman fall, seized the latter's weapon and, after reloading the empty chambers, sent six bullets after the negro, but they missed.

Crowd Starts in Pursuit

By this time a crowd had gathered at the spot where the officer fell and many pursued the fugitive on foot, but he out distanced them.

Tom Wren came up in his automobile. It was quickly loaded with officers and armed citizens and was soon speeding in the direction taken by the negro. Veering toward the Rock Island yards at Fourth street, the officers saw the negro dash into the mouth of a culvert which led under the railroad tracks. He was hidden from view after entering the culvert and they believed he intended making his last stand there. They were dismounting and preparing to close in when a muffled report came from the interior of the culvert.

Victim of Own Bullet

An investigation revealed that the negro had shot his chin and lower part of his face into a pulp with his own weapon. Whether the self-inflicted wound was intentional or accidental could not be learned, as the fugitive was speechless when picked up. Some claimed that, realizing escape was impossible and fearing lynching, he had shot himself; others that he slipped on the wet floor of the culvert and the weapon was accidentally discharged.

Lee was first carried to the hospital but soon afterward was removed to the county jail where precautions were taken against violence. Several reports that he had died were circulated, but at 7 o'clock it is known that he was still alive.

Two Boys Wounded

The two boys, Murdoch and Colton, were wounded during the general excitement near the spot where the policeman was killed. It is not known which of the boys was shot first. The Murdoch boy's condition is so serious that he has not been allowed to talk.

Bullets entered the right forepart of the Murdoch boy's body and several ranged upward into the liver and the under part of the right lung. According to the physician at the Medical College Hospital, where Murdoch was taken, the boy will probably recover.

Colton was taken to All Saints' Hospital. According to Colton's mother, the boy was shot when he made an effort to get out of the way of flying bullets by falling to the ground. He said he saw the negro aiming at a person running about two blocks ahead. Just as he dropped to the ground a bullet struck him in the back. Thinking there was no further danger, the boy said he arose and was struck by bullets from a shotgun. He was shot in the back breast, arms and head. His condition is thought to be more serious than was first reported.

Cause of Trouble Unknown

Chief of Police Montgomery said he had not been able to learn the cause of the shooting. It is not known where the negro Lee obtained the weapon. He had two loaded shells in his pocket when found.

"Lee shot the first negro in a lunch stand on Eighth street," the Chief said. "He went to the pool hall on Jones and opened fire on another negro. He ordered the crowds to stand back while he re-loaded his gun. Leaving the pool hall, Lee rushed along the street, meeting Ogletree at the corner of Eighth and Groves. Reports of the shooting came to the police station almost immediately and when we got to where Ogletree was killed, the negro had fled."

Justice Peden held the inquest over the dead policeman and Justice Maben conducted the inquiry into the deaths of the negroes.

Chief Montgomery had managed to wrestle Lee from the mob at the culvert and transport Lee to the Medical College at Fifth and Throckmorton. The police had a slight advantage over the mob in that they were all in cars and the mob, for the most part, were on foot. This lead quickly evaporated as word spread that Lee was alive and his wounds were being treated.

Dr. R. B. West emerged from the examining room where he had been administering to Lee. Chief Montgomery and Deputy Ben Thompson were anxiously waiting. "Is he still alive?" asked Montgomery.

"Yes," replied Dr. West.

"Som bitch don't know what's best for him," muttered Deputy Thompson. Montgomery shot him a quick glare but both men knew the best outcome for Lee was to have died at the railroad yards. The longer he held to life the likelier it would be that he met his end at the hands of the mob.

"Is he well enough to move?" inquired Montgomery.

"He isn't well enough for anything," said the doctor. "But he is as well as he's going to be with half his lower jaw shot off."

Chief Montgomery called for one of the officers who had been guarding the front door to the Medical College. "What is the situation out front?"

"I reckon there is close to a thousand men out there."

Montgomery grunted his dissatisfaction at the news and paced. "Tell them Lee is dead. Order them to go home."

"Yes, sir." The officer stood there for a second. He wanted to ask if the news was true but quickly decided it was best not to know for sure.

The ruse worked, and most of the mob dispersed. Montgomery, Thompson, and a few of the officers smuggled Lee out the back while the rest of the police and deputies shooed away the mob's remaining stragglers.

* * *

When the automobile arrived at the county jail with Lee, Montgomery was relieved to see no angry citizens milling about. They drove to the back and unloaded the stretcher through the kitchen door.

"Take him to the infirmary," directed Montgomery.

"Why, Chief? Why even bother to keep him alive just to be hanged?" said one of the accompanying officers.

"It is our job," Montgomery shot back. The burning in his eyes let the officer know there would be no further discussion.

This did not, however, quell the officer's burning anger. In his opinion, they should have let the mob take Lee back at the Medical College and have been done with the whole affair. More than one of the rank and file felt the same.

The Klan was a sleeping giant at the time. It was no longer a formal organization in Fort Worth, but the racial sentiments that bound the members of the Klan in the late 1800s had not subsided. A call came in to the station from Bud Daggett, an acknowledged one-time Klan member. Information was exchanged. Within minutes, word spread through the bars of the Acre and the more high-toned saloons of the north side that Lee was still drawing breath and ensconced in the county jail. It only took half an hour for the throng to gather both in front and rear of the county lock-up, and this time they were fully liquored up and blood blind.

May 17, 1913
Dallas News

Effort To Get Negro Followed By Riot
Damage To Business Houses in Three City Blocks
Estimated At $14,000.
Lee Not Seriously Shot
Four Victims of Black Slayer Are Believed
to Be Out of Danger

Special to the News.

Fort Worth, Tex. May 16. That portion of the business section adjacent to Jones, Eighth and Ninth streets, connecting about three blocks and occupied exclusively by negro merchants, tradesmen and bankers, had much the appearance this morning of a Kansas town the day after being struck by a cyclone.

Few stores had any front glass left in their window frames, the bank owned and operated by negroes in the corner of the negro Masonic Temple had a gaping orifice in front where its plate glass window had been; two saloons had their fronts completely demolished and the entire stocks and fixtures had been removed and destroyed. Barber shops, groceries, pool halls, an undertaking establishment, rooming houses and various concerns, all operated by negroes, had their glass fronts smashed and frequently their contents had been destroyed.

Saloons Suffer Most

The two saloons, one at the corner of Ninth and Jones, suffered heaviest in the loss of stock. Mobs raided them twice during the night and carried off or destroyed all liquor available. The estimate of the total loss in the negro quarter is about $8,000, although some are inclined to place it as high as $14,000.

The negro Masonic Temple is a neat structure of pressed brick and is several stories high. Many glass therein were broken and other damage was done. Numbers of small tradesmen had all their goods, which represented their total possessions destroyed by the mob. They stood in the gaping doorways of their wrecked buildings this morning and looked through doors or windows which had no glass or frames in them.

Estimate of Damage

The damaged section was roped off by the police just as it is done at a fire and the greater portion of the negro business quarter was entirely out of commission. One estimate places the damage as follows:

Building belonging to the Moore estate, Ninth and Jones $6,700

Temple Building $1,200

Dunbar Building Jones street $5,000
R.C. Houston, undertaker $300
S.S. Shepard, tailor, 409 Ninth street $25
J.J. Johnson, barber shop, 900 Jones street $200
Tom Touchett, 902 Jones street $20
One Minute Café, 307 Ninth street $15
W.H. Holland, barber shop, 305B Ninth street $10
Mexican chili stand, 305 A Ninth street $10
L. Kantovich, grocer, 914 Jones street $150
Pool hall, 912 Jones street $250
Fred Earl, tailor, 910 Jones street $200
906A and 906B Jones street $20
1310 Jones street $10
1312 Jones street $10
Church at Jones and Thirteenth streets $50
1404, 1406, 1408, 1410 and 1412 Jones street $50
315 East Fourteenth street $20
131 Calhoun street $20
Mexican restaurant 304 Eighth $10
McCampbell's barbecue stand 306 Eighth street $25
208, 310 and 312 Eighth street $30
Total $14,415

Another estimate places the total losses at just half the foregoing. Some of the property is owned by white people, although occupied by negroes. The Masonic Temple and the bank therein are the property of the most law abiding negroes in the city.

Damage to Jail Slight

Only slight damage was done to the county jail during the mob's visit last night. A number of small window panes were broken, an iron fence was overturned and there was some injury to the shrubbery. The pounding on the rear door with a battering ram did little or no damage. Sheriff Rea, who was struck by a brick thrown by a member of the mob, suffered little inconvenience from his wound today. He was at the court house attending to his duties as usual and made careful preparation to be ready in the event of another visitation tonight.

As a result of the mob demonstration, a negro minstrel troupe which had pitched its tent near Jones street and had advertised to give two performances took down its tent early last night and the performers, about twenty in number, remained in their special show car on a siding in the railroad yards.

Reports obtained today are that Tom Lee, the negro who shot and killed Policeman Ogletre and Walter Moore, a negro, and shot four other persons yesterday afternoon, is not seriously wounded, notwithstanding the statements made last night that Lee would not live the hour. It is said that the negro's wounds are not serious and that he will recover promptly.

Wounded Will Recover

Lee Murdock, the 17 year old school boy who was wounded, was removed from Medical College Hospital to All Saint's Hospital, where he is reported to be improving. David Colton, also at All Saints, will recover.

Pete Soles, the first negro shot, is thought to be clear of danger.

The two negroes wounded late yesterday afternoon in another shooting affray on Bryan Avenue are still regarded to be seriously hurt. Alice Little, the negress, is not expected to live.

Citizens Condemn Mob Action

About 100 of the most prominent and substantial citizens of the city met at the Chamber of Commerce tonight and by resolution condemned the action of last night's mob, commended the Sheriff and police for defending the jail and demanded that an investigation be held to determine why the police did not check the rioters on Ninth and Jones streets and also why officials accepted minimum fines of $1 each from those who pleaded guilty of participation in the disturbance.

R.D. Gage, vice president of the First National Bank, introduced a set of resolutions deploring mob violence, condemning officers for not checking it and proffering the services of all present to the Sheriff or Mayor to suppress mobs, but after long discussion a substitute by L.H. Burney was adopted.

Among those at the meeting were H.H. Lassiter, Leon Gross, Dr. John Rice, Burk Burnett, William Capps, Marion Sansom, Mayor Milam, J.W. Flournoy, L.H. Burney, B.B. Paddock, R.D. Gage and Paul Waples. Mr. Flournoy presided.

Many speeches were made and it was intimated that the city would have to pay the losses sustained by the riot victims.

Mayor Milam and Chief Montgomery explained that the police were engaged in defending the county jail when the mob stormed the negro business houses and banks at Ninth and Jones streets.

Many pointed questions were asked of the Mayor and Chief.

The last speaker was Police Commissioner Bob Davis, who assured those present that he was doing all he could to suppress lawlessness.

N. H. Lassiter told him that it would be a good idea for him to use every effort to suppress the hoodlum element in Fort Worth and begin when it manifests itself on Halloween night, Christmas eve and other occasions when near rioting prevails.

Among other things the resolutions contain the following:

"Resolved, That we feel that the perpetrators of last night's affair should not only be published, but that our citizens should subscribe to a fund to restore the stolen and destroyed property of innocent victims.

"Resolved, That we ask all good citizens to lend their efforts to suppress all such unnecessary and inexcusable mob violence in the future in order to protect the fair name of our city.

"We think that last night's proceedings were monstrous for a civilized community, and we know that none but a small, vicious minority of our people do or will in the least condone this action.

"Our hope lies in the vigorous prosecution of these villains, and we offer our services and funds to our Grand Jury and officers to this end.

"Resolved further, That we think the time is opportune to investigate whether the officers, whose duty it is to suppress crime on our streets and among our negroes and others, have been diligent."

May 17, 1913
Dallas News

Grand Jury Indicts Negro
Judge J.W. Swayne Instructs Body to Investigate and Act as Result of Mob Damage

Special to the News

Fort Worth, Tex., May 16. – Tom Lee, the wounded negro prisoner whose life was sought by a mob at the county jail last night, was indicted today by the Seventeenth District Court Grand Jury on the charge of murdering Policeman John A. Ogletree and Walter Moore.

The indictments were returned this morning after short deliberation.

Officers claim that the negro prisoner was removed from the jail early last evening. It is also claimed that he and two other negroes who were convicted on murder charges several months ago were taken from Fort Worth to Dallas or some other town early this morning in an automobile.

Five young men, or boys, alleged to have been members of last night's mob were brought before Justice Maben today on the charge of disturbing the peace. They entered pleas of guilty and were fined $1 each and costs, amounting to about $16. Two others were fined in the Police Court.

Impressed with the gravity of the destruction wrought by the mob of young men and boys which raided the negro business section last night and destroyed several thousands of dollars' worth of property, Judge James Swayne of the Seventeenth District Court today delivered a special charge to the Grand Jury of his court to investigate fully and return indictments against every person who participated, if names could be obtained.

Judge Swayne's Instructions

Judge Swayne instructed that indictments be returned against the offenders for unlawful assembly and rioting. The Grand Jury was taken in a body to view the ruins of the stores, saloons, shops and other buildings. The Court's charge was as follows:

"I was before you this morning and at that time asked you to return a bill of indictment as quickly as possible against Tom Lee, the negro who did the killing yesterday, and I am very much obliged to you for acting promptly in the matter. You have just returned a bill of indictment against him.

"This is as it should be. The Grand Juries of the county and the courts of the county in murder cases should act promptly. There has always been too much delay. It has been my rule and practice since I have been District Judge to never let a criminal case lag, and especially a murder case. I try them quickly, whether high or low. The Constitution guarantees them a speedy trail and it also guarantees society a speedy trail. That is my interpretation of the Constitution.

"Now, gentlemen, I have sent for you for another purpose. Since I was before you this morning privately some very estimable citizens have called my attention to the outrageous conduct of the mob on Ninth street against some of our respectable negro population. It was my lot to be one of the officials present at the jail last night when the mob attempted to take it. You know I charged you a few days ago about some outrageous conduct that had been committed by people in high places. I charged you then that no man was too high when he did wrong. I charge you now that no man is so low that his conduct should not be investigated when he is a violator of the laws of the State.

"This so-called mob last night at the jail was not comprised of good citizens, but of a lot of hoodlums—men without standing, men who were influenced by drink—and with it were a lot of hoodlum boys. There were very few among the mob who amounted to anything, except those who were from curiosity."

Purpose of Mob

"Those that composed the mob cannot say that they were not there for unlawful purposes, because, as the law directs, it became my duty as one of the Magistrates of this State to call upon them to disperse and tell them what the law is, and I did this in no uncertain terms, and after they failed to disperse each and every one of them was guilty of the conduct of the other, whether he participated in it or not.

"Their conduct at the jail and their conduct against the respectable negroes on Ninth street was absolutely indefensible. Some of the negroes who were damaged own their own property; some of them have been good citizens ever since they have lived here and at all times have tried with all their power to encourage the enforcement of the law among their race. One of the negroes whose property was destroyed, who came to Fort Worth many years ago, has, by his energy, industry and courteous treatment of all people, accumulated quite a fortune for a negro. I have known him since he was a boy. He and I were children together in the old state of Tennessee. When I went there this morning and saw the depredation committed on his property, on the bank of which he is president, and on the property of other colored citizens there, it was shocking indeed.

"At the noon hour I want you gentlemen of the Grand Jury to go in a body and see the destruction that has been done on East Ninth street. Our business people are shocked. They do not know at what time some mob may be displeased with a certain faction of our estimable citizens and there being no restraint upon this mob composed of lowly men, what restraint might there be when their property was at stake? The humblest citizen we have is entitled to the protection of the law and the protection of the officers.

"If the mob had opened the doors of the jail and gone inside, it would have been the duty of the officers of this county to have fired volleys into their bodies. As much as I regret to say that the life of citizens should be taken, yet, for the protection of society, for the protection of the officers, for the protection of our laws, it sometimes becomes necessary. Fortunately no one was killed.

"Our most esteemed Sheriff while in the discharge of his duties was struck down with a brick thrown by some cowardly cur, and yet the officers refrained from firing."

Notified to Close Up

"The police officers notified the negroes on Ninth street that there might be some trouble and requested them to close their doors at 5 o'clock yesterday afternoon. They complied with the request and left their property there without any protection save by the officials of the city of Fort Worth. Imagine their feelings when they came back this morning and saw thousands and thousands of dollars worth of property destroyed in such a ruthless manner!

"Gentlemen, investigate it! Investigate it thoroughly! It matters not who is guilty, return a bill against them. Each and every man that was in that mob at the jail or on East Ninth street is guilty of an unlawful assembly and guilty of riot. Each one who agrees to go with others is guilty of anything that anyone of the mob may have done. If the Sheriff had been killed, each and every member of that mob would have been guilty of murder. The officers of the city were not able to protect the property on Ninth street because they were up here protecting the jail. They did not expect the mob to go down there and destroy the property of respectable negroes.

"Return bills against all who were in the mob. The advertisement has gone forth of what has been done; let the advertisement go forth that the law abiding white citizens of Tarrant County do not sanction lawlessness in any way: that we protect the low as well as the high, and the high as well as the low."

Funeral of Ogletree

The funeral of John A. Ogletree, the policeman who was killed yesterday, was held at noon today from the home, 908 Missouri Avenue. Rev. E. McShane Waits officiated. The body was taken to Hawkins Cemetery, near Kennedale, for burial.

A special representation from the police department attended the ceremonies.

The pallbearers were Chief Montgomery, former Chiefs J.W. Renfro and June Polk, former Assistant Chief Edward Parsley and former Capts. Bills and Blanton. Commissioners Grant, Allen, Davis and Smith and former Commissioner Mulkey attended the funeral. Crepe was hung over the entrance to the police station today as a mark of respect to the dead policeman.

May 18, 1913
Fort Worth Star-Telegram

Lee Regrets Death of Officer; Glad He Shot Moore
Negro Slayer, Now in Denton Jail, Is Able to Talk
Is Willing to Die

"Just So They Don't Burn Me" He Says–Suffers from Wounds. Loss In Craps Cause
Prisoner Declares He Shot Himself Accidentally–Trial Here Next Week

Denton, Texas, May 17. – Huddled on the floor of his cell in the county jail here where he was brought Friday, Tom Lee, negro slayer of Patrolman John Ogletree and Walter Moore, negro, and who wounded four other men in Fort Worth Thursday afternoon, today expressed his entire willingness to pay the penalty for his crimes.

"Just so they don't burn me," he muttered. "I know I did wrong and now I'm ready to pay for it, just so long as folks down there don't burn me."

Wound Hinders Talking

Because of the gunshot wound in his jaw, it is difficult for the negro [to] talk. The lower part of his face is swathed in bloody bandages and it is with an effort that the man is able to make any coherent statement.

"I just don't remember all that happened Thursday," he said. "I knew down at the jail there was a lot of noise and shouting but I didn't pay any attention to that. Then pretty soon the officers come and put me in an automobile and brought me here."

Hears of Men's Death

Lee did not know that two of his victims are dead and two others are in serious condition until this afternoon, and then he did not express any sorrow for his action, excepting in the case of patrolman Ogletree.

"I just don't remember shooting the policeman," he said, "and I'm sorry I shot him. I didn't mean to. But that 'nigger' Moore and Pete Soles, I just had to shoot. Them two robbed me of about $100 in a game of craps the day before the shooting and I started out to get even. I'm glad I got them."

Willing to Talk

The negro's speech was thick and he interrupted himself several times by gasping from the pain of the wounds in his throat, but he appeared anxious and willing to talk. Physicians attending him are confident he will have recovered sufficiently to be returned to Fort Worth for trial next week. He is kept partly under the influence of opiates but he appears to be suffering intensely all of the time.

Sorry for Ogletree

"No, sir, I'm certainly sorry that I shot Patrolman Ogletree and I didn't mean to shoot those other two white men. That was just an accident. I don't remember much about it, because I was half drunk and was crazy mad. I'm glad though that Moore is dead."

Lee said he did not shoot himself intentionally. He says he shot himself accidentally.

"I was coming out through that sewer," he said, "when I slipped and the gun went off. I don't remember nothing more until the officers put me in that big automobile and started out of town. But I did not shoot myself intentionally."

Lost $100 at Craps

"All this trouble started when Walter Moore and Pete Soles beat me out of about $100 in a crap game. This was Wednesday afternoon and I tried to get them Wednesday night, but couldn't. So I just kept on hunting for them until I found them and then I used the shotgun. I ain't sorry for it, either, excepting for killing the policeman and shooting those two white boys. How are they getting along? I didn't mean to shoot them; they happened to get in the way."

Prisoner Well Guarded

Lee is confined in a separate cell on the top tier of cells in the north wing of the Denton county jail and he is carefully guarded. Sheriff W.C. Orr of Denton county, with two deputies, slept in the jail all Friday night, their cots being placed across the door leading to the tier of cells, in one of which the negro murderer is confined. Sheriff Orr says he does not fear any trouble in Denton but that as the negro has been placed in his charge for protection, he will furnish protection to the utmost.

The slayer of Patrolman Ogletree and Walter Moore appeared little concerned when told of the work of the mob Thursday night and of the attempts made to get him out of the Tarrant county jail.

Fears Burning

"Just so they don't burn me," he repeated over and over again. "I don't want to be burned. Those other niggers aren't worrying me none. I'm in too much trouble myself to worry about them."

Before Lee shot Pete Soles, the first victim of his deadly shotgun, he hunted all over the neighborhood looking for Walter Moore. Moore, however, avoided Lee and when the enraged negro saw Sole sitting in McGar's restaurant he shot him.

"I just walked up to him and took aim and fired," the negro muttered. "Then I got Moore and after that I don't remember nothing much. I was trying to get away and I surely did not mean to shoot that policeman. I didn't know I had shot him until you told me and I don't remember shooting the other white men. I hopes for certain that they will get well alright."

Asks about Death Plans

"But, please, mister, you don't think they'll burn me, back there, do you?" he whimpered, through the bandages covering his mouth and throat. "I'm willing to pay for what I done, but I don't want to be burned."

The negro sank back exhausted. He lies on the floor of his cell, on a pallet fixed for him by Sheriff Orr.

Sheriff Orr says Lee was up and walking about his cell for a time this morning.

Just when the Tarrant county officials will take Lee back to Fort Worth has not been announced, and probably will not be. The officers will probably attempt to smuggle the negro into Fort Worth when his trial is called and he will be surrounded by a strong guard.

Fate Doesn't Bother Him

Lee appears little concerned as to his probable fate. His only fear apparently being that the mob will get him and burn him. He smiled a ghastly sort of smile when he learned that Walter Moore was dead and expressed disappointment when told that Pete Soles probably will recover.

The interview with Lee, the first obtained since the fatal affair of last Thursday, was arranged through the courtesy of Sheriff Rea, County Attorney Baskin and Sheriff Orr of this city. Visitors to

the jail are not permitted to see the negro and he is widely separated from other prisoners, being kept in a top cell.

Guard for Trail

A strong guard of police and deputy sheriffs will surround the
county courthouse and guard the corridors and entrances Friday
when Tom Lee, negro slayer of Patrolman Ogletree and Walter
Moore, a negro, goes to trial in Seventeenth district court.

Every person who enters the courthouse Friday will be
searched for weapons.

No Demonstrations

"The first man who makes a demonstration will be thrown into
jail," Sheriff Rea said Saturday. "There will be no repetition of the
outrageous riots on Thursday night. This negro will be tried swiftly
and justice will be meted out to him, but he will be tried strictly
according to law.

"The courthouse will be guarded as strongly as necessary. If
needs be, I shall make another request upon the governor for state
militia."

How Lee Was Removed

Sheriff Rea Saturday told of the most dangerous moment of the
mob activity at the county jail Thursday night.

"It was when the back door of the jail was battered open," he
said. "The mob did not realize it, but to rush into the jail and capture the negro Tom Lee would have been child's play for them then.

"The door was open two feet. Detective Snow, Constable
Turner and I were the three only guards at the entrance. One
member of the mob hurled a brick that struck me on the top of
the head. I thought that it was all off, but Snow fired his pistol
into the air and this frightened the crowd away. It gave us time
when they scattered to close the door and barricade it."

The sheriff, describing the removal of the wounded negro
slayer of Patrolman Ogletree and Walter Moore, negro, said that
even some members of the guard about the jail were not aware
that the prisoner was being taken away.

> "Members of the state militia did not know that Lee was being
> taken out. The mob had gone. It was 4 o'clock in the morning.
> The negro was taken on a stretcher through the very door that
> the battering ram of the mob had opened, lain on the floor of an
> automobile back of the jail and hurried to Denton."

Every available officer and sheriff had been summoned to the court-house. The mob had swollen to almost a thousand. Fortunately for the few dozen officers defending the courthouse, the body had no head. The mob was angry but unorganized. Faced with a thousand drunk, angry men and boys intent on mayhem of any kind, Montgomery instructed his officers to hold the jail at all costs, left Sheriff Rea in charge, and took two men in his car to rush over to the south side of town, where the three of them fanned out, going door to door, instructing everyone to vacate for the evening. Montgomery knew if they held the jail and denied the mob Lee, eventually they would return to destroy every negro-owned home and business in the neighborhood. Some were reluctant, a few were defiant, but most took heed and fled.

When Montgomery returned from the south side he was relieved Sheriff Rea and the officers still held the jail. Judge James W. Swayne had arrived and was on the front steps attempting to quiet the mob. The mob was having none of Swayne's rhetoric.

"They will come," said Montgomery. "There is no doubt."

Rea and Montgomery stared at each other, silently hoping the other would snatch out of thin air a solution to the lynching that was most assuredly coming.

"Where have you put the nigger?" Rea inquired. "In the infirmary or a cell?"

"He's in a cell," replied Montgomery.

"Jeffers," Rea turned and called for one of his deputies.

Jeffers McIntyre was standing in the hallway with two other deputies. He turned and hurried over to Sheriff Rea. "Yessir."

"Take the prisoner down to the tunnels. Barricade yourself inside with him. Take Mather with you and have him place some boxes and whatever he can find in front of the entrance so it is not noticeable. Tell Mather to return to the rear of the courthouse. You stay with the prisoner until we come for you."

"Yessir." Jeffers hesitated in front of Rea. He seemed none too pleased with these orders.

"Now," said Rea. Jeffers turned and headed to the rear of the court-house to fetch Mather.

Rea turned to face Montgomery. "Give them time to move the nigger and then I say we let a few of them in to search the jail. I don't think they'll find him in the tunnel. Maybe that'll satisfy them and they will leave."

"Are you sure they won't find him?" asked Montgomery.

"Hell, I ain't sure of nothin' except bad things are going to happen tonight. I don't reckon we can stop that, but we can try and keep that boy alive until we hang him." With that Rea turned and went to the doors leading out to the front courthouse steps. He walked outside to confront the mob and stood beside Judge Swayne.

"They are not listening to reason, Sheriff," said Swayne.

"Drunkards rarely do, Judge."

The mob mostly milled around. Most carried rocks and seemed to contemplate what to do with them. Sheriff Rea rightly concluded they would figure out soon the only thing to do with a rock after a while was to chuck it.

"Now listen, men," Rea began. "The man y'all are looking for is not here."

Boos, cuss words, and shouts of "Liar!" rose from the crowd.

"We took him to Dallas for safety. I assure you in due time he will know the justice of a noose." Rea spoke with a stern authority, but the mob would have none of the story. The curses grew louder, and the mob turned restless.

A teenage boy, eager to earn and prove his manhood, leaped up the steps and turned to face the mob. He held in his left hand a thick rope already noosed. "We've no need to wait! I've brought justice with me!" he shouted, raising the noose high over his head.

The mob let out a roar and began to surge up the steps. Sheriff Rea raised his own hands above his head and walked down the steps towards the young man. Stopping two steps above him, Rea began to shout, "Hold on! Hold on! I can prove the prisoner is not here! Hold on!"

The boy turned at looked up at Rea. "How do you propose to do that?" he asked.

"You can come in and see for yourself," said Rea. A few other men began to walk up the steps. Rea put out his hand to signal they stop. "Just this man here," said Rea. "As he seems to speak for all of y'all."

Everyone froze for a moment. The teenager, flush with the power of authority and supposed respect, turned to face the crowd. "No worry, men! If that nigger is in there, I'll drag him out!"

A general roar of approval went up from the crowd.

The boy enthusiastically turned from the crowd and look up to Rea. Rea stared back with cold blue eyes that showed no whites. A little of the bravado seeped out the young man's shoes.

Rea turned and began to walk back up the steps. "Come along, son," he said. The teenager followed, trying to gather back the courage as he climbed the stone steps.

As Rea and the teenager entered the jail, Rea called to one of his deputies. "Take this . . . " he paused, "man down to examine the cells and the infirmary."

Before the deputy could comply, the teenager spoke up, "Naw, I want to see every room on every floor. Y'all ain't gonna fool me. Y'all could have him anywhere." He spoke just a little too loud.

"Fine," Rea waved him off with his hand, "I don't give a shit. Just make it quick. I'm going in my office and having a whiskey. You can walk this whole jail or you can join me. The result will be the same." Chief Montgomery and Sheriff Rea walked off toward Rea's office, leaving the teenager and officer standing and staring. The young man was tempted to have a free whiskey but followed the officer when he took off down the hall.

As Montgomery and Rea entered Montgomery's office the sheriff offered, "That boy couldn't find his ass with both hands."

"This might work," replied Montgomery.

Fifteen minutes later the officer and teenager returned. The young man looked a might sheepish. "I see that noose is still empty," said Rea.

"Yes, sir. That nigger don't appear to be here anywheres."

Montgomery slapped the table with the palm of his hand. "Now go tell the rest of those hooligans we're telling the truth, he's tucked away soundly in Dallas, like we said."

"I will."

The three men walked outside and the young man, the rope hanging limp at his side, told the crowd Lee was not to be found. To Chief Montgomery and Sheriff Rea's dismay, the mob would not accept the answer. Maybe they realized they had sent in a neophyte, or maybe they were just hell-bent for blood. Either way, they began to throw rocks and sticks at the officers atop of the jailhouse steps. The young man scampered away, leaving the noose behind.

"What more do y'all want?" asked Montgomery. "We let you search the jail from top to bottom."

"Let me go! That boy don't know nothing,'" shouted one of the men several steps up.

"Aye!" shouted another. "Let a few grown men in! We'll see how that goes!" shouted another from farther back.

Rea and Montgomery exchanged glances. They really had no choice. Either they let a few more in and risk they find the tunnel or just start firing into the mob. Things were turning south quickly.

"All right, all right!" shouted Rea above the din. "Three men. Three men only. But on one condition. Once they search the jail and find nothing, which is all they'll find, you men break up and go home peaceably."

Shouts of "Aye, aye" floated from the mob. Three men came forward, the first man who spoke up and two others standing directly behind him.

The five men climbed the steps and entered the jailhouse.

"Let's do this shit again," said Rea as he motioned the same officer over to accompany the men on their search.

"Yes, sir," replied the officer.

The three men looked around the jail like they had never been there before, which was actually true for two of them. The third had spent a few nights sleeping it off but still tried to look official.

After the search party headed toward the cells, Rea and Montgomery returned to Rea's office. "Maybe we should have gone with this bunch," said Montgomery. "They show a might more rawhide wisdom than the boy."

"I considered doing just that but thought better of it," replied Rea. "I don't want them comparing stories with the boy, should he stick around. Besides, if they find him, they find him. That would change everything anyway."

"You got a plan if they find the tunnel?" asked Montgomery.

Rea sighed, reached down, opened the bottom left drawer on his desk, and pulled out a bottle. He motioned for Montgomery to fetch two glasses from a file cabinet against the wall. "Truly, and between you and me . . . I sure as shit do not."

The two men sat in silence, sipped their whiskey, and waited.

The three men returned, empty handed, about fifteen minutes later. "The nigger really ain't here," said one. He seemed resigned and ready to call it quits.

"I ain't convinced," said the second. He seemed resolved to continue. "Y'all have done pulled a fast one somehow, some way. I'm set on that."

Rea bowed up to the man. "The fast one we pulled was spiriting him to Dallas. Like we done told you."

"I know what bullshit smells like," said the second man.

Montgomery jumped in, "You didn't find him because he is not here! Now get out there and tell those folks to go home before someone gets hurt bad!"

The three men left the jail and rejoined the mob. Rea and Montgomery watched from the top steps as they talked to the gaggle of men on the lawn. The first man had just walked off shaking his head. The other two, surrounded by the mob, spoke and gestured animatedly, occasionally turning and pointing up the steps. They did not appear to be persuading the mob to disperse.

Over the next hour or so, the mob's energy ebbed. A few hundred or so wandered off. For a while it seemed the mob would die of lethargy. As the minutes ticked away, for every man that deserted, two joined, and the mob began to swell. The men coming in were more drunk and itching for a lynching than the ones wandering away.

New agitators arrived, the shouting and cussing increased. The mob began to boil, and this time there would be no calming them down. All of a sudden, thirty or so men rushed the steep steps in front of the courthouse with a wrought iron fencepost turned into a makeshift battering ram. The officers held the high ground and though outnumbered, managed to keep their backs from being pressed against the large courthouse doors.

For almost fifteen minutes the scrum ebbed and flowed up and down the steps. A few of the mob left the mass of men with bloody and swollen faces. Clubs, sticks, rocks, billy clubs, and leather batons were raised, dropped, and flailed. One of the officers, Deputy Estes, broke from the mass holding one of the mob by the shoulder and crotch, lifted him above his head and tossed him off the top of the steps into a treetop. Estes, a barrel-chested man with tree stumps for forearms, now apart from the mass of men, could see the police were slowly losing the fight. He drew his revolver and fired twice into the air.

The mass of men went stock still and silent.

"I'm done!" shouted Estes. "And will shoot the next bastard that takes a step up these stairs!" Estes cocked his revolver and glared at the mob. No one moved.

Finally the mob retreated down the steps. The four holding the fence post looked especially sheepish. For a few minutes the mob moped around the lawn, unsure of what to do next. The officers on the steps tried to look stern and defiant while desperately catching their breath and resolve. Several officers had been beaten severely. Officer Ike Boyd sustained two blows to the head from flying rocks; the second knocked him out cold. He was dragged into the jail and taken to the infirmary. He would recover but spent the rest of the night in a mental fog. The head injury would deny him the glory of retelling the event from a firsthand perspective, as he lost all recollection of the night.

Word began to circulate through the crowd that Lee had been taken to Dallas and that a mob was gathering there to storm the Dallas jail and lynch Lee. This news seemed to satisfy many of the men and the mob thinned considerably.

Even though word had spread of Lee's departure, the jail still held four negroes, and the crowd was beyond feeling the need for vigilante justice and was more set on satiating a primal bloodlust.

Begrudgingly accepting that Lee was gone, the crowd began to shout for the heads of two other negroes held in the jail on murder charges. Paul Fowler and Ernest Harrison were being held under a death sentence for the murder of Robert Knetsch.

None in the mob, however, seemed too keen on charging headfirst into the barrage of nightsticks wielded by the officers. Enough men were ambling around the courthouse lawn with bloody brows and swollen eyes to dissuade any newcomers from such foolhardiness.

They needed an easier target for their vengeance, and they were suddenly gifted with easy pickins. A street car rattled by not half a block away carrying four black men on their way home from work. They must not have known the situation or surely would have taken a wider berth home. The men were spotted by a few of the mob on the periphery, and they hollered and hooted until more than a hundred gave chase to the trolley.

They caught up on East Belknap and surrounded the trolley and began to violently rock it back and forth. They tipped the trolley on its side and climbed in and pulled the negroes out by hair and legs. The four men stood no chance against the mob and were beaten unmercifully. The majority of the mob was unable to get close enough to inflict injury and soon turned their attention south. The mob, now intent on simple destruction and mayhem, marched south on Commerce Street headed for the negro businesses and homes clustered around Ninth and Jones.

Sheriff Rea and Chief Montgomery could do nothing but stand on the courthouse steps and watch as the lynch mob morphed into a race riot. Montgomery took little solace knowing he had at least cleared out and warned residents to vacate their property. There were still enough stragglers on the lawn that the officers could not abandon the jail and attempt to quell the riot. They would simply have to let the riot run its course.

Montgomery entered the jail and called first the north side and then the south side stations. He ordered every man to the courthouse immediately. He had now gathered every officer in the city, on duty and off, to the courthouse. Seventy-five percent of Fort Worth was now completely unguarded and unprotected.

He quickly formed a flying squad and personally led the men down Commerce in pursuit of the mob. Sheriff Rea and his men stayed behind to guard the jail from the remnants of the mob. For good measure, Rea put in a plea to Austin for the governor to call out the state militia for reinforcements. The officers had fought fiercely but were battered and weary. They needed help and they needed it quickly. There was some discussion about calling in the Texas Rangers, as was normal protocol; however, Rea convinced Governor Oscar Colquitt that the situation called for a little more than the Texas Rangers "One Riot, one Ranger" motto.

＊ ＊ ＊

As soon as Chief Montgomery and his officers arrived in the Acre they fanned out and began, forcefully if necessary, to clear the streets.

"Now, boys, we're your friends," Montgomery shouted. "And we need your help. You aren't doing any good by this. You're not getting the right kind of revenge. I want you boys to go home quietly."

Montgomery led the line of officers into the mob. Most heeded the chief's warning and fled. Those that did not clear out on their own were shoved or found their noggins on the wrong end of a policemen's night stick.

By midnight the Acre was quiet. It was completely destroyed and partially aflame, but it was quiet. Back at the jail, however, the mob's clamor began to rise back up to a raucous pitch.

Around one o'clock fifty men from the Fort Worth Fencibles, who had last been called to service for the Spanish-American War, came marching double time up to the jail. The guard lined up in front of the jail, bayonets attached to Springfield rifles pointed toward the mob.

"No more, boys!" shouted Major Calvin O. Elliot, commander of the Fencibles. "I'm running in any man still here after five minutes."

A few of the more sober of the mob moseyed home, but many if not most defied Major Elliot, although at a good distance from the bayonets. Five minutes passed, but the major did not back up his threat, as the mob seemed broken of fighting spirit.

Inside the Rea's office Chief Montgomery, Sheriff Rea, and a few others assessed their predicament.

"We might make it," said Chief Montgomery.

"What is the situation out back?" inquired Sheriff Rea to an officer walking up from the rear of the jail.

"Mexican standoff, for sure, but quiet," came the reply.

"Even if things hold, we need to move Lee," said Montgomery. "We can't function like this, and that mob isn't going away until he is dead or gone."

"Agreed," said Rea.

"Let's see about smuggling him out of here," said Montgomery. "I think the best plan is to move him to Denton and put out the word he is in Dallas. Throw them off the trail twice."

"Sheriff Rea," called an officer in the doorway. "The attorney general is on the phone asking to speak with you, Sir."

"Be right there," Rea replied. Turning back to Montgomery he said, "You attend to Lee and I'll take the call. It is likely the governor wanting an update on the situation." The two split up in different directions.

*　*　*

Officer McIntyre sat in the tunnel with Lee with only the nightmare of his imagination to fill his head as to the goings on outside. It was damp and dirty, and the two only had about three feet of light thrown by the dim hurricane lantern. Lee moaned and wept from the pain. At least four times McIntyre thought he was in death throes, but Lee continued to whistle breath through the wound in his mouth and jaw. It crossed McIntyre's mind to smother him and be done with the whole trouble. It would only take a second.

McIntyre heard footsteps, which always sent his heart racing, then he heard the unmistakable voice of Chief Montgomery on the other side of the barricaded door. There soon followed three quick raps on the door.

"Open up, McIntyre!" shouted the chief. McIntyre rose and moved the barrels and crates and swung open the door. The chief and two officers entered. "I take it the prisoner is still alive?"

"Yes, Chief," replied McIntyre. "He isn't in the best shape."

"I would not figure so." Turning to the other officers, Montgomery said, "Grab the stretcher, men. Take him to the back exit.

"Go get some food and stretch your legs," he told McIntyre. "It ain't over yet. We still need you."

"Yes, sir. Thank you," McIntyre replied. He almost ran out of the tunnel.

*　*　*

"Is the car outside?" Chief Montgomery asked as he approached the eight officers gather around the back door.

"Yes, Chief," replied one of the men.

"How does it look outside?"

"Quiet but not all clear, I would say. There are twenty, twenty-five men loitering about, last time I checked," answered a second officer.

"How many of our men on the other side?"

"Six," replied the second officer.

The two men carrying Lee rounded the corner behind the chief and approached.

"What y'all going to do with me?" cried Lee. He was difficult to understand, talking with only half a jaw. Every breath and word caused his excruciating pain. "Don't take me out there! It ain't Christian! Don't let them folks burn me! Please!" Lee wept. Seconds later, he had passed out from the pain.

"Well, that's a blessing," said Montgomery. He walked over to make sure Lee had passed out and not died. "You three," Montgomery pointed to the first two men and a third, "are coming with me. We are taking a trip. Give these men a break." The chief motioned to the two men carrying Lee. Two of the three men exchanged places with the stretcher-bearers and readied themselves to make a break for the waiting auto.

When the door opened all the officers walked outside and lifted Lee off the stretcher and into the back of the chief's official automobile. The three officers got in the auto, two in the back with Lee and one in the front. The chief slid behind the wheel, put the already idling auto in gear, and sped off.

The mob had, by now, turned into mere onlookers.

May 30, 1913
Fort Worth Star-Telegram

Alleged Rioter On Trial For Burglary
Negro Saloonkeeper, Joe Patterson Testifies
Against Jack Jobe.
Mob's Work Described
Witness Denies Having Trouble with Ogletree, Slain by Tom Lee

Joe Patterson, negro saloon keeper, on the witness stand in District Judge Buck's court Friday, described the scene of devastation that greeted his eyes late at night May 15, when he went to his East Ninth street saloon to inspect the wreckage wrought by the mob following the murder of Patrolman Ogletree by Tom Lee, negro.

Patterson was the first witness in the trial of Jack Jobe, alias Grundy Jobe, barber, charged with the burglary of Patterson's saloon. It is alleged that Jobe was a member of the mob that broke into Patterson's saloon and the nearby saloon of Hiram McGar, negro, lugged away whiskey, cigars and other merchandise and destroyed liquors and bar fixtures.

Fined $500 Wednesday

Jobe was found guilty of selling whiskey without a license in county court Wednesday. He was fined $500 and sentenced to thirty days in jail. Another charge of unlawful assembly still stands against him in the county court.

Jobe is represented by Tom Bradley of McLean, Scott, McLean & Bradley; R.E. Bratton, ex-county judge, and A.C. Heath, Bratton's law partner.

Patterson said that he had been in the saloon business for eight years and he told of how he had saved his money and invested it in property. His saloon on East Ninth street, he testified, represented the accumulation of eight years in business. The mob totally wrecked it.

Assistant County Attorney Baldwin asked Patterson if he knew John Ogletree, the murdered policeman, in his lifetime, and he answered that he did.

"Did you have any ill feeling against him? Baldwin asked.

Denies Trouble With Ogletree

Bradley vigorously objected to this question and to questions of a similar nature, but Judge Buck permitted the answer. Patterson said he never had any trouble with the policeman.

The negro said that the mob took 'everything loose' in his saloon, carrying away even a suit of clothes. He said that every negro in the settlement had left late in the afternoon on orders from the police. The rooming houses over the stores and saloons, he said, were deserted when the mob was in the neighborhood.

Judge Buck had to rap for order several times during the course of the examination of Van Childers, negro porter in the barbershop of A.L. Benson, 105A Main street, where Jobe was employed.

Negro Causes Laughter

The negro's answers to some of the questions caused boisterous laughter and Judge Buck ordered Deputy Sheriff Wood to bring the next offender before him for contempt of court.

Childers said Jobe appeared in the barbershop early the morning after the riot. Jobe had four quarts of whiskey and a quart of wine, he said, and the negro said he bought a quart of whiskey from him for 50 cents. He said Jobe told him he got the liquor "mud." He said Jobe asked him where he was the night before and when he told him he was at home, Jobe said, "It's a good thing you were."

"Why did you go home early that night," Baldwin asked.

"Ah jes natchelly suspicioned there was goin' to be somethin' doin'," the negro answered, and the spectators shook with glee.

"You drink all the liquor you can get, don't you?" Bradley asked on cross-examination.

Knows When He's Got Enough

"Naw, sah." Childers answered. Ah knows when Ah's got enough, and Ah goes home."

B.F. Barlow, charged with theft of whiskey from Patterson's saloon in connection with the riot, was found not guilty by a jury in county court Friday. Barlow has only one leg and carries a heavy wooden crutch with a wrought iron "heel." A witness testified that he saw Barlow burst in the end of a whiskey barrel with his crutch, but that he did not see him take any whiskey away.

City Detective Tom Jackson testified he saw Barlow on a car with two pints of whiskey and a quart of wine. Jackson said he asked Barlow where he got so much whiskey and Barlow answered that he got it where the negro saloons were wrecked.

1913-1914

THE WOMAN OF NO MAN'S LAND

— 1913 —

June 24, 1913
Fort Worth Star-Telegram

Speight Investigates Escape of 7 Women
Delivery of Monday Night Furnishes Police Mystery—
None Yet Rearrested.

Assistant Chief Speight, in charge of the police department during the absence of Police Chief Montgomery and Commissioner Davis, who are at the Galveston convention of the Texas City Marshals and Chiefs of Police Association, Tuesday began an investigation into the escape of seven women Monday night from the city jail.

Night Sergeant Little reported that when Mounted Officers Traxler and Bills went to the women's ward at 11:30 p.m. they found the doors of the separate cells for white and negro prisoners wide open.

The sole remaining occupant of the ward, a negro woman, said that she was asleep at the time of the escape and did not know how the doors were opened. The prisoners escaped by pushing a screen from a window on the west side of the ward. Only one of the women is white. She is Bessie Williams, who escaped two weeks ago from the jail in a similar manner. None had been arrested Tuesday at noon.

"What in tarnation is going on in this jail?" Assistant Chief Speight paced with purpose in front of the three beleaguered policemen. Although he had posed a question, no one dared answer. Speight was lathered.

"You lawmen are aware of the difference between a jail and a hotel!" Speight drew the "aw" in lawmen out long for emphasis. Finally his angry energy waned and, exasperated, Speight walked behind his desk and sat in his wooden chair. It creaked like a stuck pig from his force and weight. He continued to drill Night Sergeant Little and Mounted Officers Traxler and Bills with an ice-cold stare.

To a man, the three officers wished Speight would continue to yell. Silence meant Speight was thinking. Likely, he was attempting to come up with the absolute worst punishment and/or assignment for the trio. The silence stretched from seconds to well over a minute. Evidently, Speight could not think of something merciless enough to impose on his three minions.

Eventually he closed his eyes, drew a deep breath, and slowly exhaled. With his next breath Speight exclaimed, "Go now and find these women and bring them back. Especially the Williams woman. The six niggers, I do not much care, just bring at least six darky women back to the colored women's ward." Little, Traxler, and Bills stood frozen, not sure if the dressing-down was truly over. They were too afraid to move.

"Now, you imbeciles, now! Before I throw you all in jail for impersonating police officers!"

After the three bulls exited his office Speight opened his left-hand desk drawer, pulled out a half-eaten chaw of tobacco, and took a healthy bite. After chewing vigorously and thoughtfully a half dozen times, he turned his head and spit. His aim and concentration were off kilter and he missed the spittoon by a full six inches, high and to the right. He continued chewing and dropped his head in his hands.

"Shit fire," he said.

Speight did not enjoy being in charge.

June 27, 1913
Fort Worth Star-Telegram

Key, Shaped from Spoon, Opens Jail Doors for Women

The mystery of open doors in the women's ward at the city jail, permitting the escapes of seven women Sunday night, was solved with the arrest Thursday night at Belknap and Houston streets of Bessie Williams, one of the escaped prisoners.

Bessie was taken in custody when she left her place of refuge in "Battercake Flats" to visit a restaurant. At the city jail she took Mounted Police Traxler into her confidence.

"You treat us women prisoners pretty fair," she told the policeman, "and I'll come clean. I opened those doors myself. I did it with this."

"This" was a rude key, ingeniously fashioned from a teaspoon handle. Bessie showed Traxler how she reached through the bars of her cell and unlocked the door with ease. Once in the 'runaround' that borders the cells, it was the work of a moment to open the door of the adjoining cell in which several negro women were confined. The woman surrendered her 'key' and another similar unfinished implement on which she had been at work.

Bessie Williams has a record as a jail breaker. Several months ago when confined in the county jail, awaiting trial on a charge of theft from person, she escaped twice within a few weeks. A spoon was her principal tool. She used it to dig through the west wall of the building.

* * *

Bessie trailed the man since he stepped off the train at the T&P shortly after noon. The mark was middle aged and well dressed. He carried a cane in one hand, and in the other he toted a shiny new leather case with the initials "MPS" sewn on the side. The case was small and Mr. S. carried no other luggage, so he was likely in town only for the day or was returning from a short trip.

Bessie discreetly followed the man through town. He made no stops or acknowledgments but headed directly for Battercake Flats. Since he made his way into the Flats directly he likely was not a local; he was too well dressed to live there, which gave Bessie hope she had chosen well. Once in the Flats he beelined for Potters Grocery and Mercantile, which was not as Bessie had hoped. She had preferred Mr. S would head for a saloon or even one of the female boarding houses where she could have fleeced him after he had gotten good and drunk.

No matter, he was in her bailiwick now, loaded for fun in the Flats or the Acre with a gold pocket watch chain hanging from his vest pocket and likely a fat wallet, both of which Bessie planned on lifting.

As soon as Bessie stepped into Potter's Grocery and Mercantile, Abe Potter, old man Potter's son, spotted Bessie and quickly approached.

"You need to scat, Bessie. You have no business here," he said, moving from the back counter toward Bessie waving his arms and making a show like the mayor in a parade.

"I have business here like any other, Abe." Bessie's ire was up. Abe wasn't too good to visit Bessie or one of the other soiled doves in the back alleys or shotgun shacks of the Acre, but they could not do business in his daddy's store? Where did he think his daddy's store was, Main and Exchange? Hell, no, he was on Franklin Street, and his money came from the drab rabble of the back alleys and saloons surrounding his mercantile. She was about to school young Abe on a thing or two about manners and courtesy. For a moment the mark from out of town simply became a wide-eyed bystander.

"I got a right to be in here, Abe, as much as any!"

Abe had figured, and rightly so, that his well-heeled customer was a mark for Bessie and was not having him fleeced on his floorboards before he could get to him. "Not today, you don't. I said out!"

The two met in the middle between the corn meal and molasses and began to scrap. Abe swung and missed, and that figured to be his one and only chance as Bessie wheeled, pulled a shred of metal from somewhere on her person, and dug a hunk of flesh from poor Abe's neck.

At the first sight of blood the mark hugged the wall all the way round to the door and fled shouting down Franklin Street. With this commotion a crowd began to gather in the doorway and in the street. With her afternoon now wasted, Bessie became double wild and pounced on poor Abe with all the fury of a gulf hurricane.

By the time Officer Traxler made his way through the crowd and into Potter's Grocery, the place was a wreck, and a plucked hen was in better shape than poor Abe.

August 15, 1913
Fort Worth Star-Telegram

Woman Jail Breaker "Beats" Police Case
Bessie Williams, Who Defies Locks with Spoons, Acquitted
on Charge of Disturbing Peace.

Bessie Williams, queen of jail breakers, "beat" a case in police court late Thursday. She was tried on a charge of disturbing the peace in a Franklin street grocery store. The acquittal was a triumph for Bessie.

Several times the woman has picked her way out of both the city and the county jails. Once she dug out of the county jail with a pewter spoon; once she unlocked the cell door in the woman's ward at Central police station with a key she had fashioned from the handle of a spoon.

A specially made lock has been fitted to the door of the woman's ward at Central police station because of Bessie's escapes.

September 27, 1913
Fort Worth Star-Telegram

Where, Oh Where Is Bessie? She Escapes Eighth Time
It's Getting to be Mere Routine News When Prisoner Flees.

Looking for something newsy to read? Turn to the market page and read the Savanna naval stores quotations.

This story is nothing but a formal report that Bessie Williams has escaped jail again.

Bessie's last previous escape was Sunday. That was her seventh escape since she dug out of the county jail with a pewter spoon last January. She was captured Monday.

"Put me in your old jail, she jeered at the policeman who had her in tow. "When I get ready to leave, you'll see me going."

Chained in her cell.

The police decided they wouldn't let her escape again, so they hoisted a ponderous chain—one that clanks like a medieval dungeon chain, and secured it with a padlock on Bessie's cell.

When the women prisoners were fed Friday afternoon at 1

o'clock, Bessie was in her cell and the chain had its old familiar
clank. At 3 o'clock Turnkey Maner went into the women's ward to
lock up a prisoner just arrived.

When he emerged, despair was written o'er his face.

"Bessie's Gone"

"Bessie's gone," he said in much the tone of a child crying over a
lost doll.

Was there excitement, confusion, panic, hustling and bustling
and calling out of reserves? Nay. Desk Sergeant Newby sighed,
turned to a motorcycle officer and asked him quietly and politely
if he'd kindly go out and try to find Bessie.

Bessie's still gone, though. She sawed a link of the clanking
chain and then she had easy sledding. The west window through
which she had escaped Sunday had not been repaired and Bessie
walked out of the jail on Monroe Street in broad daylight.

Where Bessie gets her saws no one knows. Picking locks,
though, is child's play for her. She can fashion a key out of
anything that is metal. Pewter spoons are her favorite engines of
escape. Bessie is charged with vagrancy.

※ ※ ※

Assistant Chief Speight sat alone in his office poring over the police ros-
ter. All this talk of a new jail had the commissioners breathing down
Police Chief Rea's neck. Every man and every penny needed to be double
justified. When he looked up from his desk, Jailer John Moore was standing quietly in the doorway.

When Moore saw the startled look on Speight's face he said, "Sorry,
Assistant Chief. I did not wish to disturb you."

"Well, you have." Startled or not, Speight was happy to be distracted
from his chore and shuffled and set aside the papers. "What do you
need?"

"You told me to tell you when Bessie was back. Vagrancy. Again."

A low, terribly sad groan escaped from Speight's throat. "The lock
didn't hold her... The chain failed . . . have we at least repaired all the
holes and damage she has done?"

"Yes, Sir," Moore replied. Speight continued to stare down Moore.

He shuffled his feet and added in a low whisper, "Mostly."

"Mostly?" Speight repeated.

Speight stared through Moore like he wasn't there for several moments. Moore was awfully uncomfortable.

"Shit fire." Speight rose from his desk and paced back and forth slowly. "I will not have her drag us through the papers again. I will not."

"We searched her and found no spoons or objects of any kind," Moore offered.

"You always search her and you never find anything and yet she always escapes." Speight continued to pace. "If Bessie lights out again Rea will be a bear with a sore head and will come down on me." Speight stopped pacing and stared at the wall. "Who is over at county tonight?"

"I do not know," replied Moore.

"Well, dammit, find out. Then transfer Bessie out of here and over to county jail. I want her gone before daybreak. Understand? We will let county make headlines for once."

"Yes, sir."

"And in the meantime, Bessie is not to be left alone for a moment, hear me? Do not give that woman the time it takes God to skin a minnow, understand?"

"Yes, sir," Moore repeated. Jailer Moore then turned on his heels and briskly walked away.

Speight continued his thousand-mile stare. "Just hope she stays the night." After a moment or two his gaze returned to the paperwork on his desk. He sighed. "Som'bitch."

December 8, 1913
Fort Worth Star-Telegram

Bessie Williams is Buffeted About 'Twixt Two Jails

Bessie Williams, who has escaped jail so many times she has lost the count, is too much for the city. She landed in the city prison Saturday night on a vagrancy charge, but was transferred to the county Monday morning by Patrolman Coffey.

"We can't do anything with her so we brought her up here to get rid of her." Coffey explained as the county court complaint was being filed against Bessie. It also was signed by Deputy Sheriff Williams.

Bessie has not decided how long she will remain the guest of
the county jail this time. Her trial will not come up this week and
her visit may last until her trial, because she has no spoons with
which to dig out of the antique prison.

Bessie came walking up to the front of Mamie's house more than a little
worse for wear. The door abruptly opened to reveal Homer Joyce, not
Mamie. Bessie was surprised but did not show it.

"I remember you," said Homer.

"I do not know you," replied Bessie. "I am looking for Mamie."

"Ma!" Homer said. "You have a caller." Homer stepped aside as Mamie
walked out.

"I declare, Bessie Williams, as I live and breathe. What brings you to
my door—or don't I know it?" Mamie drained the remainder of a glass
of Jake and eyed Bessie.

"I was looking for Annie."

"You are looking for a place to flop and we both knows it. Annie lit
out like a Mayfly in June and won't be back." Mamie eyed Bessie up and
down as Bessie swayed slightly on the porch. "You can just keep walking,
Missy." Mamie turned to walk away but was stopped by Homer.

"Now hold up, Ma. That ain't no way to treat a woman in need."
Homer and Mamie eyed each other and briefly but efficiently spoke
the unspoken language of family. Mamie was none too pleased and
stormed into the house. Homer turned and said, "Come on in, Bessie."
Homer stepped aside and Bessie cautiously walked up the steps and
through the door.

"Mamie and me were about to go out looking for some dough. You
look like you could use a little scratch. Wanna come along?"

"How do you mean?" asked Bessie. She still swayed and looked
droopy-eyed, but her mind began to click.

"Mamie mooches drinks off some stewbum, then gets him to the
alley thinking he's in for a little more, if you know what I mean. Then, I
smash and roll him. It's easy pickin's darlin'."

"This is a waste, Homer," said Mamie. "She's two bit and smashed at
that."

"She may be a little worn, Ma, that is true." Hesitantly, Homer offered, "But she is a might younger than you and likely can pull men out

of them tap rooms quicker, allowing us to hit more marks."

Mamie bristled, but Bessie's eyes caught fire and she stalked toward Mamie. "I been rollin' dopes all by myself for longer than you know, Mamie. I never needed muscle and don't need any now."

Homer stepped between the women. "Easy, Bessie. Nobody said you needed help. It was just an offer. With all three of us workin' we can make a lot of money fast. Split it between us, fair and square. What do you say?"

"I do not work with others," said Bessie. She hesitated and swayed. "But I am in need of a place to rest my head. Perhaps I can help y'all score a little scratch tonight in return for board."

"Fine idea, Bessie," said Homer. "That sounds capital, right, Ma?"

Mamie snorted like a rutting pig and walked away.

✳ ✳ ✳

Bessie sat at the back of the White Rat pool hall bolt upright on her usual three-legged stool. Undisturbed and motionless, she waited for a mark. A man carelessly flashing too much cash or a watch was a target as long as he wasn't a regular or lived nearby. Locals were usually off limits for Bessie, as revenge had a way of catching up to a woman in the Acre. However, any fella in town on business, pleasure, or just passing through was game in a hunt.

The White Rat was a dingy dive, poorly lit in the daytime and dark as pitch at night. The three nicked and scarred pool tables were as level as Travis County, and most of the tables, as well as the bar, began their life as wooden crates or boxes that were broken up and cobbled together to make furniture. The barkeep let Bessie sit, without drink, hunting her mark, as long as after she found one she spent a fair share of the take on his rathskeller.

Alice Odell, a short, stocky bawd from Franklin Street, wandered in off the street looking for Bessie. Alice had managed not to drink enough of her earnings when she was a young woman to lease a house of soiled doves and for the past three years had managed to stay off her back and scratch together a living from the toils of other women.

In the past month one of her women had lit out for Oklahoma and another had killed herself rather than spend another night in Alice's shack. As a result, cash flow had been meager lately, and Alice was about to take to the mat again when she read about Bessie's escapades in the papers and figured she would make a star attraction. It had not taken her long to learn she would likely find her at the White Rat.

When Alice walked in, every hooch hipster in the place turned to look at her. She paid no never mind and beelined for Bessie in the back.

Approaching Bessie, Alice said, "Good afternoon, Bessie."

She was stopped in her tracks five feet away when Bessie coldly replied, "I do not know you."

"Well, that is right, we have never been properly introduced. Let me fix that now, my name is Alice Odell and . . . "

Bessie quickly cut her off. "I know who you are. But I do not know you. What do you want from me?"

A bit flustered, Alice tilted her head and slightly smiled. "Then you know I hire only the best and most diligent girls to work with me in my boarding house."

"You prey and use innocents and addicts to fuck derelicts and drunken wasters in your shitty bawdy house. That is what I know."

Fire flickered across Alice's eyes, but she held her temper. "Sometimes, Bessie. Sometimes I do if it makes my scratch. But I know better than to take you for one of those types of women." Alice paused, regained her composure, and continued. "You have gained a fair bit of notoriety in the papers, Bessie." Alice reached into her handbag and produced a wad of clippings. Bessie looked at them with surprise. "Did you not know? You have become quite famous." She handed the clippings over to Bessie, who began to slowly read through them. "And not just local, neither. There are stories there from Dallas and I hear tell as far away as San Antonio and even a few out of state. Fame has found you, Bessie Williams."

"I do not take to being confined."

"Not many do, Bessie. Not many do." Bessie handed the clippings back to Alice. "But 'taint many can do much about it, like you. No ma'am, you have grit and determination."

"I just do not accept it. I have to git out or I will suffocate. I would die."

"Let us get down to brass tacks." Alice looked around the White Rat disdainfully. "How long you been sitting here? Two . . . three hours or more? Just hoping for a mark."

"What of it."

"It is a waste of your time, Bessie, that is what of it." Alice was building steam. "If you was to come ply your trade in my house, and do not look at me in that way, I know you got light fingers. Come work in my house and the marks will come to you." Alice waved the handful of clippings in front of Bessie's downturned eyes. "Plenty of pickins once I let word the famous jail breaker Bessie Williams is at Odell's. Come on, Bessie, leave this mare's nest and come with me. You and me both will soon be stepping in high cotton for sure."

Behind Alice and Bessie a burly, unshaven man wearing the work clothes of a railroad grader erupted into the White Rat. "Clyde Miller, you son of a bitch! You cannot hide from me!"

And with that declaration the grader marched to the bar as everyone but the helpless Mr. Miller scattered. With his right hand Miller reached for a glass on the bar and raised it to strike his oncoming assailant. His eyes, however, betrayed fear and resignation to an unfavorable outcome in the impending melee.

In less than a minute the beating was finished. "Let that be a lesson," the grader declared, and with that, he left the White Rat. Mr. Miller lay bloody and torn up. Bystanders stepped over him on the way back to their drinks at the bar. The barkeep wiped spilt drink off the bar and offered to refill glasses. "Can someone get word to," he looks over to the prone Clyde Miller to check he is still breathing, "the almost widder Miller to come fetch her husband?"

"Aye," said a man at the end of the bar as he finished his shot and slammed the glass on the bar. "It is on my way home, and I should light out anyways."

Alice turned and looked at Bessie. "That hardly happens in my boarding house, and all the men a-calling have money to spend."

"You do not own me," affirmed Bessie.

"Of course not. You work when you please, come and go as you will. You just give me a fair cut."

"And I do not work on my back."

"Of course not. That is understood."

Bessie looked around the White Rat and pondered the out-of-the-blue offer. "Maybe I will come tonight."

"Fine, Bessie, that is fine." Alice stuffed the clippings back in her handbag. "You know where I am."

"That is a fact."

And the bargain was made. Alice Odell turned and left the White Rat, careful to walk around the slowly moving Mr. Miller (now turned over, half on his knees), so as not to get blood on her dress.

1914

January 15, 1914
Fort Worth Star-Telegram

Bessie Williams in Again; Fight Causes Capture

Bessie Williams is in the county jail again. This time the noted woman jail breaker is hardly in condition to try to dig her way out of her cell, even if she had a spoon. For both of her eyes are nearly closed as the result of a free for all fight in Alice Odell's rooming house on Franklin Street on Wednesday night.

Bessie was not jailed alone. Deputy sheriffs arrested the Odell woman, Nellie Hendricks, Tom Jett and John Burke. Complaints of drunkenness and vagrancy were filed against all of them.

Deputies Alderman and Henderson worked all night in the Trinity river bottoms. Alderman said this was the beginning of a campaign to clean out the bottoms.

Bessie's time at Odell's rooming house had been profitable for both. Alice played on Bessie's notoriety, and her traffic had almost doubled. The clientele, for the most part, toted in with more money and left more with the girls. If they happened to lose a watch or wallet during their stay, well, accidents happen.

With free room and board and a fairly steady flow of eligible marks, Bessie had managed to stash a great deal of her earnings. Relations between Bessie and the other girls were constantly strained, but Alice took no guff and managed to keep the peace, for the most part. Girls that couldn't take the arrangement and resented Bessie's special treatment soon found themselves back on the street or headed out of town.

Bessie did not stay in any one place long, no matter how fat the pickings were. She had learned long ago there was no such thing as a safe harbor, and it was better to leave on your own terms than be beaten and shown the door. She had planned her exit almost as soon as she first walked into Odell's bawd house. Bessie had saved enough to lay claim to a small shack in "No Man's Land" and keep a place of her own for the first time in her life. Problem was, Bessie did not know how to end a situation quietly or peaceably. Her departure from the boarding house was to be no exception.

Alice was out for the evening, tying one on in the Acre, when Bessie walked into the boarding house and spotted a mark. But he was already with one of the other girls, and when Bessie moved in to lay claim, the woman snapped. The other woman was new and a morphine addict short a dose. She ripped into Bessie with a vengeance and the other girls, seeing an opportunity to strike, jumped in and laid the wood to Bessie.

The mark bolted and the tussle rolled out into the street. By the time the police arrived Bessie was a mess, but the other girl was missing teeth.

Since the police were already in the Flats, pretty much in force, they called for every black Maria and off-duty copper and swept the area for every vagrant, soiled dove, sporting man, and stew bum they could find. When Alice stumbled home she was caught up in the raid, and after finding out her boarding house was empty and closed and her main attraction beaten and jailed, she flew into such a rage it took three officers to subdue her and haul her off.

Matron Hargrave had been brought onto the women's ward to make changes. The all-male police force had always found the women's ward to be a strange and foreign place. When Cowtown was a small frontier burg with scant women residing there at all, however, and even fewer inhabiting the jail facilities, it had been a minor issue. But times had changed. At the turn of the century Fort Worth's population was a manageable twenty-six thousand, mostly Anglo, but with the Swift, Armour, and Libby meat-packing plants opening in 1902, the population exploded to over seventy-three thousand by 1910. Not only had the sheer numbers exploded, but now there were enclaves of African American, Mexican, Czech, Polish, Irish, and Chinese and other ethnicities all over town.

Gone were the days of a few soiled doves, drunks, and itinerants, popping in for a quick stay. Dozens of female inmates could be packed into the ward at any given time, and the men found them to be increasingly meaner, tougher, and just plain ornery, and since they were second-class citizens to begin with, well, the male policemen simply found better things to do than pay attention to them. As to the colored women . . . the all-white, male force had even less bother with them. Thus, enter Matron Hargrave. She could relate and, in a manner of speaking, lay down the law to these women in a way they could understand.

Only problem was, when it came to Bessie, Matron Hargrave's results were exactly the same as they had always been.

1914

TOM LEE

Tom Lee was born Tom Lee Young. Tom Lee Young, however, had been convicted of robbery in Ennis and did three years in the Texas penitentiary. Tom Lee Young had also killed two men, one accidentally in a barroom fight he had not even started and the other in a jealous rage over another man's wife. So, after leaving Huntsville and moving to Fort Worth to get a fresh start and live with his brother, Tom Lee Young was left in the dust and it was Tom Lee who headed north to Fort Worth. Tom Lee tried to leave the record and reputation of Tom Lee Young behind in Ennis and he had for awhile, but all it took for the short fuse and bad temper of Tom Lee Young to resurface was one perceived slight and a bad decision to undo the good work of Tom Lee.

Tom Lee lay on his bunk in the jail cell that served as his last home. His blood pressure rose almost every time he blinked. He was sorely afraid to close his eyes, even for the quarter second it took to blink.

Tom Lee Young was four when he went with his father to cut his uncle down from a tree. It was his first glimpse of a lynching, and his father wanted him to learn early. He was seven when the Klan came and dragged the neighbor man out of his house, beat him for a solid hour, then covered him in tar and lit him up. It seemed to Tom Lee Young that the neighbor man screamed for an hour before he died. He huddled in the back of the house with his mother and brothers and sisters while his daddy stood behind the front door silently holding an axe.

Tom Lee had to live in the here and now. Every time he closed his eyes he saw the mob and pictured his beaten, dismembered, bloody body swinging from a tree, or worse, covered in tar and set aflame.

Sitting in the cell and listening to the sound of the gallows being tested was a much preferred fate to what he would have met at the hands of the mob. His jaw and cheek bone, what was left of it, wracked his body with pain, but the pain disappeared and was replaced with numbing fear whenever he thought about what would have happened if the mob had ruled.

March 8, 1914
Fort Worth Star-Telegram

Tom Lee Jokes and Blows Smoke Rings in Death Cell
"If the People Want Me to Go, Alright," Negro Slayer Says When Told Pardon Is Denied.

Lying on a comfortable cot in his guarded cell Saturday afternoon, Tom Lee, negro slayer of Walter Moore, another negro, and Patrolman Ogletree, sent large rings of cigar smoke to the low ceilings and paid little attention to the statement that the board of pardons had refused to recommend that his death sentence be commuted to a life term.

Lee smoked on in silence for several minutes and apparently did not hear remarks addressed to him. Suddenly he was all attention for just long enough to say "If the people want me to go, it is alright."

A few minutes later he angled his top-shaped head through the small opening in the cell door, held his cigar in one hand while he slipped his other thin hand through an opening and then resumed smoking.

Presently he looked up at the gallows, where he is doomed to die Monday unless the governor stays his execution, and remarked to Bessie Miller, a negress confined in the women's ward across the corridor, that he would take his last trip up the steps Monday.

He seems to be the least perturbed person about the jail; sleeps most of the afternoon and for part of the night; eats heartily and laughs and jokes with the prisoners who are allowed run of the jail.

Jokes With Negro Girl

"A whole match?" Lee inquired as he broke the end off a match and handed it to a negro girl who passed by his cell and asked for a light. As he accommodated the negress, he laughed and remarked that he would be able to give her only a few more.

Lee had hope until Saturday that the governor would save his neck. Before he was told that the board of pardons had refused to recommend commutation he pulled a letter from his pocket and told a reporter that the letter expressed his only hope. It was a brief notice from the governor's secretary, stating that his petition for commutation had been referred to the board of pardons.

If Lee hangs Monday he will be the first negro of Texas to suffer the death penalty on a technical charge of killing another negro.

Sheriff Rea stated Saturday that in the event there is no inter-ference he will carry out the execution as prescribed by law. The law provides that any legal execution must take place between 11 A.M. and sundown. The sheriff said it would take place as soon after 11 as possible.

Trouble Over "Crap" Game

Tom Lee went to McCampbell's barbecue stand, 300 East Eighth street, May 15, and shot Pete Soles, a negro with whom he had trouble the night before following a "crap" game. He then went to McGar's pool hall, 911A Jones street, and killed Walter Moore, another negro. Near Ninth and Grove streets he killed Patrolman John Ogletree. He claimed he shot the policeman in self-defense.

Lee was captured by policemen only after he had shot off his chin. He was removed hastily from University Hospital to the county jail and was smuggled out of the jail and taken in an automobile to Denton early the following morning and remained in jail for several days.

A mob battered the doors of the county jail the night before Lee's removal to Denton, but a squad of police assisted Sheriff Rea's deputies in keeping it out of the building.

The mob played havoc in the negro colony on East Ninth street, destroying plate glass windows and fixtures in saloons and stores.

"I tell you, gentlemen, this cannot stand." Judge Swayne's voice was simmering about two short degrees from a boil.

Swayne sat in Mayor R. F. Milam's office with Sheriff Rea, Chief Montgomery, Judge Hugh Bardin, and Justice of the Peace T. J. Maben, along with Marion Sansom, J. L. Terrell, H. H. Lassiter, Burk Burnett, William Capps, J. W. Flournoy, L. H. Burney, B. B. Paddock, and Paul Waples. The group of city, legal, and business leaders had been discussing strategies for keeping the lid on the citizenry and keeping the city out of libelous issues for half an hour.

"We cannot profess to be a modern city of industry and attitude and let these pikers off with trifling fines and a nod and a wink," argued Swayne. "Burning and looting businesses in any part of town, negro owned or white is an affront to be dealt with. We will be a laughingstock and it will affect business, if that is your chief concern, over justice."

"The city is still a tinder box, Judge, and negro homes and businesses are still smoldering, damages the city may be held liable for, I remind you, and now we are told Lee cannot be tried first degree for murdering Ogletree," said Burk Burnett. "It seems to me now is the time to tread lightly. Half these men are Klan folk and we need the Klan to keep a lid on them."

P. D. Paddock pricked his ears at the mention of the Klan. "Now let's mind our manners and our words, gentlemen," he said. "Judge Swayne, I know most of these men, as do you. They are, for the better part, hard-working citizens. I know many of them personally, as do you, Judge. They have employers as well as families depending upon them. Sometimes a man's blood boils and nothing can cool it down. It seems to me like a good time for understanding and a little Christian charity."

"What I know, gentlemen and what I believe in, what I have sworn to uphold, is the law. Fair and just. I cannot be shaken from this stand." Swayne's voice trailed off on his last sentence. He knew he was beaten. No amount of breath or persuasion would change the direction of the city and its businessmen.

March 9, 1914
Fort Worth Star-Telegram

___

Lee Dies Gamely; Smiles Until End
Negro Laughs and Smokes as Straps Are Being Adjusted
Baptized In His Cell
Widow, Father and Brothers of Slain Officer See
Condemned Man Executed

___

Tom Lee, negro slayer of Walter Moore, another negro, and Patrolman John Ogletree, trotted up the steps to the gallows in county
jail Monday morning and joked up to the very minute Sheriff Rea
fastened the noose that hanged him around his neck.

While he was being strapped, he turned to Rev. J.H. Winn,
negro pastor of the St. James Baptist Church, and asked for his
cigar so he could get his last "draw." He bowed to the 150 that witnessed his hanging and said he was going like a "game little man."

The trap was sprung at 11:29 and Lee was pronounced dead
in ten minutes.

The officers who helped Sheriff Rea execute Lee said they
never witnessed a hanging where so much nerve was displayed.

While Lee was getting his last shave and massage he admon-
ished the negro barber to give him a good one and not interfere
with his smoking too much. He laughed and joked with Deputy
Sheriff Alderman and after he was put back in his death cell read a
bible and winked at Albert Appleton, the day watch.

Surrounding the jail were hundreds of people, including many
negroes.

Baptized in Cell

Rev. Winn baptized Lee early in the morning and held a short
prayer service in his cell.

Lee was convicted of killing Walter Moore, negro, and is the
first man in Texas to hang for killing another negro. He shot
Moore May 15, 1913, and on the same day shot and killed Patrolman Ogletree.

Lee shot Pete Soles at McCampbell's barbecue stand, 300 East
Eighth street. He had had trouble with the negro the night before
following a "crap" game. He then went to McGar's pool hall, 911
Jones street, and killed Walter Moore. Near Ninth and Grove
streets he killed Patrolman Ogletree. He claimed that he shot the
policeman in self-defense.

After his chin was shot off Lee was captured by policemen and
hastily removed from University hospital to the county jail and
taken in an automobile to Denton early the following morning.

Mob Sought Lee

A mob formed at the county jail the night before. A large squad
of police assisted Sheriff Rea's deputies in keeping the mob under
control.

The mob sought vengeance by playing havoc with the negro
colony on East Ninth street, destroying plate glass windows and
fixtures in saloons and stores.

Among the crowd who witnessed the execution were Patrolman Ogletree's widow, his sister, Mrs. Mable Tatum; his father and
three brothers. There were also many policemen present.

Lee's family and near relatives visited him in the county jail a
few hours before execution. He told them all good-by without a
sign of weakness.

Colquitt Refuses to Interfere

Sheriff Rea received a telegram from Governor Colquitt early
Monday, which read:

"I decline to interfere in Tom Lee case. Let law take its course.
(Signed) "O.B. Colquitt."

Lee's body was turned over to Jeffrey's Undertaking Company.

1914-1915

THE WOMAN OF NO MAN'S LAND

— 1914 —

March 27, 1914
Fort Worth Star-Telegram

Bessie Williams, Come on Back to Jail and Behave

Bessie Williams, champion jail breaker, is gone from the city jail and eleven of the twelve others who were in the woman's ward at the same time Thursday are still at large.

Bessie did not really break jail. All she had to do was to saw a little chain that held fast the exit to the street from the run around. Matron Hargrave left the prisoners in the run around to eat supper. The escape was discovered shortly after 8 p.m. Thursday.

Minnie Stewart was recaptured by Motorcycle Officer Langdon shortly afterward. Another escaped prisoner was taken up by Patrolman Dills later in the night.

Bessie Williams has the reputation of breaking every jail she has been locked in. She twice took French leave from the county jail and has left the city jail numerous times before. She can pick a lock., chisel a hole through a wall, or saw the bars. Bessie says she just never was made to be locked up.

Bessie had not made her living by prostitution since Effie died. She made her way by wits, muscle, and pure-dee gumption that some called orneriness. Even though she avoided prostitution as much as possible, Bessie was still a soiled, undesirable woman by all standards. If a woman was not married or under the care and protection of her father or closest male relative, she was socially undesirable.

As far as Bessie was concerned, marriage was a confinement worse than prison. When her father abandoned her in the Acre she had decided she needed no man, just marks.

Now, if a man turned over his bank roll of his own accord, well, easy was easy and did not come often for any woman, especially a woman living in No Man's Land. Bessie might, if she was feeling right and the roll was big enough, show him a little kindness.

Jack Thompson was just such a man. He had met Bessie, or rather, Bessie had met him when he was on a business trip to town and made a traipse through the Acre. Jack kept coming back, and Bessie kept obliging him by taking his money, which he freely gave her. Thompson became more than merely taken with Bessie and had moved his family from their home in Lampasas to Fort Worth a mere month after first laying eyes on Bessie. He settled his wife and two children into the most respectable hovel on Bridge Street so he could more effectively court his mistress. Thompson took a job at the Armour Meat Packing plant but was haphazard in attendance and performance. Every minute with his family or at work was a moment stolen from time with Bessie, as far as he was concerned. The Thompson family struggled to make ends meet and only survived with monthly checks from Maggie Thompson's father, who hated his son-in-law but detested the prospect of his daughter leaving the wastrel to return to his home with fatherless children in tow. A man's reputation was more important than life itself, and to have a divorced daughter living at home with her children was more than a financial burden. It was a colossal embarrassment that could not be hidden or fixed unless Maggie could find another man to remarry, and any man willing to marry a divorced woman with children was likely worse than the useless son-in-law he had now.

It was midafternoon on a Tuesday when Jack Thompson walked into the saloon, wide-eyed and looking frantic. He had been fruitlessly searching for Bessie since noon, and the spring thunderstorm had soaked him from hat to knee. From the knee down he was covered in mud and horse shit. The man was a sight.

Upon entering the saloon he immediately spotted Bessie sitting in the back, talking to Homer Joyce.

"Bessie!" he waved and began to walk toward the couple. "I have been looking . . . "

Bessie abruptly rose and exited through the rear door. Thompson physically drooped. Homer smiled, rose from his seat, and approached Thompson.

Upon reaching him he clapped Thompson on the back and said, "There, there, fella. Go on after her, a woman likes that." Homer smiled broadly, knowing full well Bessie would not like Thompson to chase after her and would like as not whup the tar out of him if he did.

"I been chasing her all day," Thompson said, more to himself than Homer.

Before Homer could reply, Maggie Thompson, Jack's wife, darkened the saloon door, eyes afire. "J. U. Thompson!" Maggie screeched. "What the hell are you doing in this saloon instead of earning a day's wage for your wife and children!" Every man in the bar laughed at poor Jack as he slowly slinked back to Maggie.

June 6, 1914
Fort Worth Star-Telegram

Bessie Williams Once More Escapes
Five Other White Women Make Their Way Out of City Jail.

Bessie Williams, the woman who laughs at locks and steel bars, sawed her way to liberty from the city jail again Wednesday night for the 'steenth time, and is now at large and enjoying that liberty which obscurity from the police only will give her.

Five other white women wedged their way to freedom through the 12x12 hole which Bessie's steel saw had cut in the cage Wednesday night. They were Alice Odell, Dot Shay, Maud Smith, Nellie McFadded and Josie Hill, all of whom were either serving 'time' for vagrancy or awaiting trial.

After sawing through the steel cage, the women made their exit from the building by breaking through a steel screen to a window.

They worked noiselessly, and their escape was not discovered until Thursday morning.

Bessie Williams, whose home is in "Battercake Flats," is the champion woman jail breaker in the world, the police say. She is always getting arrested for something or other. She has broken out of the city jail more times than the police can count.

The cage and cell in the woman's ward at headquarters are locked now by brand new and powerful steel locks for the reason that Bessie showed the police on many occasions that the other locks were just playthings. She has made her escape many times by picking the locks. She picked locks with her hair pins, shoe buttoners and even spoons.

Bessie has broken out of the county jail almost as many times – by picking the locks, sawing bars and digging her way out with a spoon.

Wednesday night Bessie cut the steel bars as smoothly as if they had been made of paper. Two women in the jail refused to make their escape.

As Bessie was being led into the courtroom, Jack stepped out of the crowd and wrapped her in a warm embrace. Bessie stood straight as a board. She let no man embrace her without permission, but with her guard holding one arm she was not sure how to react. Jack slipped a small blade into the fold of Bessie's blouse, awkwardly but without notice.

"Anything for you, Bessie. Anything." Jack looked at Bessie like a love-sick hound dog. Bessie moved on without expressing any emotion. The guard on her arm seemed relieved no outburst had occurred.

"I'll be there for you when you get out," Jack said. Bessie continued walking, showing no response.

"Court is now in session," wailed the bailiff. "Honorable Justice Maben presiding."

Justice Maben took his seat and shuffled the stack of papers in front of him. When he looked up and saw Bessie, he slumped slightly. Looking up from the papers he said, "Bessie Williams, arrested for theft of person." He paused. "How do you plead *this time*, Bessie?"

Bessie shrugged her shoulders and shuffled her feet.

"Thirty days or $25." Justice Maben banged his gavel. "Although we both know you will neither pay the fine nor do the time."

Bessie was removed from court, the saw blade safely tucked away.

June 14, 1914
Fort Worth Star-Telegram

Haven't Caught Woman Who Sawed Jail Bars
Bessie Williams Successfully Eludes Police Since Escape
With Five Other Prisoners.

Bessie Williams, the white woman who sawed out of the city jail, at the same time liberating five other white women, is still at large. Police have visited all her old haunts in an effort to recapture her.

Information has been given Mrs. Hargraves, the matron, that someone slipped Bessie a steel saw while she was in the courtroom the day before she made her escape.

Bessie moved about the house in a rare state of elation, moving from one room to another cleaning the walls and baseboards with a rag that had long ago been white. Occasionally she would put down the rag and drag the meager furnishings around the room, pausing and stepping into a corner to consider the new arrangement.

She had been in the house less than two months. It had taken weeks to drive out the larger varmints and critters, but curs no longer wandered in to nap, and the nest of opossums under the porch had been vanquished after a brutal and somewhat bloody skirmish. She had patched the walls with scrap to make them mostly whole, and the roof was, miraculously, intact when she moved in.

No one owned a home in No Man's Land. You simply moved in if it was vacant, or vanquished whoever was there before you, if you could. There were no named streets or city services. No plats in city hall that neatly mapped out property lines and boundaries. No Man's Land was a hodgepodge of shacks, hovels, and lean-tos. Garbage, piss, and shit were tossed out a window, if tossed out at all, and rats and worse vermin outnumbered people a hundred to one or more. Puddles of green scum calf deep dotted the landscape, and nothing grew from the poisoned earth except Dallas grass. Nothing killed or even discouraged Dallas grass.

Yet, Bessie veritably glided about her house in this cesspool, happy to finally have a place and a stake of her own. She had no idea of the hurricane blowing her way.

The highest point is the best vantage to view the deepest depth . . . but no one ever looks.

Maggie Thompson was in a rage. Even the meanest feral dogs and children scampered out of her way as she made straight through No Man's Land looking for Bessie. She had begged and pleaded to no avail with her husband, Jack Thompson, to leave Bessie be. The man was smitten. Her only avenue was to remove the target of his affections, and she aimed to do it. When she ran into Abe at Potter's Grocery and Mercantile, her shoes and skirt were ruined from mud and human and animal waste and fluids. He told her where to find Bessie.

By the time she walked up the front porch a small cadre of women and children and even a few layabouts had massed behind her. In this part of town people were mostly inured to fights and mauls, but a good ruckus always drew a crowd. The denizens of No Man's Land could smell a good fight, and the odor of a doozy of a donnybrook hung in the air.

"You will leave my husband be, Bessie Williams," Maggie shouted from the front yard.

Bessie walked out her front door holding her broom and simply stared at Maggie. "I do not know who you are, but I chase no man. If he comes, he comes on his own."

"I am Mrs. Jack Thompson, you cheap whore, and if you will not respect my marriage I will beat the fear of God into you."

Bessie did not wait for Maggie to come to her but raised the broom and came at her swinging. Between them there were less than two hundred pounds of women in the fight but there was surely more than a ton of fury.

Poor Maggie Thompson never stood a chance. Bessie was much more accomplished and experienced as a brawler, and she had the broom as a weapon. Truly, it was not as much a fight as a simple, pure beating. Maggie, to her credit, would not stay down. Bessie would whack her with the broom, knock her down, and kick her mercilessly, but Maggie always managed to regain her stance before immediately being whacked back into the dirt and muck.

The hooting and hollering of the crowd eventually attracted the attention of patrolling officer Peter Howard. Howard was a veteran officer whose service on the force dated back to the wild and wooly days of the 1890s. He saw his duty as a police officer as protecting "decent" citizens. In his mind there were no decent citizens in No Man's Land. When he heard the noise from the crowd screaming at Bessie and Maggie, he ambled up and quickly assessed the situation as being needless of interruption. Beatings, knifings, shootings, and murders were commonplace and seldom solved. This was likely to be another one. He tried but failed to keep his shoes and trouser cuffs mud, muck, and shit free.

Eventually, Maggie stayed down and Bessie lost interest in kicking her. Officer Howard disbursed the crowd, and Maggie dragged herself back the way she came.

August 7, 1914
Fort Worth Star-Telegram

Testifies Against Wife; Is Accused
J.U. Thompson Works Up Vagrancy Charge
for Himself by Action in Police Court

J.U. Thompson of Bridge and Franklin streets, took sides against his wife, Maggie Thompson, in favor of Bessie Williams, noted character, while on the stand in police court Friday morning, and thereby worked up a charge of vagrancy against himself.

His wife and Bessie Williams had a fight. Thompson came into court presumably as a witness against the Williams woman, but on the stand he laid all the blame on his own wife and attempted to exempt her opponent. Other witnesses reversed his testimony.

The wife took the stand and told some things about her husband. In dismissing the charge of assault against her, Prosecutor George Polk ordered the arrest of the husband.

Bessie Williams was fined $5 and costs.

Bob Higdon sat at the Thompson dinner table eating his biscuits and gravy. Jack sat silent in the chair across from him.

With biscuit in mouth and gravy on his beard, Higdon said, "Jack, do you know who bought the fixin's for this meal?"

"You did, sir."

"That is right." Higdon was about down to sopping up the last of the gravy with the last half of biscuit. "I make money raising and selling cattle at market. Do you know how much money I'm making sitting on my ass here in your kitchen?"

"No, sir."

"Shit diddly squat! That is how much. Instead of earning my living and yours, I'm down here talking my daughter into staying with your sorry ass. Now you listen to me. You will keep your wife happy. You will keep shoes on your children's feet like a God-fearing Christian man, and you will keep your whoring out of the newspapers! Am I clear!"

"Yes, sir."

Higdon grunted and no more believed Jack than he believed in Santa Claus. "I head back to Lampasas tomorrow and you will get one more check on the first of next month and that is all. Do not make me travel back to Fort Worth until the Fat Stock Show next February!"

August 17, 1914
Fort Worth Star-Telegram

Well, Well, Well! Bessie Has New Way to Escape

Bessie Williams, the most arrested woman in Fort Worth, got additional fame as a jail breaker Sunday night when she dug a twenty pound stone out of the wall in her cell, and battered down an iron door to freedom. Two other women got their liberty along with Bessie. The escape is supposed to have been made about 10 o'clock Sunday night.

City and county jails are patched in half a dozen places where Bessie has sawed through them in the past year, but battering down an iron door—a feat heretofore considered next to impossible—is a new method of escape not only for Bessie, but for all jail breakers.

Bessie Williams has the reputation of having broken out of jail more times than any woman in the world.

When Bessie got her supper Sunday night she is supposed to have held back a spoon. With this spoon she gouged the big stone out of the wall. Then she went to work on the iron door.

Assistant Chief Speight, Night Sergeant Little, Police Chief Montgomery, Patrolman Coffey, and Deputy Sheriff Fitch stood silent in the run of the women's ward. All eyes were lowered to the iron door and large stone lying on the floor.

In the cell behind them and to their left, the door was slightly ajar and a large, gaping hole was in the wall where the stone had been. Chips, dust, and masonry bits were scattered on the floor. In his lowered hands Speight held the lock and chain futilely used to contain Bessie.

"If we just gave her the money we spend to keep her in here and repair the damage she does, she likely would have no need to thieve and whore, and our jail would not be torn down stone by stone," said Speight, more as a thought to himself than general conversation. "Before much longer we will be guarding a hovel. All the bars and beds will be gone. Washed down and floated away in the Clear Fork."

Speight drew a heavy breath, closed his eyes, then dropped the lock and chain. "I do not know what for," he exhaled, "but put it all back the way it was." No one moved, let alone spoke an acknowledgment.

Speight and Police Chief Montgomery walked over the iron door and left the run. Night Sergeant Little, Patrolman Coffey, and Deputy Sheriff Fitch looked from the iron door to the hole in the wall then back to the door.

"Frank," said Night Sergeant Little. "Go fetch the toolbox." Patrolman Coffey nodded and left.

*　*　*

No marks were ever allowed in Bessie's house. She preferred to keep business away from her home and private asylum. However, there were different kinds of marks, and exceptions were made on occasion.

Bessie had known John West for several years. He could be considered more of a benefactor than a run-of-the-mill mark. West worked for Swift as an inspector and from time to time brought Bessie scraps of gristle and bone. Their relationship was simple, clear, and unemotional.

West had lost his parents at age eleven. His father was killed in a railcar accident, and his mother had died of consumption four months later. Relatives had made it clear John was not their concern, and he had grown up on the streets like Bessie. Well, not exactly like Bessie; life on the streets for a boy old enough to have at least a little muscle on his bones was quite different from a girl of tender years.

Both had developed similar emotional detachments from people, places, and things that made their relationship feasible. Without thinking about it Bessie knew she could let John into her sanctuary without worry or threat.

John had shown up at Bessie's three days ago with an armful of Jake, and the two had been on a bender. John knew how long he could miss work before he would no longer be welcome at Swift and was throwing up through a window when Jack Thompson walked in the front door. Bessie lay on the bed, full-blown gone in a stupor.

When John entered the room still wiping the spittle from his mouth, he found Jack sitting on the bed with Bessie's head in his lap, slowly caressing her cheek.

"What in the Sam Hill," John muttered.

"You do not take care of her," Jack said, glaring up at John.

"Of all the souls in this world needing took care of, she is not one of them." John took slow but deliberate steps toward a chair across the room that held his shirt. Bessie stirred. She came back to consciousness with a jerk and leapt from the bed.

"Jack Thompson, you Bedlam fiend! What in the hell are you doing here!" She screamed. Jack reflexively drew his arm in front of his face but Bessie threw no blows.

"Get out of here!" Bessie screamed.

"But Bessie," Jack said, barely audible.

"Leave my house! Now!"

Again, speaking low, his head lowered, Jack whimpered, "I have money for you."

"Good. Leave it, then git!"

Jack slowly stood from the bed, reached in his pocket, and left two dollars and change on the bedside table.

"I mean it, Jack Thompson. I'm in no mood for you," said Bessie.

As Jack reached the door John muttered, just loud enough for Jack to hear, "That ain't no real man."

Jack tensed, stood straight but said nothing. He did, however, walk with a little more purpose.

August 29, 1914
Fort Worth Star-Telegram

Refuse Bail in Killing
Woman Attempts to Swallow Broken Glass after Tragedy
Shooting in House
Jack Thompson Waives Preliminary Hearing on Murder
Charge.

Jack Thompson, a horse trader, giving his address as Lampasas, was formally charged with murder Saturday morning, following the death late Friday of John West, 125 Maple street, from four pistol shot wounds. Thompson appeared before Justice Maben and waived examining trial and was remanded to jail without bond. J. J. Hurley, his attorney, would not say what his defense would be.

Bessie Williams, who is famous as a woman jail breaker, having escaped from the city jail only ten days ago by hammering a big steel door off its hinges with a rock, which she dug out of the wall, was a witness to the killing.

She was in the house, 125 Maple Street, Friday afternoon with West, whom she had known for several years, when Thompson came in, she said, in a signed statement. She had also known Thompson for a long time, she said. Both she and West tried to get Thompson to leave the house, she added. Finally West and Thompson quarreled, and Thompson left the place. In a few minutes, she said, she looked up and saw someone in the doorway. The shooting followed and West, who was sitting on the bed, fell back dead. Three bullets went into his chest, and a fourth struck him in the groin.

Small boys followed Thompson to the Delaware bar on Main Street, near Fourth. One of the boys tipped off his whereabouts to Patrolman Aiken. Thompson was leaning against the bar when Aiken stepped up behind him and grabbed a pistol away from him. Motorcycle Officers Langdon, Glosson and Davison, who had been in a chase for Thompson, came upon the scene a few minutes later. Thompson was sent to jail.

Sanitation Officer Ben Dollins was the first to arrive on the scene of the shooting, riding in a Robertson ambulance. He found the body of West sprawled on the bed, his head wrapped in a towel.

Woman Eating Glass

Bessie Williams was sitting on the side of the bed. She was scream-ing and was eating glass. Blood was flowing from her mouth where the glass had cut. She had taken a whiskey bottle and broken it, and then put the smaller pieces in a thick teacup and was pound-ing the glass into a powder. While officers were wrapping the body of West in a sheet, the woman poured the broken glass into her hand and then put it into her mouth. She tried to swallow parts of it, but couldn't and was forced to spit it out again.

West's body was sent to the Robertson's morgue. Bessie Wil-liams was sent to jail, but she threatened to break down the cell and officers put her in the dungeon on the men's side of the jail.

The county attorney's office took a statement from a woman in the Maple street neighborhood who said Thompson "shot up" her house about an hour before the killing of West. She said Thompson came into her home and demanded that she fix him his supper. She refused, she said, and he then took out his pistol and fired two shots into the floor at her feet.

Times had been hard since Jack Thompson killed John West. Bessie's fame was now much more a hindrance than help. When she walked down the street people pointed and whispered. Every bar, mercantile, or hotel she entered, the whispers started immediately, and within minutes everyone knew who she was and what had happened. Marks fled her like the flu. Her small bankroll disappeared quickly in a constant haze of whiskey and Jake.

Homer Joyce had been steadily coming around Bessie's house for weeks, and Bessie had eventually let him in. He was the only person, besides lawyers and police, who would talk to her, and as much of a loner as Bessie was, she was hungry for any personal contact.

Homer had mistakenly thought the murder and its infamy would attract wealthy marks to Bessie, and they could go on a rolling spree like before. He was wrong. Instead they simply sat around Bessie's house all day getting drunk and high.

"We are a couple of skunks, Bessie. You and me," slurred Homer. "Skunks what can't control our spray. Just sprayin' our stink on everyone, everywhere, every which a way." Homer sat at the kitchen table staring out the back door. Lost in his philosophy. "We stink."

Bessie sat on the stoop outside the back door, a bottle of hooch between her knees. "Aye, maybe," she said. Staring out over the muck and chaos of No Man's Land, she watched children play, dogs hunt rats, and everyone dodge the puddles of standing green slime. There was a tinge of sadness in her eyes. Sadness was a rare and unwelcome emotion for Bessie. "But some people need spraying, as you say. I have never done anything to anybody that did not hurt or intend to hurt me first." Bessie dropped her head and considered the hooch. "We should walk up to the White Rat and get more drink."

"We should walk to the courthouse and get married," said Homer. "We deserve each other."

Bessie sat a bit longer, saying nothing in reply. She was tired, sad, and soul-beaten. Maybe Homer was right. Images of Effie's bony, blue-gray corpse had been haunting Bessie's alcohol-induced delusions for weeks, and it made her prickly to the marrow.

September 23, 1914
Fort Worth Star-Telegram

Cupid Wounds Bessie

Bessie Williams, noted jail breaker, had a new name when she was brought into police headquarters Tuesday night on a charge of disturbing the peace. She introduced Homer Joyce, charged jointly with creating a disturbance, as her husband. They had been married only a few days, she said.

Bessie was placed in the woman's ward as usual. She created such a racket, however, that Motorcycle Officers Langdon and Glosson transferred her to the dungeon in the male ward. Thirty minutes later Glosson heard the "swish-swish" of a saw, and, tiptoeing to the jail door, he found Joyce at work on the dungeon lock. He was trying to liberate the woman. The saw measured seven inches in length.

The Joyce family had a hard session in police court Wednesday morning. Fines were assessed as follows: J.C. Joyce, the husband

and father, fined $25 for assault; Mamie Joyce, wife and mother, $8.95 for disturbing the peace; Bessie Joyce, the new member of the family, $8.95 for disturbing the peace; Homer Joyce, son and husband, discharged.

Bessie was not exactly the demure, blushing bride type. She was not used to taking orders from anyone, especially a drunken man she supported with her pickpocket skills. J. C. was constantly goading Homer about his out-of-control, bossy wife. After a while Homer could stand it no more. Homer did not drink for courage; he needed no excuse to get liquored up, but one afternoon when he was about blind drunk he lit into Bessie out of the blue. Taken by surprise and mostly drunk herself, Bessie spotted Homer seventy-five pounds and never stood a chance. The beating was quick and vicious.

The walloping left Bessie unconscious. Homer sat on the floor of the living room attempting to get control of his shakes. After almost an hour he managed to rise and limp out the door to return to his mother's home. The marriage vows, never seriously taken, were now completely forgotten.

A short while later Bessie regained consciousness and managed to wave down a boy passing the house to fetch the police. Upon arrival Officers Langdon and Glosson found Bessie passed out in the dirt patch that passed as her front yard.

"Ma'am," said Glosson.

"Is that Bessie Williams?" Langdon asked. The two officers stood over Bessie, her face swollen and disfigured from the beating. Her clothes were ripped, tattered, and caked with blood and mud.

"Maybe," said Glosson. "Hard to say."

Bessie stirred but could not rise. Glosson kindly offered his nightstick for Bessie to grab in order to steady herself and rise up.

"That man," mumbled Bessie. "That man beat me for no good reason."

The two men looked at Bessie, then to each other, then back to Bessie. Glosson offered, "Must have been something you said."

Bessie mumbled unintelligible curse words at Glosson. "You let a snake into your house, then are surprised when you git bit. Only a woman," he said.

The two men looked at each other and nodded in silent male astuteness of the female's unfathomable unsophistication.

When she finally rose to her feet and steadied herself, the officers walked Bessie to the station and booked her. It was the kind, gentlemanly thing to do.

October 19, 1914
Fort Worth Star-Telegram

Bessie Finds Hubby and Policemen Find Bessie – Bruised Up

Bessie Williams, the champion woman jail breaker, who two days ago was married to Homer Joyce, apparently is destined to go without bliss in her marriage. Motorcycle Officers Langdon and Glosson got a call to a house at Second and Calhoun streets Sunday afternoon. They found Bessie Williams there.

The woman was bleeding from two cuts on her head and was crying. She pointed to a broken chair nearby and between sobs explained what had happened. She said the chair had been broken over her head. Then she pointed out the door and with more sobs she detailed the flight of the man who had struck her.

The police have not yet found the assailant.

Beaten and broken in mind, body and spirit, Bessie sat silent in her cell. She spoke to no one and looked no one in the eye. At first Matron Hargrave checked Bessie's cell every fifteen minutes, then every thirty minutes. Eventually she just made her regular hourly rounds of the women's cellblock. Each time she walked by Bessie, sitting curled up in the corner, she could not help but feel more than a little surprised Bessie was still present and accounted for.

"What you waiting for Bessie," said Dot Shay. "Let's git gone from here." Dot, along with the other woman sharing a cell with Bessie, Maud Smith, had already been the beneficiaries of two of Bessie's escapes. When Bessie did not reply, Dot looked at Maud.

Maud shrugged and said, "She don't look right to me."

"She is fine," Dot said. "Ain't you Bessie?" Again, no reply from Bessie. "Bessie got a fire in her belly, just burnin' to git out of here." Dot looked anxiously at Bessie.

"Leave her be, Dot." Maud settled into her cot and closed her eyes. "We ain't going no place but the work house in the morning."

Bessie sat perfectly still on her cot, staring into the ether like a corpse staring into heaven.

"Damn. I think someone done stole her rudder," said Dot.

October 20, 1914
Fort Worth Star-Telegram

City News Ticker
Bessie Williams in Toils Again.

A complaint charging theft from the person was filed in Justice
Maben's court Monday against Bessie Williams, famous for her
numerous escapes from jail, who is also one of the principal witnesses in the Jack Thompson murder case, to be tried this week in
the Seventeenth district court. She waived preliminary hearing and
her bond was fixed at $750.

Lonnie ran around waving the chicken bone wildly above his head, the
mange-infested cur running and barking angrily behind him. Lonnie and
the cur had been playing this game of keep-away for several minutes
when Jack Thompson came walking up the street. He stopped in the
middle of the neighbor's yard and planted himself firmly.

"Come out you son of a bitch!" he shouted to the shack.

"I said come out and face me, John West, and I mean now!"

Lonnie stopped dead in his tracks and watched the man. The cur
jumped at the chicken bone he held above his head, just out of the mot-
ley cur's reach. As the neighbor's front door cracked, Lonnie tossed the
chicken bone toward the backside of the house. The cur chased it. Lonnie
was fixated on the man in the opposite yard. He was holding a small
caliber revolver. Lonnie was little, but growing up in the Flats, a child
learned early to recognize when action is brewing. If you did not learn
this lesson early, you likely did not grow up at all.

Lonnie recognized Bessie but laid eyes on John West for the first time
as he stepped out onto the porch.

Swaying more than standing Bessie shouted, "What are you doing
back here, Jack?"

Jack, the pistol-wielding man in the yard, answered by raising his gun
and firing repeatedly into the staggering body of the man on the porch.

Bessie made a wailing sound Lonnie had never heard emit from
woman, man, nor beast. The man in the yard fled down the street. The
man on the porch staggered back into the house. Bessie followed.

Lonnie decided to follow the action and ran after the man.

One block over and two blocks down he saw a policeman and shouted for him to follow.

"There has been a shooting," Lonnie excitedly exclaimed.

October 21, 1914
Fort Worth Star-Telegram

Boy, 8, Chief Witness in Murder Trial
Lonnie Cox, though Badly Frightened,
Describes Killing of John West.

Lonnie Cox, a badly frightened little boy, who was not sure about his age, but seemed from his testimony to be about 8 years old, an eye witness to the shooting of John West by Jack Thompson on Maple Street, August 31, was the first witness for the state against Thompson, who was placed on trial for murder Wednesday morning in the Seventeenth district court.

It was his first experience in a courtroom and his answers at first were hardly audible even to the stenographer, but he soon gained more confidence and told the story of the killing in detail. He said that he was standing at the door of his father's home at Fourth and Maple streets when he saw Thompson walk along the street and stop and shake hands with West, who was standing on the porch of the house where the shooting occurred. He said that the shooting started immediately after they had shaken hands and that he heard four shots. West staggered back into the house and Thompson went around the house and on up Fourth Street toward town. He ran to the house at once, followed by his brother and others, and found West on the floor dying. The only other person in the house, he said was the woman, whom he described as West's wife, but who he also knew as Bessie Williams, although he could not remember the name until it was suggested by the county attorney. He also was unable to remember West's name until it was suggested, although he said he had heard it. Ben Le Get, attorney for Thompson, objected to allowing either of the names to be suggested.

Less trouble than was expected was experienced in obtaining a jury. Although no special venire had been ordered, the selection of the panel was completed by 11:15. The jurors chosen were Frank Huster, H.C. Johnson; S.K Garland; W.G. Geer, N. Hukill, G.B. Coke, J.M. Hiett, A. P. Willingham, E.P. Alford, E.J. Routt, G.F. Conant and W. L. Anderson.

In questioning jurors the state was careful to inquire whether there were any who had prejudices against the death penalty for murder, while the defense asked all prospective jurors whether they were prejudiced against a plea of self-defense in a murder case, indicating that that would be the line of defense.

"It ain't right the way Jack follows you around like a puppy, Bessie," John said while putting on his shirt.

"Ain't no harm, John; besides, he pays often enough." Bessie sat clutching the edge of the bed. Two gunshots rang out in the distance, but neither Bessie or John paid any heed.

"Alls I'm saying is it ain't proper behavior for a man to act all hang-dog over a whore."

Bessie flew into a righteous rage and leapt off the bed. "I ain't no whore, John West!" She flew into him landing three blows, two to the body and one to the head, before he could defend himself. John's weight was shifted to his Jake leg and the two tumbled to the floor, shaking the entire house.

"Hell fire, woman, I meant no affront." John rolled on top of Bessie and managed to grab both her wrists. "I know you are different from these other bawds but, hell, Bessie, you ain't exactly a proper lady either."

Bessie quit struggling and the two lay on the floor catching their breath.

From the front yard an angry, slurred voice cried out, "John West, you son of a bitch, come out here!"

John rolled off Bessie and she jumped to her feet. "That bastard is back!" She ran out the front door. John lay flat on his back and drew a heavy sigh. He awkwardly rose to his feet and limped out the door.

Moments later shots rang from the yard. West staggered back through the door, and the house shook again as the corpse of John West dropped to the floor.

October 22, 1914
Fort Worth Star-Telegram

Witness Prides Self on Her Jail Breaking Record
Bessie Williams Tells Court She Broke Out of County Prison Twice and City Jail So Many Times She Lost Count.

Bessie Williams, who seemed to take considerable pride in her record as a jail breaker, told the somewhat lurid story of her life on the witness stand in the Seventeenth district court Thursday morning in the trial of Jack Thompson, horse trader, charged with the murder of John West at her house on Maple Street, August 31.

She said that she had made her escape twice from county jail and so many times from the city jail that she had ceased to keep count of them. Most of the cases made against her had been for theft from person, she testified. She said that she could not tell how many times she had been arrested on that charge, but that she never had been "stuck" for it.

Her story of the killing varied materially from those of both Thompson and Lonnie Cox, the small boy who gave the most important testimony of the witnesses introduced by the state in making its main case. She was put on by the state in rebuttal after Thompson had told his own story of the affair.

She was questioned about her relationship with both West and Thompson and said that the quarrel grew out of the fact that Thompson had visited her during West's absence. She confirmed Thompson's statement of his visit to the house just prior to the killing, of the drinking of the greater part of a quart of alcohol and a pint of whiskey, and of the trouble which started between West and herself.

She declared that after that trouble West put Thompson out of the house and that the latter walked away, returning half an hour later and opening fire on West, without warning just after he had passed the house. She said that he was at least ten or fifteen feet away from the porch on which West was standing when the shots were fired.

Thompson and the Cox boy both said that he was on the porch when the shooting occurred. Thompson claimed that West was chasing him with a knife and the boy said that the men had shaken hands just before the shooting. She denied both statement and also those made by Lonnie Cox in regard to her lack of clothing when he arrived.

Thompson claimed that he had been told of threats West had made against him, but said he knew no reason for them and denied any intimacy with the Williams woman. He said that he had gone to the house in a buggy with West on the afternoon of the shooting and that he was there continuously from that time until the shooting. He denied that he had gone away to get a pistol. He said that he had the revolver with him all the time and made a practice of carrying it.

Jack Thompson sat in his cell staring at his uneaten dinner. Slowly he picked up the spoon from his plate and closely examined it like he had never laid eyes on such a utensil. He turned the spoon and scrutinized it from every possible angle. He dropped the hand that held the spoon into his lap and turned his gaze to the jail cell door. He felt more than a little ashamed to still be in jail almost two weeks after being arrested. Bessie had busted out of this very building on numerous occasions with little more than a spoon and gumption. Jack had the spoon but was still in jail. It bothered him that apparently he lacked the gumption.

The door at the end of the run opened and Jeff Daggett burst through, quickly followed by attorney Ben LeGett. Both men walked at a pace more akin to a slow trot than a walk.

"If there is so much as one hair harmed on my client, there will be hell to pay!" said LeGett. "Do you understand turnkey? I said hell to pay!" Ben LeGett was not a man of few words. LeGett loved to talk, especially in front of jurors, and it mattered little if he stayed on point or even had a point. Actually, as far as LeGett was concerned, the more points the better and to hades with coherence.

Daggett wheeled on the point of his boot and pushed his thick, barrel chest against LeGett. If he had been three inches taller the two men would have been nose to nose. As it was they were more chin to nose.

"Listen to me, you loud-mouthed buzzard. This is my cellblock, and I'll treat him as I treat him, and you will say or do nothing about it. One more word out of you and I'll take you back the way we came, and he can sit in here until hell freezes over."

LeGett turned it down a notch. He was new in Fort Worth and had not yet gotten the lay of the land. He did not know who this mulatto fellow was, but his last name was Daggett, and if he was any relation to Bud Daggett, or for that matter, any of the Daggetts of Fort Worth, his first case in town would be his last, and most likely a fatal loss for his client.

"Easy now, Mr. Daggett. No need to get your back up. I am merely inquiring as to the health and well-being of my client." LeGett smiled sweetly as he verbally patted Jeff on the head.

Taking a deep breath, Jeff stepped away from LeGett, turned, pulled his massive key ring from his waistcoat, and opened the cell door. As it swung open he said, "You can see for yourself the man is doing finer than the other he shot down in cold blood."

"Unproven allegations," said LeGett. "Unproven allegations."

Jeff closed and locked the cell and as he walked off yelled, as if to no one, "You get ten minutes and not a minute more."

Jack rose from his cot but did not move. LeGett crossed the cell, hand extended, and introduced himself. "Ben LeGett, Mr. Thompson. Your generous father-in-law, Bob Higdon, retained me in your defense." It took a second, but Jack raised his hand to shake. LeGett looked at Jack's outstretched hand with a confused look on his face. When Jack looked down he saw he was still holding the spoon.

"My apologies," said Jack. He placed the spoon on his untouched dinner tray.

"You do not have much of a stomach for jailhouse grub, I take it," said LeGett.

"No, sir."

"Let us get down to brass tacks, Mr. Thompson. We do not have much time. As I understand your situation, we have a clear case of self-defense." LeGett set his leather case on Jack's bunk, popped the brass latch, and rummaged around for his note pad and pen. "Mr. Higdon informed me you have had past dealings with the Williams woman, a soiled dove intent on rendering asunder your most sacred bond of matrimony, and that West was a scoundrel in cahoots with Williams in perpetrating this unholy deed." LeGett was quickly gathering righteous indignation and about ready to unleash hurricane-force rhetoric.

"We shall defy and challenge all the records of mankind, all the horrid imps of Dante's Inferno, and all the records of hell to produce a meaner man than John West. Down and downward, forever hellward, was the trend of his degradation."

Thompson could do nothing but stand in awe of LeGett's rhetoric. For a brief moment he felt as if he could walk immediately from his cell, following LeGett and his preaching, past all the guards and police straight to freedom, for who could stand in the way of such fervor?

"We will prove, beyond all doubt and reason, that West was a monster of depravity, and your actions against his sophistry were certainly more effectual than the sacramental wine or catnip tea. We shall make judge and jury understand that to prevent and to punish with death the crimes of this monster of depravity comes to us with divine sanction and was often practiced by those who are conspicuous in the lineage of the Savior."

The sermon ended, and LeGett turned to Thompson. Slipping from the piety of the preaching, Thompson did not know whether he should applaud or shout amen.

In a fatherly tone LeGett addressed Thompson, "Jack West had publicly threatened you, and when you approached him to defend yourself, he made a threatening move and you, of course, rightly felt your life was in imminent danger, so you fired . . . Three times."

"Four . . . I think. I do not rightly remember."

"You do not have to rightly remember. We will determine everything you need to remember. Have no worries, Mr. Thompson. I have defended, successfully, dozens of such cases. Many, thinner than yours. At least you dispatched Mr. West face to face. I have had numerous clients who defended themselves by shooting their attacker in the back."

LeGett sat on the bunk and began to take notes. "Now, in your own words, tell me exactly what happened on the day in question. I will clear up any misremembrances. Also, if you have any witnesses I can add to the list I have already begun, that might be helpful."

❋ ❋ ❋

"The Williams woman has done doubled the cost in damages than she has paid in fines for her offenses," Commissioner H. C. McCart disgustedly declared. "It is clearly financially undesirable to arrest the hellion."

"We cannot let her walk the streets stealing and whoring with impunity," said Commissioner T. A. Altman.

"Of course not, but she has her hands in the city treasury far more than any drunken rogue," replied Commissioner McCart.

"Bessie or no Bessie, we have no choice but to issue bonds to build a new jail," said Commissioner T. J. Powell. "This woman has merely shown us the obvious. The jail has rotted to the core. It is a lean-to in a hurricane."

All the commissioners slumped in their leather seats contemplating raising taxes mere months before an election. Each considered their own damage control options. None were in serious jeopardy of losing their district elections. Fort Worth was, like most Texas towns, securely in "good ole boy" control, and each commissioner had the firm backing of the city fathers. Still, the public tongue-lashing and backroom disapproval would be fierce and discomforting, at the least.

"There is one other remedy," said Commissioner Altman.

"And that would be . . ." said Commissioner McCart.

"Lock the Williams woman up and throw away the key. Convict her of a felony crime and send her to prison. Let her tear down the state penitentiary for a change." There were a few moments silence as the council mulled the suggestion.

"The woman is a menace," Commissioner Altman continued. "She preys mostly on travelers in town for a day or two who leave their money in our coffers. Stories of coming to Fort Worth and being rolled by soiled doves are surely not the reputation we want spread across the rest of the state and beyond. Bessie should have been dispatched to the state pen years ago."

The men looked at each other in silent agreement.

Commissioner Powell mused, "There is one other way to save a little money before sending her away for good."

"And that would be?" said Commissioner McCart.

"If we arrest her two or three more times, she will have demolished the jail of her own accord and save us the trouble and expense of tearing it down ourselves."

No one was amused.

November 19, 1914
Fort Worth Star-Telegram

County Jail in Real Peril Now;
Bessie's In Again

It will have to be a rush job if the repairs to the county jail recently authorized by the county commissioners are completed in time to do any good. Bessie Williams is in again and the chances are that by the time she gets through there will hardly be enough left of the ancient structure to be worth repairing. Bessie has a reputation as a jail breaker to sustain and it is not to be supposed that she will let any opportunity like this one slip. Testifying as a witness in a murder case in the district court recently, she said she already had broken out of the county jail twice and the city jail so many times that she could not keep count of them.

Bessie's present incarceration is due to her failure to appear in the county criminal court Thursday morning in the case against her husband, Homer Joyce, based on a complaint, which she had filed, charging him with aggravated assault. When she failed to appear, an attachment was issued for her and she was brought into court by Deputy Sheriff Casey. Judge Brown fined her $25 for disobeying a subpoena of the court and as she was unable to raise that much money on short notice she was sent to jail. Joyce was acquitted.

She denied positively Thursday that Joyce had struck her, as was charged in the complaint, and said she was drunk when she filed the charges against him. Asked as to how her face happened to be so badly bruised, she said that was the result of a Halloween celebration, when she and another woman were masquerading in men's clothes.

Bob Higdon sat at the bar and downed his third whiskey. He was to have met with LeGett over forty-five minutes ago. Higdon reviled lawyers and city folk in general. Their demeanor, manner, and sensibilities were foreign to him. In Higdon's mind anyone who did not make his living with his hands or from the back of a horse was suspect from the get-go.

LeGett entered the dark saloon and bee-lined to Higdon. "Good day, sir," said LeGett. "How do you fare?"

"I tire of the train ride from Lampasas to Fort Worth. When will this business be over?"

"In a gnat's life, Mr. Higdon." LeGett took a stool next to Higdon and ordered a whiskey from the barkeep. "Truth be told, cases are usually won or lost during voir dire, and I have that well in hand. However, if you wish there to be absolutely no doubt as to the outcome of Mr. Thompson's trial, as I believe you have stated on many occasions, then there are a few witnesses that could stand to recount events in a more favorable way." LeGett and Higdon locked eyes for several moments. LeGett smiled. Higdon scowled.

"It sounds, Mr. LeGett, as if you require more money."

"Not for myself, Mr. Higdon." LeGett paused. "People often have different recollections when their pockets are full rather than empty." LeGett took a slip of paper from his breast pocket and slid it down the bar to Higdon.

Higdon slapped his hand loudly on the paper, picked it up off the bar, and slipped it into his wallet. "I'll see to it myself but this business needs to be concluded." With that, Higdon rose and left.

LeGett lingered a few more hours in the saloon.

1915

January 27, 1915
Fort Worth Star-Telegram

Woman Is Charged with Taking Bribe
May Kelley Is Alleged to Have Secured $25 For Promise Not to Testify Against Jack Thompson.

As a companion case to the two filed last week against Bob Higdon, charging bribery and attempting to bribe witnesses in the Jack Thompson murder case, information was filed in Justice Maben's court Tuesday against May Kelley, charged with receiving a bribe as a witness. She waived preliminary hearing and her bond was fixed at $1,000.

Higdon, who is Thompson's father-in-law, is charged with paying May Kelley $25 not to testify against Thompson and offering a like amount to Bessie Williams. Both women did testify in the case, although May Kelley was a very unwilling witness and had to be brought into court by the sheriff.

Mayor R. F. Milam was under pressure from doctors and health officials to do something about the disease-ridden conditions of the river bottoms, better known as No Man's Land. The police were also chewing his ear off, as the area was as infested with crime and lawlessness as much or more as disease. He was late to his own meeting and walked in to find Police Commissioner Davis, Chief Montgomery, City Physician Hays, Harry Adams of the Board of Health, Dr. S. G. Bittick, city pure food inspector, and Ben Dollins, sanitation officer, already present, seated and solving the considerable ills of Fort Worth.

"As this meeting has already come to order, I suppose we should get down to business, gentlemen," Mayor Milam said. He slid into his chair at the head of the long oak table. Everyone exchanged greetings and pleasantries with the mayor.

"As I have said, repeatedly, I might add, the abhorrent health conditions in No Man's Land and to a somewhat lesser extent, Battercake Flats, is a danger to the city as a whole. We cannot ignore the situation any longer as it is putting all of the good citizens of Fort Worth in peril. I'm sure everyone remembers the meningitis outbreak of 1912, and I am equally sure no one wishes a repeat," concluded Dr. Hays.

"Aye," said Mayor Milam, "but what to do about it."

"I can send in the mounted," said Chief Montgomery. "Evacuate the people and raze the shanties."

"We've done this before," said Mayor Milam.

"And vagrants sweep back in like the floods," said Ben Dollins. "The real danger of No Man's Land is not the unsanitary conditions, it is the unholy condition of whites, blacks, Mexicans, and wanton women that present the real danger. Reverend Norris said as much not two Sundays ago. Disease is born from sin, and there is sin aplenty down there."

"Well, something must be done," said Mayor Milam. "Located so near the courthouse and other respectable businesses, it is an eyesore and affront to the nose on most days. It is bad for commerce and believe you me I get an earful."

"When children fall ill and mothers point to you, Mayor, is when you will get an earful," said Harry Adams, doctors Hays and Bittick nodded in agreement.

Mayor Milam rapped his knuckles on the thick table and declared, "Montgomery, Davis, sweep the varmints out. Shoo or arrest the people, shoot the curs and level every shack and shanty. And keep sweeping until everyone stops returning."

"Yes, Mayor," replied Montgomery.

"With pleasure and godspeed," replied Davis.

"I will need a thorough inspection of the area to see what type and quantity of supplies are needed to completely sanitize the area," said Dollins.

"That sounds like a sentence that comes just before a request for additional funds, Mr. Dollins," said the mayor.

"Most likely," replied Dollins.

At least he was honest.

March 29, 1915
Fort Worth Star-Telegram

"No Man's Land" Will Be Made Holocaust by Police Inspectors Order Immediate Steps Taken to Cleanse Squatter District in Eastern River Bottoms.

City health and police officers were candidates for the bathtub when they finished an inspection of "No Man's Land," the free rent district of the east side river bottoms, Monday morning. They were Police Commissioner Davis, Chief Montgomery, City Physician Hays, Harry Adams of the Board of Health, Dr. S.G. Bittick, city pure food inspector, and Ben Dollins, sanitation officer.

To devise a way to cleanse the district was the object of the trip. They hit upon the following plans:

To drain the district of water.

To saturate many houses with oil and burn them.

To arrest many "squatters" in the district and force them to seek new and more sanitary quarters.

These plans will be carried out as soon as possible.

"No Man's Land" was cleaning up when the inspection party arrived Monday morning. Residents had heard they were coming, and a half a dozen of them had rake and broom.

Good Enough for Father

The inspectors found a two roomed house, where a 4-month-old baby was fast asleep in a chair while his mother was washing dishes. The father conducted them through his home.

"This place is good enough for me," said the husband. "I pay a dollar a month rent. I ain't responsible for this slough out here, and all them tin cans and stuff. I didn't put them there, did I?"

"You don't expect to raise that baby in a place like this, do you?" asked Harry Adams.

"I expect to, friend," was the reply. "This is the finest baby I ever seen."

Adams admitted that it was a mighty healthy-looking baby.

The inspectors passed a dozen or more houses which had been more than half torn down by squatters for firewood.

In one house they found a woman with a broken leg in bed with a dog. The windows were closed up with slabs of tin. The house contained three rooms, but the front one only was occupied. The flooring had been torn out of the others for firewood. A stifling smell floated over the house, and Harry Adams wondered how the dog managed to live in it, much less the woman. A heating stove rested on three tin cans.

The officials hurried past another house because of the stench.

Pays No Rent.

One woman—just released from jail for vagrancy—had just cleaned up her combination kitchen-bedroom for the coming of the inspectors. She had been warned. She did not pay any rent, she said—did not know who owned the house. She did not attempt to work.

"How do you live?" asked the chief.

"My husband sends me money," she said.

Dollins pointed out a dilapidated house, without doors and windows, where he said John West was killed by Jack Thompson seven months ago. It was the home of Bessie Williams. Bessie was then a squatter in "No Man's Land," but she has since moved to other quarters.

The inspectors spent two hours in the district, wading through piles of filth and rubbish, and jumping over green-scummed pools of water.

News of the city's plan to level and drain "No Man's Land" spread through the ghetto like the overflowing Trinity after a spring thunderstorm. People bustled about packing their meager belongings and stealing what they could from neighbors. Bessie cut through the frenzy like a hot knife through soft butter. She had not been back to her home since the murder of Jack West, but she would be damned if the city would tear it down.

She began to scream one hundred yards away, and even the feral dogs gave her a wide berth. The people in her path near about levitated out of her way.

She hit the porch in a feverish fury, ripping boards, planks, and plywood with the strength of four good-sized railroad men. At first a few children wandered over to watch the destruction, but in sight of twenty minutes men and women alike had stopped their desertion and crowded around to watch as Bessie tore the house to the ground with her bare hands.

By the time it was over there was nothing left standing of the only structure Bessie had ever known as home. She stood in the middle of the wreckage looking barely human. Her hair was sweat soaked and tangled. Her clothes ripped where the sharp angles and nails of the house had futilely fought back against their attacker. Every inch of exposed skin was covered in dirt, mud, and slime. Her breath was labored and heavy.

Bessie tilted back her head, opened her mouth, and raged at the heavens, her fists clenched at her sides. It was not a human sound that rolled up from her belly.

The children scattered, the women wept, and a tingle ran up the spines of the men in the gawking crowd.

No one was around when Bessie finally walked away.

June 2, 1915
Fort Worth Star-Telegram

Death Penalty of Messenger Boy's Slayer Affirmed

The death penalty imposed on Clint Williams, Fort Worth negro youth, for the murder of Oscar Scroggins, messenger boy, near Polytechnic, was affirmed Wednesday by the court of criminal appeals at Austin.

Other important Tarrant county criminal cases affirmed Wednesday were: Horace M. Collins, Jr., given 35 years for the assault and robbery of J. H. Greer and Marion Long last September; R.B. Lustess, forty-five years for pandering; Jack Thompson, ten years for murder and Ed Roan, four years for burglary . . . . . .

After one mistrial Jack Thompson was convicted of killing John West, a horse trader, in August 1914. The killing occurred in a house occupied by Bessie Williams, notorious jail breaker in the No Mans Land district in the east bottoms . . . . . .

June 19, 1915
Fort Worth Star-Telegram

Flood Area Cleaned, Say City Workers
137 Pieces of Furniture Received From Dallas Dealers

Sanitation work in the recently flooded Trinity river district was virtually completed Saturday, according to Dr. Webb Walker, city physician in charge of the work, and G.C. Clynch, his assistant. Walker reported health conditions good in the face of disease bearing conditions caused by the flood.

The last place visited by the health workers was in and around Trinity Park, where little trouble is expected. Valley View was finished up Saturday. Battercake Flats was sprinkled and cleaned Thursday and Friday. A solution of formaldehyde was used to disinfect houses. Lime was poured on the soggy ground and crude oil in the pools formed by the stagnant water.

There were 137 pieces in the carload of household goods received through the charity of Dallas furniture firms. They were as follows: 28 mattresses, 12 rocking chairs, 4 wash stands, 4 dressers, 5 tables, 5 couches, 15 beds, 1 cot, 26 springs, 9 pillows, 6 quilts. Of the articles received 74 were turned over to the North Side Emergency Club for distribution.

All of the household effects and food received by the Relief Association and the Emergency Club failed to meet the demands of the flood sufferers. Chairs, mattresses, pillows, quilts and food are the main things needed.

Of the four dressers received, two were sent to the North Side and two were distributed by Mrs. Louise Gabard, investigator for the Relief Association.

"I had a terrible time with a blind man because I couldn't supply him with a dresser," said Mrs. Gabard Saturday. "What a blind man wanted with a dresser I don't understand."

1915-1916

PETER HOWARD

— 1915 —

Fort Worth was growing by every measurable indicator. Businesses popped up and expanded weekly. The population grew daily with people coming from all directions by foot, by rail, by horse, and wagon; even a few arrived by automobile. The smoke hung in the air thick with brown dust and black soot. What hung in the air that couldn't be seen could certainly be smelled, as the aroma from the meat-packing plants covered everything as thick as molasses on flapjacks.

The word had come down Saturday night from on high that one hundred men, as able-bodied as could be mustered, were needed by daybreak Monday for road crews. The city fathers wanted the dirt roads, especially those on the north side and sprawling out from the courthouse, to be red-bricked as soon as possible. A smog-filled skyline and red-bricked streets were signs of prosperity and wealth.

"We have less than sixty in the hoosegow, boys," said Night Sergeant Willows. "Grab a paddy wagon and head to the Acre and Battercake Flats and clean out at least another sixty before sunup."

Officer Peter Howard sighed and adjusted his holster. Going with the boys assigned to the Acre was better than walking Battercake Flats alone, but raiding bawdy houses and saloons in the Acre was no Sunday picnic.

Officer Peter Howard had far too much seniority to be walking the beat in Battercake Flats, having joined the force in 1897. He tended to settle disputes the old way, using a decisive rap upside the head with his club. His manner and language were a bit coarse for a cushy beat in Quality Hill. He viewed his job as protecting the white citizens of Fort Worth and keeping coloreds and other minorities in their restricted districts. What the Mexicans and coloreds did to each other, well, that was of little concern. As long as they left the respectable citizens unbothered by their poverty and sin, Howard let them be.

Howard didn't mind walking the Flats, but he had been through some close scrapes and requested to be given a partner. His superiors had not seen fit to grant his request. Actually, they had tried, but the two officers they approached said they would rather quit than walk the Flats at night, alone or with Howard. So Howard came to walk the Flats alone with no aim other than to keep the violence and alcohol-fueled crimes contained in the district.

The night had progressed without much undue excitement. A few of the drunks had put up more fight than necessary and were bruised and would be sore still on Monday, but still fit for the road crew. The policemen did as they were bid and had made seven trips to jail with the paddy wagon brimming with drunkards and layabouts. They were on their last scoop and were funneling men from the White Rat Saloon when Howard stepped through the door with Laura Gilbert, a well-known soiled dove who mainly worked out of her house in Battercake Flats.

Night Sergeant Willows shouted, "Leave her be, Howard, no room for women when we're in need of every man we can fit in the wagon."

"You heard the man," slurred Gilbert. "Leave me be, you dumb dick." It was a wonder Gilbert's alcohol-soaked breath didn't ignite the oil lamps and set the entire Acre aflame.

"The bitch took a swing at me," bellowed Howard. "She's going to jail if I have to tie her to the back of the wagon and drag her the whole way."

Gilbert was a whip of a woman, and when Howard shoved her to the back of the paddy wagon, he lifted her clean off the ground and was about to shove her in the back when Gilbert began churning her legs like she was peddling a bicycle at breakneck speed. Howard lost his grip for a moment, and Gilbert's right heel caught Howard in his privates. Before he lost his wits Howard tossed Gilbert into the back of the wagon, then immediately balled up and fell to the ground.

Everyone, the officers and the drunkards and Jake fiends in the back of the wagon, guffawed at Howards plight. Howard rolled on the ground, unable to breathe. It took him a full five minutes to regain his composure. When he finally recovered his ego was shrunk but his privates were swollen. The other officers gave him hell and would continue to do so for days.

* * *

Three days later Howard was walking west down Franklin Street, one of the few streets bordering Battercake Flats that actually bore a name. It was a little after 9:00 p.m. and, as usual, Howard wore a pistol on each hip as he walked his beat. He was specifically headed in this direction on Franklin because he aimed to lay eyes on Laura Gilbert, and her house was midway down what generously could be called the block. Gilbert had served her time after the Saturday night assault on Howard, and he meant to make her pay for his abuse.

The night had been quiet for the Flats. In August the heat created a feast or famine of activity. Sometimes the humidity coming off the Trinity created a suffocating blanket that made it difficult for residents to even move, let alone get up to no good. Other times it seemed to make them so ireful Howard felt like he was breaking up a brawl or knife fight every ten paces.

In the purple and orange dusk of sunset Howard could see Gilbert standing outside her house speaking to a short, slightly built man he did not recognize. Gilbert flashed her eyes in Howard's direction, but the man seemed to purposefully turn his head away.

This raised Howard's suspicion and he picked up his pace.

"Doing a little business, Laura?" asked Howard.

"I'm minding my business," Gilbert retorted. "Can't you leave me be?"

As Howard approached, the man turned to look Howard in the eye but could not seem to bring himself to look any further than Howard's chest. He was small, no more than five foot five, and his complexion and features showed he was likely of mixed race. The only thing lower than a Mexican or black man, in Howard's opinion, was a man of mixed blood.

"What have we here?" said Howard to the man. "What are you, Mexican or colored?" The man seemed nervous, but Howard was not particularly worried, as he seemed jittery and afraid.

The man did not answer Howard's query.

"I asked you a simple question," said Howard. He inched closer to the man. Howard towered over him by a good six inches.

"I'm part colored," came the eventual reply.

The man spoke with a heavy Mexican accent, affirming Howard's suspicion that he was mixed.

"Arms out, I'm going to search you," said Howard. It was obvious to the policeman that a man of mixed race, standing in the street with Gilbert, a known prostitute, had to be up to unlawful activity.

As Howard reached out to pat him down, the man quickly knocked Howard's hand away and stepped back from the officer. "Naw, you don't search me," he said. "You have no cause."

Howard quickly pulled his revolver, "Hands in the air," he commanded. The man complied. "Turn around." Howard reached out and spun the man around. With his left hand Howard reached for his handcuffs. They weren't there. The station did not have enough cuffs for every officer, and Howard had forgotten to take a pair with him when he left the station. He cursed briefly under his breath. It was only a mild inconvenience, however, as he firmly had the drop on the man.

"Just march yourself on up the hill ahead of me," he commanded, giving the man a shove to get him started.

Howard and the man began to walk up the hill. Howard held the man ahead of him at arm's length, holding onto the man's jacket as they trudged. After a few steps the man began walking at an odd gait, more on the balls of his feet, sort of bouncing. Howard was an old hand arresting people with something to hide. He knew the exaggerated gait was meant to dislodge a weapon from the man's waist and slide down his pant leg.

Howard forcefully jerked the man around and attempted to search his waistband. He quickly found what felt like a blade, but the jacket prevented him from grabbing it cleanly.

"Dammit, I knew you were armed!" Howard cursed. He jerked the man off balance and threw him to the ground. The man landed on his stomach but managed to flip onto his back before Howard could pounce. Howard pinned the man down but still could not grab the weapon. The man grabbed Howard's wrist. The only sound in the night was their labored breathing.

When Howard and the man fell to the ground, Gilbert turned her gaze to her house. A shadow darted around the corner. As Howard and the man grappled, the man drew breath and let loose a quick, two-note whistle. At the signal, a second man darted from the side of the house and in a lick was on Howard's back.

The second assailant wielded a skinning knife and repeatedly stabbed Howard in the back and neck and chest. Howard was outnumbered but was a much larger man than either of his assailants. The wounds would have been much more severe and numerous had Howard not fought so gamely. He managed to hit the second assailant in the temple with the butt of his revolver and knocked him off his back. The first man pushed Howard over, decided he had enough, and lit out up Franklin Hill. Howard, bleeding profusely and out of breath, lay helpless, flat on his back, blood soaking his uniform and clouding his eyes. The second assailant, regaining his whereabouts, also gained his footing and followed after his friend.

Gilbert, watching the struggle, ran towards the three men shouting, "Kill that som bitch, you worthless cusses, kill him!"

Howard regained his composure, rose up on one knee, and fired one shot at the two fading men. At the sound of the gunshot, Gilbert yelped and ran for the cover of darkness between two houses.

Howard was alone and bleeding out in the dirt. In the quiet of dusk, a stray dog wandered by, stopped momentarily, sat, scratched his fleas, licked his balls, and then trotted off down the hill into the darkness of Battercake Flats.

As Howard shakily struggled to his feet, a man, Wesley Williams, walked up from behind. He had been crouched in the shadows, watching the entire affair. He had come to Franklin Street to do business with Laura Gilbert, but the fight had begun when he turned onto the street. He would get no satisfaction from Gilbert but, just so the trip was not a complete loss, he walked over to Howard and picked his hat and both pistols up off the ground. Howard paid no heed as Williams walked away.

Howard's eyes were glazed and his black pupils crowded out the blue. He gamely rose to his feet and slowly shuffled one foot after another, making his way up the hill to Houston Street.

W. F. Jenkins was pushing his watermelon cart down Houston on his way home when he noticed Howard walking up Franklin Hill. Jenkins had passed two officers not twenty yards back up Houston, so when he saw Howard, covered in blood, he turned and shouted for help. Officer Loren E. Carlisle and special officer Callie Harding heard Jenkins shouting and came running.

Carlisle was the first to reach Howard. "Who cut you, Pete?" he shouted. Harding was right behind. When he saw the shape Howard was in he threw up in his mouth. "Jesus, Mary," he said.

Neither officer thought to render aid. When Jenkins approached he pulled his bandana from around his neck and attempted to stop the bleeding. Howard was leaking from too many wounds to stanch. Jenkins clumsy attempt to stop the bleeding was more about instinct than aid. None of the men had any emergency medical training, and after one look, all three had come to the same conclusion.

"A yellow nigger from Waco and a negro woman," came Howard's weak reply. "Get old Laura, she'll tell you what happened."

Other officers arrived and went into Battercake Flats to find and question Laura Gilbert. Howard was loaded into a horse-drawn cart and taken to City Hospital on Fourth Street.

August 17, 1915
Fort Worth Star-Telegram

---

8 Suspects Held in Police Murder; Blood Is On One Officers Believe Negroes and Not Mexicans, Responsible for Stabbing Patrolman Howard to Death

---

Practically abandoning the theory that Mexicans were responsible for stabbing Patrolman Pete Howard Monday night on Franklin street, the police Tuesday afternoon had under arrest eight negro suspects. Many of these had been frequenters of the "Battercake Flat" district, which is reached through Franklin street. Officers now are working on the theory that a plot existed among negroes to get rid of Howard.

A negro, arrested by the police at Fourth and Calhoun streets Tuesday morning, wore a bloody shirt. The fact that he had a quarrel with the patrolman Monday afternoon over the arrest of a negro woman was the original cause of his detainment, however.

Dr. Lewis C. Crabb placed the blood stain under examination Tuesday and declared it was human blood.

Negro Sets Up Alibi.

The negro said his shirt was stained with blood while cleaning doves which John Scott, Belknap and Pecan streets, killed Sunday. Scott bears him out in regard to the doves.

The negro had a further alibi from Scott's sister with regard to his whereabouts at 10 o'clock Monday night.

The blood test will be completed, however. Blood from the shirt was compared by Dr. Crabb with blood from a chicken and there was no resemblance. Tuesday afternoon he obtained blood from Howard's body and will compare it with the shirt stain.

At least a dozen negroes were examined Tuesday morning, but none of them are charged directly with the murder.

Howard was killed with a knife and two persons evidently were implicated. His throat was laid open and he was stabbed in the breast and the back in eight places, and slashed on the arm. A shot from Franklin street was Howard's alarm for help, but it came too late.

Accuses Man and Woman

Investigating the shot, W.F. Jenkins, a peddler, ran down Houston street to Franklin, and met the patrolman staggering up the hill. Patrolman Carlisle and Special Officer Callie Harring were next on the scene.

"Who cut you?" Carlisle asked him.

"A nigger from Waco and a negro woman," said Howard, barely able to talk.

The wounded man continued:

"Get old Laura – she knows all about it. I fired my pistol and hit him over the head, but they took them away from me."

By "old Laura" it is believed he meant Laura Gilbert.

The police found the woman coming up Franklin street in company with Jim Turner, a negro employee of Cantrell Brothers' stables. Both were sent to headquarters, but were released when they told their story. The woman was rearrested later, and is now being held.

Charges Mexicans Guilty.

The woman insists two Mexicans killed Howard. She saw them from her porch, 200 feet from the scene, she said.

"First, one Mexican comes up to my house and asks where some Mexicans lived," she said. "Then Mister Pete come up and goes to talking to us. He looks at this Mexican and says: 'What are you, Mexican or a nigger.' He says, 'I'm part nigger.' Mister Pete says: 'Let me search you,' and he runs his hand around the man, but the man jumps back.

"The man says: 'Naw, you don't search me,' and grabs Mister Pete's wrists. Mister Pete jumps back and draws his pistol. Then he says to the Mexican: 'You just march up the hill there ahead of me,' and he holds the pistol at the Mexican's back and they start up the hill.

Calls His Partner.

"A little ways up I can see them rolling in the dirt. I don't know which one is on top. Then I heard the Mexican whistle for his partner and goes to saying something in Spanish, and I can see the other Mexican come up from under the bluff. They fight there and I hear a pistol shot. I don't know where the Mexicans ran to—they must have gone under the bluff. Mister Pete walks on up the hill."

Belle Holmes, another noted negro woman police character, who was in Laura Gilbert's house at the time, is also being held by the police.

Patrolman Carlisle said Belle Holmes and Laura Gilbert threatened to have Howard killed a week ago. They made these threats because Howard had arrested them. He was with Howard at the time, and says the threat was made when the women were being placed in the patrol wagon. Two dozen witnesses heard it, he says.

At police headquarters Laura Gilbert on that occasion told police officials that Howard was 'jobbing' her—arresting her for nothing. Police paid no attention to this.

Franklin street is a part of the famous district known as "Battercake Flats.' Policemen have dreaded this beat because of the number of bad negroes and other characters who made Franklin street their headquarters. It has been the scene of dozens of cutting scrapes and shootings during the past few years. Among the recent killings are those of Pearl Carter and "Snow Belle" Gilbert.

Howard Buried Today.

The funeral of Patrolman Howard will be held today at 4 o'clock from his residence, 906 Fournier street. Policemen in uniform will attend. The services will be under the auspices of the Woodmen of the World. He was also a member of the Eagles.

In respect to his memory there was no session of the police court Tuesday morning.

August 17, 1915
Dallas Morning News
Patrolman Howard Stabbed to Death

Officer Dies Before Making Statement Of Affair
Negro Woman Is Held and Officers Are Searching for Two
Mexicans Well Known in Fort Worth

Special to The News.

Fort Worth, Texas, Aug. 16. – Peter Howard, a patrolman of the city police force, was stabbed tonight at 9:40 o'clock on Franklin Street, two blocks northeast of the courthouse. He died thirty minutes later at St. Joseph's Infirmary, where he was taken in an ambulance of the Spelman Undertaking Company.

At the hospital he was found to have received seven knife wounds in the back and a pistol wound in the neck.

It is not known who stabbed and shot him or what trouble led up to the affair. Those of the neighborhood heard a shot and cries for help. Howard was then found struggling up the river bluff, down which Franklin street runs. To those who first reached him he tried to tell something of a negro man and a negro woman. At the hospital he was too weak to give any information that would be instrumental in catching the assassin.

No one could be found who saw the affair. A negro woman, Laura Gilbert, who was taken in charge by the police, said that Patrolman Howard had two Mexicans in charge.

Could Give No Direct Account

According to those who first got to Howard, he stated that a negro man and a negro woman were connected with the affair. At that time he was so weak from loss of blood, after running up the bluff, that he could give no connected account of the trouble that led up to the cutting.

Howard was first reached by W.F. Jenkins, who has a watermelon wagon about two blocks from the scene of the affair. Jenkins said that he heard one shot. After that came cries for help. Jenkins then ran in the direction of the cries. At the top of the bluff he met the injured patrolman. It was then that Howard made the statement concerning the negro man and woman.

A squad of policemen hurried to the scene when the alarm came in. Near a telephone pole about half way down the bluff they found first traces of blood. This was strung out at various places along the bluff.

At this point Franklin street is very dark, there being no street lights for several blocks in either direction. The district there is known as "Batter Cake Flats." It borders on the river.

Bloodhound Sent For

An order was sent for a bloodhound and an effort is being made to locate the criminal by this means. Policemen over the entire city have been instructed to look out for two Mexicans. Names of two Mexicans with whom the police are familiar with given by the negro woman, who was held. Other negroes of the street verified her story that the Mexicans were seen there tonight.

Howard had served on the present police force since this administration went into office April 15. Previous to this he had served eight years in the same capacity. He was 41 years of age, and lived at 900 Fournier street. He is survived by his wife and one daughter, Mrs. Laura Dees, who resided with him.

Dallas Officers Notified

Dallas police officers were ordered to look out for two Mexicans who killed Officer P. Howard in Fort Worth last night. The order was issued here following a request from Chief Bailey of Fort Worth. He gave a description of the two men alleged to have done the killing. All incoming trains and interurbans were closely watched last night.

After Howard had been hauled by ambulance to City Hospital, the six policemen now on the scene began their investigation.

"Whoever did this most likely headed down the bluff or back into the Flats," said Officer Broiles.

"It's pitch black in both directions," said Patrolman Grace. All the men nodded. None were eager to conduct a search in either the Flats or the bluff and river bottoms.

"Hogkins, call back to the station and get some bloodhounds down here," said Broiles. "Take two men and search the bluff when they arrive."

"Will do," said Hogkins. He headed to the call box to request the dogs.

"Come on boys, let's see if we can't backtrack Howard's steps." The four officers headed down Franklin Hill, fanning out parallel to the street at arms length. They followed the blood halfway down the hill. "Yonder is Laura Gilbert's house," said Broiles.

It wasn't long before Battercake Flats was swarming with police and sheriff's deputies. It is difficult to say who was more skittish, the officers or the denizens.

August 17, 1915
Fort Worth Star-Telegram

Asks "Protection" Against "Gangs"

A.J. Cohen, merchant at 109 Houston street, appealed to the city commission Tuesday for protection from the gangs that are said to infest the neighborhood of his store.

"I am not surprised," he said, "that poor Peter Howard was butchered up last night. The people around there are afraid to open their mouths. Niggers, white men and Mexicans are all mixed up there. They are loafing around so much that a decent citizen is afraid to pass there. There is fighting every night. The police can't do any good."

Police Commissioner Hurdleston asked him if he ever had brought his complaint to police headquarters and he said he had not.

"Well," the commissioner said, "it is just such citizens as you that help these conditions along by not reporting them properly."

When word of the attack on Howard reached the station, every officer of both the city and county leapt into action. Officers and paddy wagons fanned out into the Acre, Irish Town, and Battercake Flats, rousting every person of color unlucky enough to be found on the street or in one of the usual loafing places.

For the next two days a steady stream of suspects were brought to the city jail and forced into the bull pen, which quickly swelled to suffocating proportions.

"Jumping Jehoshaphat, Benny," exclaimed Officer Shanks. "What am I supposed to do with these sons a bitches?"

Officer Benjamin F. Harmon entered the jail room containing the bull pen with another line of fifteen suspects rousted from Irish Town. "Don't know, don't care, Shanks," came the dead reply from Officer Harmon. "I ain't slept nor ate since I can't remember when and I's just told to round them up and bring them in." Officer Harmon stood looking at Shanks. Both men were too exhausted to muster a good argument.

Shanks knew Harmon was just doing his job, but Shanks's job was past untenable. The twenty-five-by-twenty-foot bull pen was well past capacity. Arms and legs flailed through the bars. Shanks could see men who were passed out but remained on their feet because there was no room to fall. The smell of piss, shit, vomit, sweat, blood, and lord knows what other bodily fluids mixed into a smell that could not be described. Shanks had already vomited twice. The jail smelled worse than the human waste-filled Trinity and the Armour killing floor combined. The last time Shanks had opened the door, eight men had been flung out, not of their own accord but from being decompressed by the swinging iron bars.

Harmon signed over the suspects, turned, and trudged out to fill the paddy wagon again, as he and others had done since Monday night. Officer Nowlin entered as Harmon exited and addressed Shanks. "The DA and Judge Maben are ready to start processing the suspects and witnesses."

"Thank goodness," Shanks murmured.

"Which ones is the suspects and which ones is the witnesses?" inquired Nowlin.

Shanks stared at Nowlin contemptuously. He hated rookies. "Just take these fellers soon as I write down their names."

August 18, 1915
Fort Worth Star-Telegram

Identifies Negro as in Trio That Killed Cop
Officers Raise $357 Reward for Slayer's Conviction—Dead Policeman's Hat Not Yet Discovered.
$357 Reward Now Offered for Slayers

A reward now being raised among police and city hall employees as a bonus for the conviction of the murderers of Patrolman Peter Howard, had reached $357 at noon Wednesday. The reward does not apply to officers alone but to any one giving information leading to the capture of the guilty parties. Circulars giving notice of the reward and descriptions of the two Mexicans now sought will be circulated broadcast by the police.

Wesley Williams, 23, a negro who was arrested late Tuesday at 406 West Bluff street by Detectives Snow and DeJordy, was a member of the trio that killed Patrolman Pete Howard on Franklin Hill Monday night, according to a statement of a negro woman witness now being held at police headquarters.

Whether or not Williams inflicted any of the fatal stabs on Howard, the woman could not say, as she was too far away to see plainly.

Other Mexicans

The woman's first story involved only two Mexicans in the murder. Then in a new statement, made to George Hoset, assistant county attorney; Detective Chief Blanton, Police Chief Bailey and others, she said three men did the work, and named Williams.

Williams, she said, was with the two Mexicans when they came down Franklin street and stopped in front of a negro house. While they were talking there to negro women, they saw Patrolman Howard coming toward them. Williams and one Mexican dodged under the house—it is built on pilings over the bluff on Franklin Hill—but the other Mexican stood his ground and faced the officer.

Mexican Resists

The officer began to talk to the lone Mexican and the women. He asked the man his name, where he was from and whether he was a Mexican or a negro. The Mexican said his name was Luis, he was recently from Waco, and he was part negro. Then when Howard started to search him for arms the Mexican resisted and grabbed Howard's arms. Howard drew his pistol, put the Mexican in front and started marching him up the hill.

Then near the top of the hill the woman said she saw both Mexican and policeman fall to the ground in a tussle. The Mexican shouted in Spanish and whistled and the second Mexican and the negro climbed over the bluff and ran to his assistance.

Followed by Pals

The second Mexican and negro, who had been hiding under the negro house, had run up the hill under the bluff when Howard and his prisoner started in that direction.

Police say they are positive the plans for murdering Howard had been in preparation a long time, and were not hatched on the moment.

Half a dozen negro witnesses are still being held. All others were released Tuesday night.

Slayer Left Hat

One of the Mexican murderers lost his hat in the attack on the patrolman, but grabbed the wounded man's own hat and wore it away. Howard's police wreath was attached to his hat.

A woman nearby says she heard one of the assailants shout: "Get my hat, Williams."

The Mexican's hat was taken to the home of Roy Childress, negro, 406 West BluffSstreet, by Wesley Williams ten minutes later. Williams told Childress two Mexicans had murdered "Mister Pete" and then showed him the Mexican's hat.

Williams said he was on the porch of a negro house on Franklin street after the attack, when a negro woman came out and tossed him the hat. Williams said he did not know what to do with it.

Sent Hat Away

Childress said he made Williams take the hat away.

"Don't let that hat stay here," Childress said he told Williams.

Williams then left with the hat, saying he would take it back to Franklin Street. It was subsequently found in a negro house on that street.

Williams admitted to being at the negro house with Laura Gilbert and other negro women and two Mexicans when Howard came up. At first he denied being there. He still says he did not hide from the patrolman, but said the other Mexican dodged under the house.

Both Williams and Laura Gilbert told investigators that the Mexican, Luis, whom Howard attempted to search, was carrying a big pistol. They saw it they said. That was why he refused to allow Howard to search him.

Williams is being held in a cell at headquarters. He has not been confronted with the testimony, which the negro woman witness gave against him.

Pistols Not Recovered

The police have not been able to find trace of either of the two pistols, which were taken away from Howard, or his hat. A 45-caliber six shooter shell, loaded, was found on the scene of the assault by Policeman Turner. This evidently came from the Mexican's pistol, because Howard carried two automatics.

Convinced of the correctness of his alibi, the police late Tuesday released a negro who had been arrested as a suspect in the Howard murder case because he had blood stains on his shirt.

The blood test, which was being conducted by Dr. L.C. Crabb, was consequently dropped. It was shown that the blood stains on the negro's shirt had come from a dove, and as the blood of this bird bears the closest resemblance to human blood of any other fowl or animal the stains on the shirt were easily mistaken for human blood.

Mayor Tyra called an all-hands-on-deck meeting of all city and department heads, assistants, and select business and civic leaders. To the relief of all present, Mayor Tyra was calm and unflustered. "I'm going to state the obvious, gentlemen. This horrendous murder needs to be solved quickly and beyond a shadow of a doubt." Ayes and affirmations all around. "As I understand things a mighty fine reward of $500 has been raised. I have reached out to the governor asking state funds to be added but was declined." Heads were shaken and tisks were offered. "My last report from the department gave little hope solid leads are forthcoming." More head shaking. "I need an arrest and I need that arrest to stick." The mayor looked around the room. There were no eyes willing to meet his gaze.

Things were beginning to get uncomfortable when Captain Claud Canterbury, leader of the local Texas National Guard, spoke up. "I'm certain the brave men of law enforcement are tireless in the execution of their duty to apprehend and convict the dirty cowards that murdered Pete Howard, but I would like to offer three companies of National Guardsmen to assist in any way needed or necessary."

"I'm not sure the National Guard has any standing in this matter, Captain Canterbury," said Judge Swayne.

"If this really is the beginnings of the Plan de San Diego, it would hold in good stead to have the guard already deployed," said Assistant Chief Cantrell.

"The Plan de San Diego is hogwash and every sane man knows it," shot back Swayne.

His ire up, Cantrell retorted, "Tell that to the good citizens of Columbus, New Mexico, Your Honor."

"Every time a Mexican so much as wipes snot on his sleeve, you folks make it out to be a revolution, and it just ain't so."

Mayor Tyra cut his eyes to the judge, but before he could draw breath Captain Canterbury spoke up. "Captain Harrison and I were discussing just last week that the Guard are past due training exercises." He paused, then continued, "This presents a good opportunity for the men to hone their skills and knowledge for when they are actually called into service." He turned to Cantrell. "And it cannot hurt to show the Mexicans in the Flats, two are ready and able." He then turned to Judge Swayne. "They will solely be deployed for training and teaching purposes."

The judge folded his hands across his chest, shook his head, and sat back in his chair.

August 18, 1915
Fort Worth Star-Telegram

---

3 Cops Will 'Clean Out' Negro Dives

The First steps to 'clean out' Franklin Hill were taken Wednesday morning when Bicycle Patrolman McKinney, Herring and Brothers were sent into that district. Fifteen negroes, including seven women, were jailed on charges of vagrancy before noon. The raids will continue Wednesday night.

Franklin Hill was policed by two men Tuesday night. Heretofore only one man has been detailed to this beat. Policeman "Dad" Aiken has been assigned as regular patrolman from that beat, but he will be given an assistant each night until the district is cleaned of undesirable inhabitants.

Dad Aiken was feeling more than a might full of himself. He was about to lead a small band of patrolmen into Battercake Flats, and they were more than a little afraid of what the night had in store for them, so Aiken had pulled out his soapbox and let loose. "I'm guessing I don't have to tell you fellows to swing free and easy," Aiken paused and looked each man in the eye. "These aren't like the nice and polite folks y'all are used to dealing with on the north side or up on Quality Hill." He raised his voice for emphasis, "These darkies will sooner kill you as look at you." Each of the men's eyes were as round as platters. This pleased Aiken greatly. "We have been charged with clearing the Battercake Flats of all undesirables, but the question is do you know how to spot an undesirable?" He raised up and waited to see if anyone would venture a guess.

No one did.

"They're in Battercake Flats, you imbeciles," he shouted. They laughed. "No decent man, woman, or child would be caught dead the wrong side of Franklin Hill. If you see someone, rap them upside the head and haul them to the pokey."

The men laughed and headed into Battercake Flats for a night of beatings with full hearts and pure souls, secure in the knowledge they were doing the Lord's work.

August 20, 1915
Dallas Morning News

Three Murder Charges Filed In Howard Case
Negro and Two Mexicans Are Implicated
Former Is in Jail, While Search Is Being
Conducted for the Others

Special to The News.

Fort Worth, Texas, Aug. 19.—Charges of murder were today filed against Wesley Williams, negro, Joe Estoppa and Luis Flores, Mexicans, in connection with the killing of Peter Howard, the patrolman, Monday night on Franklin street.

The negro is now in jail and has admitted that he was with the two Mexicans just before the policeman was killed. He denies any knowledge of the affair and states that he left the pair when patrolman Howard was seen coming down Franklin street. At first he denied knowing that the two Mexicans were in town.

Efforts of local officers are now being directed to catching the two Mexicans. More than 1,000 circulars, giving descriptions of the two men were mailed to city and county officers of Texas and Oklahoma today.

New evidence secured today has led the police and detectives to believe that a plot to murder the policeman was laid two hours before the attack. Another negro woman has been found, who says she passed Williams and the Mexicans Monday night about 8 o'clock. The three were standing in front of a house on Franklin street and she stopped for a moment and talked, according to her story.

August 22, 1915
Dallas Morning News

Posse Searches River Bottoms for Suspects
Hunt for Mexicans Thought Hiding There Futile
Efforts Still Being Made to Find Two of Three Men Indicted
in Howard Case.

Special to The News.

Fort Worth, Texas, Aug. 21. – Police, members of the Sheriff's office and citizens formed a posse this afternoon and searched the river bottoms for two hours in an effort to locate some Mexicans, believed to be those wanted in connection with the murder of Peter Howard, the policeman who was killed last Monday night on Franklin street.

A report that two Mexicans had been seen there caused the search, which was without result. One Mexican was caught and sent to headquarters, but was turned loose after detectives had satisfied themselves he was not wanted.

Efforts are still being made to locate the two Mexicans who were indicted yesterday, along with Wesley Williams, negro, in connection with the murder of Howard.

September 5, 1915
Dallas Morning News

Report Louis Flores Held at Georgetown
One Of Two Mexicans Indicted in Howard Murder Case.
Telegram from Sheriff There Says Will Have Joe Estapa, the Other, "in Thirty-Six Hours."

Special to The News.

Fort Worth, Texas, Sept. 4.—A report to the police department this afternoon was to the effect that Louis Flores, one of the Mexicans under indictment for the killing of Policeman Peter Howard two weeks ago, is now being held at Georgetown. The Sheriff there further stated that he would have the other Mexican, Joe Estapa, who is under indictment on the same charge, "within thirty-six hours."

Two members of the detective department were sent to Georgetown tonight to bring the prisoner here, if he proves to be the right man. A reward of $400 is offered for the capture of the two Mexicans.

The Sheriff here stated this afternoon that he had no information concerning the Georgetown prisoner, other than what was furnished in the message to the Chief of Police.

September 6, 1915
Fort Worth Star-Telegram

Murder Suspect Arrested on His Way to See Girl
Martin Flores Freely Admits Part in Fight in Which
Policeman Was Killed—Denies Doing Stabbing.

Martin Flores, alias Louis Flores, brought back from Georgetown
Sunday, accused of having a part in the murder of Policeman Peter
Howard on the night of Aug. 16, freely admits that he was present
when Howard was killed, but denies that he struck the blows
which ended the officer's life. Flores was arrested while on his way
to Tyler to see his sweetheart.

According to his story he had just arrived here on a freight
train in company of Joe Estapa, also sought in connection with the
killing, on the morning before the crime. Both were wanted by the
police here at that time and they dropped off at Sycamore Creek,
remaining in hiding from 2 a.m. until after dark, when they
worked their way up through the bottom and went to the home of
Laura Gilbert.

Flores said he was standing there drinking wine with Estapa
and Wesley Williams, when Howard approached them.

"He put me under arrest, pulled out his gun and was marching
me up the hill," said Flores. "I had a gun and was trying to work
it loose with my elbow. He saw what I was doing and felt the gun.
Then he hit me over the head and knocked me down. I whistled
for Joe, who had dodged under the house.

"I was lying there on the ground under the officer, trying to
keep him from shooting me. The next thing I knew the officer let
go and ran. Joe took hold of me and pulled me up off the ground. I
heard someone running down the hill, but didn't know who it was.

"I went on down the hill with Joe and hollered to Wesley
Williams to get my hat."

The hat and Howard's two pistols are still missing.

Didn't Know of Stabbing.

Flores declares he thought at the time Joe had struck the officer
with a rock and did not know that he had been stabbed until Joe

told him of it later. A wicked looking dirk, which he admitted was the one used in the cutting, was found on Flores at the time of his arrest.

He said he and Estapa remained on the north side for three days and then went to Dallas, catching an interurban car at Cleburne Junction. From Dallas they went to Beaumont, Houston, San Antonio, Kennedy and Sinton, where they separated, Flores going back to Granger, where he was arrested, while Estapa said he was going to the border.

Flores started for Tyler to see his sweetheart, but at a small town in Williamson county met a Mexican whom he knew only by the name of Julian. He was getting up a cotton picking outfit of about 100 Mexicans and Flores hired out to him to pick cotton, intending only to work long enough to get money to go on with his trip.

He made a trip to Granger and met there a Mexican named Blanco, with whom he had had trouble before. Constable Ed Allen of Granger already had talked to Blanco about Flores, and he immediately notified the officer. Allen placed him under arrest, but he denied his identity, giving his name as Jesus Costa. He was taken on to Georgetown, however, and was identified by another Mexican who was in jail there. He then admitted his identity. He says that his name really is Martin Flores, but that his name was given in by the arresting officer as Louis Flores the first time he was arrested here and that he has since been known in Fort Worth by that name.

Flores says he has made a living by gambling since he left here and gave the officers some interesting information about the manipulation of cards. He said he was in Granger to buy four decks of cards and some sandpaper and showed them how it was used. If a deck is to be used for poker the aces and kings were taken out and the ends of the rest of the deck sandpapered enough so that the aces and kings would be just a trifle longer than the other cards when replaced in the deck. He said that on his own deal it always was possible in that way to give himself or his partner four aces or four kings. He had $9 in money when arrested.

Judge Swayne and county attorneys Reuben S. Phillips and Marshall Spoonts had been in the judge's chambers for over an hour. Swayne had heard the two had turned down LeGett's plea deal of a guilty verdict in exchange for life without parole, and the judge had wanted to know why the deal had been rejected. "I see no reason to expend the time or monies of this county on a trial seeking the death penalty when it is not clear and evident Flores even took part, let alone struck the killing blow."

Phillips had refused a seat and seemed primed for a fight. "The good people of Tarrant County thirst for justice, and we believe the Mexican should swing from a rope not rot in a cell at the state's expense."

The judge turned to the more experienced attorney, "Spoonts?"

"With all due respect, Your Honor, we feel confident we can elicit the death penalty from a jury."

"Are you as confident in his guilt as you are in the verdict?"

"We have no doubt Flores instigated Howard's death by his actions."

"Whether or not he struck the blows is of no consequence to you, Phillips?"

"A good man died," Phillips continued. "One of the city's finest, and justice must and will be served."

1916

April 15, 1916
Fort Worth Star-Telegram

Flores Convicted of Killing Cop; Given Life Term

Lewis, alias Martin, Flores was convicted of the murder of Patrolman Pete Howard, and his punishment was fixed at life imprisonment by a jury in the Seventeenth district court Saturday.

The first ballot after the jury retired Friday about 3:40 p.m., was on "guilty or not guilty." The result was 11 to 1, one of the jurors favoring manslaughter. On the next ballot, however, he voted with the others.

Then balloting on the sentence began. Six of the jurors favored death, three favored life imprisonment and the other three were for lower sentences, one wanting to give the prisoner only five years.

Asked for Testimony.

After the jurors had balloted for about an hour and a half Friday, they returned to the courtroom to have read the portion of the defendant's testimony wherein he said "we done this murder."

When the jury retired Friday night it appeared hopelessly divided, but almost the first effort to agree Saturday morning was successful. Attorneys in the case were notified about 9 o'clock, but the jury was not brought in until about 9:30 because the defendant was not ready to come to the courtroom from the jail.

He sat alone when the verdict was ready, and appeared careless of what it was. He smiled slightly an instant later, however. His attorney, J. Ben LeGett said he had not decided whether an appeal would be taken.

Attorneys for Flores offered before the trial was started to plead guilty and take a life sentence for their client, but the county attorney refused to make such an agreement.

Father in Court

None of Patrolman Howard's relatives were in the courtroom when the verdict was returned, but Mrs. G. Frank Coffey, widow of Police Captain Coffey who was killed on the North Side, was one of the listeners.

Flores' father, George Flores, advanced to the railing and talked to the prisoner a few minutes after the verdict was returned.

Arguments in the case were closed by County Attorney Spoonts Friday afternoon.

Officers' Widow Scores Verdict

Mrs. Pete Howard, widow of Flores' alleged victim, created a scene when she arrived at the court house about half an hour after the verdict was returned. She first attacked the jury bitterly and then complained of the actions of Judge Swayne. Swayne refused to discuss the matter with her.

Judge Swayne was about fit to be tied. The case was over and done with, a life sentence, which could have been agreed to without cause for a trial, had been reached and now Ben LeGett was filing appeals against his client's wishes to further tie up and delay the case. "I've about had it with lawyers, LeGett. I have spoken with Flores, I have his wishes hand writ, and you are going to further this? Is that what you are telling me?"

LeGett held his ground. "I believe the verdict to be unjust, Your Honor."

Swayne seethed.

LeGett continued, "I do not believe Flores struck any blows, and he did not intend for Howard to be killed. I think manslaughter is called for at worst."

Swayne continued to stare at LeGett.

"Flores does not have full comprehension of the law or his untenable situation," the lawyer continued. "I am merely trying to give a full and vigorous defense, which is his due and my charge."

"I believe you, LeGett, but I also believe this goes nowhere, and the wishes of Mr. Flores should be honored. Sometimes fighting for justice is not worth the effort."

May 15, 1916
Fort Worth Star-Telegram

Louis Flores Is Sentenced; Lawyers Agree

Louis Flores, Mexican, one of the slayers of Patrolman Pete Howard eight months ago received his sentence of a life term in the penitentiary in the Seventeenth district court Monday morning and is being prepared for the trip to Huntsville.

Flores had appealed his case, but Saturday he asked Judge Mike E. Smith permission to withdraw this appeal and take the sentence. His appeal was not granted until his attorneys had consented. Their consent was given Monday morning.

"You are sentenced to hard labor for a term of not less than five years nor more than your natural life," the judge told him.

Flores said nothing, but returned to his seat and resumed puffing on a cigar.

1915

THE WOMAN OF NO MAN'S LAND

December 15, 1915
Fort Worth Star-Telegram

"No Man's Land" Is Raided By Police
Squatters Ordered Out and Some Arrested
on Charges of Vagrancy.

Squatters were driven out of "No Man's Land" in the river bottoms, Tuesday afternoon by a squad of mounted police who raided that district. Some arrests on charges of vagrancy were made.

Squatters have been ordered out of that land several times before, but each time they returned. Shacks in that district have offered free rent to negroes and whites for years.

1916

June 14, 1916
Fort Worth Star-Telegram

In the Courts

Forty-Eighth District Court
Hon. Bruce Young, Judge

State vs. Willie Clark, theft from person: defendant pleaded guilty, punishment fixed at five years imprisonment, with suspension of sentence.

Bessie stood in the box in Judge Young's courtroom. She was dirty, unkempt, and dazed from lack of sleep. Her mind, however, was spotless. Perfectly clean and free of any thought, static or white noise. She had been arrested, arraigned, and sent to trial so many times in her life she knew where to go, where to stand, and when to nod, by rote.

"Bessie," Judge Young said. "The police, prosecutors, courts, and indeed, the entire city have reached the end of the rope with you." He twirled his gavel absentmindedly as he continued, "I should end this farce now, as I have been instructed, but . . . " Young paused a long moment and looked intently at Bessie. "Mrs. Joyce."

"Williams," Bessie interrupted insistently. She had seemingly awakened from her stupor. "My name is Bessie Williams," Bessie firmly stated.

"Yes," replied Judge Brown. "I know who you are, but the indictment says Joyce, and I seem to remember a marriage to a Mr. Joyce, a while back. Has there been a divorce? Is there some mistake?"

"The marriage was a mistake. I am and always have been Bessie Williams."

"Yes, well," Young stumbled, "as I was saying. I find you guilty as charged and sentence you to five years imprisonment." Again, Judge Young paused. "And hereby suspend the sentence. But next time, Bessie, you will find yourself in a wagon headed to Huntsville the next time you set foot in this or any court in Tarrant County. Do I make myself clear?"

Bessie did not reply but shrank noticeably in stature. Judge Young took this as a yes, banged his gavel, and the bailiff called the next case as Bessie was removed by a marshall.

An hour later Bessie was released from the courthouse into the cool spring afternoon. Fort Worth bustled in anticipation of the end of the workday. A few cars and trucks rumbled through the streets, fighting and startling horses and mule-drawn wagons. The sound of blaring horns and neighing equines filled the afternoon streets and boulevards. Pedestrians traversed the streets as they pleased, and electric streetcars trudged the main thoroughfares packed well beyond safety and comfort. The soot from the Swift and Armour meat-packing plants on the north side permeated the air but slowly dissipated as Bessie made her way south towards the Acre.

Bessie wandered aimlessly as afternoon faded to evening, then dark of night. Saturday ticked by without Bessie taking rest or nourishment.

No one noticed or bothered Bessie as she meandered through town. Finally, early Sunday morning, with the sun still burnishing the Atlantic but heading her way, Bessie found herself at the corner of Fourth and Throckmorton. Artificial light from the large neon sign of the First Baptist Church illuminated her face.

Bessie Williams stood in the street until the church bells tolled, then she slowly walked inside the mammoth church with all the other sinners.

1916-1917

SOMEBODY OUT THERE NEEDS KILLING

— 1916 —

Kid Yates stopped into the Pickwick Saloon a few blocks from the jail before heading home after his shift. The establishment was a favored spot for many on the force just completing their night or day's long shift and more than a few about to take up their beat. Detective George Chapman stood alone at the bar, four quick whiskeys already burning in his belly.

Yates walked up, ordered a beer and a shot, and waited silently. Chapman glanced in his direction. "I sorely needed you, Kid Yates, down in Cabbage Patch last night," muttered Chapman. Yates did not acknowledge Chapman's remark but had his full attention on the barkeep who, Yates reckoned, was moving awful slow with his task.

"Now I ask you, Kid." Chapman stood tall, turned and gestured to Yates with his index finger. "Why is there a no-good ofay trash sitting in the slammer without a mark on him, when he done cursed and threatened at least four fine officers all the way to the pokey?" Chapman paused, the fog of whiskey briefly clouding his rant. The barkeep set Yates's drinks before him. Yates glared as he slapped his money on the bar.

"There was a day," Chapman bellowed, "when threatening an officer of the law would purchase you a ride to the infirmary before the pokey, by God almighty!"

Yates grabbed his drinks and turned to leave the bar. He had come in for some peace and quiet and was not interested in listening to Chapman's rant. He was tuckered, and in his mind, Chapman's yelling was as displeasing to his ears as the sniveling and yapping he would hear upon his arrival home from Bessie and Selma.

"Where you off to, Kid? I thought you of all people would appreciate the need to teach a Brass Ankle manners."

"George, I have no hankering to hear a boozegob mouthing off."

"Truer words, Kid, never been spoke. But it is hard in these days for a man of the law to proper do his business. What with higher ups reforming good lawmen into being poons."

"You are only a poon, George, when you act like one. A real man cannot be made a poon. Simple as that."

Chapman stared at the bar and considered Yates's words. It took a might for their meaning to stumble through the alcohol fog of his brain, which was none too sharp to start with.

"If somebody out there needs killing, ya ought to do it and be done. Beatings are for teaching a lesson and only useful on women, children, and dogs. A full-grown man is too old to learn, and most often than not just needs to be put down."

Yates turned back to Chapman and returned to the bar. He placed both drinks down on the oak. "If you can make sense, I'll listen." Chapman nodded in affirmation. "Tell me your tale."

"Not terrible much to it really. Me and two others arrested a feller off his chump for carrying illegal. He was also drunker than a coon on payday and when we was carting him off he threatened to kill me, right there in front of God and the police." Chapman shook his head at the audacity of the situation. Yates just stared Chapman in the eyes. "Now, you know as well as I, Kid, when a coward threatens your life a man takes heed and replies."

Yates drained his beer and slapped the glass on the bar. "He'll be out before supper. Do you know where he will be this afternoon or at least his whereabouts?"

"I have a fair idea," replied Chapman.

"Well, Chapman, somebody out there needs killing. I will meet you at two o'clock and we will settle up with this man." Chapman stared back at Yates. For one brief moment a sober thought trickled up in his brain and wondered if talking to Yates had been such a good idea after all.

It was quickly beaten down by the whiskey.

Arrangements were made, then Kid Yates strolled home to take care of his daughters, see to chores, and catch some sleep.

December 22, 1916
Dallas Morning News

Tex Wallace Shot And Killed In Dance Hall
Policeman and Detective Are Charged With Deed.
Wallace, Recently Arrested, Is Alleged to Have Threatened Police Officers Several Times.

Tex Wallace, aged about 40, was shot three times and instantly killed about 4 o'clock this afternoon in a dance hall at 1302 Calhoon Street. According to witnesses five shots were fired, three of which took effect in Wallace's body one entering the right ear, one the right arm and the other the right hip.

Wallace was arrested last Saturday night on a charge of carrying a pistol. It is alleged that he had threatened policemen on several occasions.

Policeman J.K. Yates and City Detective George W. Chapman went to the office of Justice of the Peace Moore immediately after the shooting where they were placed under bonds of $1,000 each and charged by complaint with the killing of Wallace.

According to their statements they were entering the place at 1302 Calhoon in which Wallace was standing, when he made a move as if to get a gun from his pocket, and the shooting immediately began.

Justice of the Peace Emmett Moore was called to conduct the inquest, but did not complete the evidence and returned no verdict tonight.

Wallace had lived in Fort Worth for several years and is survived by his wife, who lives at 314 Ross street. His wife was present at the time he was killed. The body is being held at Spellman's undertaking parlor.

1917

Ed Parsley, Jacob Washer, and Worshipful Master Malvern Marks sat behind the closed door of the smoking lounge of the Masonic Lodge. Marks and Washer had called Parsley to the bastion of Fort Worth business to discuss problems they were hearing from local businessmen. No other building in Fort Worth better represented the seat of the establishment of the city.

"Dammit, Parsley, how can one man who thinks he is the reincarnation of 'Longhair' Courtright give a town of our size and industry a black eye across the entire state of Texas!" Jacob Washer shouted. "Hell man, we're for smoke! You can see the efforts of progress surrounding our city from miles away in all directions."

"Yates is clearly throwed off, Washer, that is plain as day," replied Parsley. "Hell, I know we cannot have him running all over Fort Worth acting judge, jury, and especially, executioner. Do you truly think I do not know that?"

Washer was spitting ten penny nails and would not stop his rant. "No business wants him walking by their establishment because people move out of his wake like the Red Sea parting before Moses! Every time he kills someone," Washer pivoted and pointed a finger to the sky for emphasis, "which is a regular occurrence, Fort Worth loses business. I am convinced of it! We look like a bunch of frontier yahoos dishing out frontier justice!" He paused, but only because he was out of breath, not because he was out of shout. Parsley stared back at him, his eyes steady and even. Marks sat, end of the table, looking wise and weary.

"Hell, do not mistake what I am saying." Washer had caught his second wind. "You know I gave my fair share to keep a roof over his children's heads when his oldest got ruined in Dallas. That was truly a nasty bit of business, and I always support our own. But Yates is past his time. We need order in Fort Worth. Times have changed, and business has changed. Hell, when that dandy from Dallas started all the sleeping panther shit, it did not bother Fort Worth one iota. Hell, Paddock went and put it on the paper's masthead for God's sake, but we cannot have out-of-town people and businesses with money to bring to Fort Worth afraid of being shot in their chairs for the slightest misstep."

"If we fire him, he will be unhirable to any other business. He has no other skills other than policeman," Parsley noted.

"That is my point! Are you not listening to me? He has no skills as a peace officer in this day!" countered Washer.

"Like it or not, he still has friends on the force and in the community. This must be handled carefully."

"True enough. He is not, after all, the only man in town that thinks it is still the frontier half a stone's throw west," Marks muttered.

"It would not be smart to have him making a fuss this close to the election." Parsley interjected.

Washer thought for a few moments. He silently conferred with Marks with a dart of his eyes. "Very well. Election day will come, but then Yates has to go."

"Agreed."

The three men sat silently for several moments. Parsley understood his part in this meeting was played. He rose, shook Washer's hand, nodded to Marks, and exited. Washer and Marks shifted their conversation to other civic matters.

A few moments later, Parsley was on the street heading back toward the station. As he walked, he rubbed the bridge of his nose and forehead and contemplated why he had ever left walking a beat to get involved in the political side of police work. It was often bloodier than the floor of the Armour killing room.

April 16, 1917
Fort Worth Star-Telegram

Third of Old Police Force Held Over by Davis Regime

Police Commissioner Parsley retained about one-third of the present force in the list of officers submitted to and approved by the new city commission at its first meeting Monday morning. Of the higher officers Assistant Chief Loughry and Detective Chief Jackson are retained. Loughry was appointed a motorcycle officer and Jackson remains on the detective force, where he has been for the last eight years.

Mrs. Ed Cogdell was appointed police matron, succeeding Mrs. Emma Richardson.

Following is the entire list:

... Mounted Officers—E. T. Williams, John Brown, J.K. Yates, J.B. Sprinkle, Will Lawrence, J.L. Holden, G.G. Davis, Joe Defee, W.A. Young ...

Kid Yates burst through the doors of the White Elephant like, well, a raging bull elephant hell bent on trampling anything in his path. He stomped straight to the bar and slapped his palm heavily on the smooth wooden surface three times.

"Beer and a chaser!" he shouted. There was no need for the palm slapping and raised voice; he had everyone's attention, including the bartender, as soon as he threw open the door. Yates decided if the good citizens of Fort Worth were going to treat him like a raging bull and scurry from his path, then by God he was going to act like one. He did not realize his shift in behavior was minor.

A group of men at the bar moved away as Yates approached. One neglected to grab his newspaper as he slid away. Yates glared at the men as they moved and noticed the paper lying folded on the bar.

"Have you read this rag?" he yelled at no one and everyone.

"Politics! Pure dee bullshit politics!" Yates grabbed the paper and waved it around his head.

"I am a detective, God dammit! A rank I earned walking the bottoms and Hell's Half Acre, dealing with the scum of this city so those bastards up on Quality Hill did not have to get the shit of this city on their precious, polished boots."

The bartender placed Yates's beer and whiskey on the bar, reaching and placing them down at arm's length so as to stay as far away as possible.

"And now they place me on mounted duty?" He paused as if to let this horrid insult sink in to the minds of everyone in the room. "I have to buy a horse and tack to slop in the mud on the South Side?"

He paused again before shouting, "Horse shit! That is horse shit."

Yates picked up his whiskey, turned, and stared at his fellow patrons as if he actually expected them all to nod in agreement.

"A man what has principles will not stand for insults to his position and integrity." He tossed back the shot.

April 21, 1917
Fort Worth Star-Telegram

4 Policemen Named By Parsley Resign

Four policemen sent in resignations to the city commission Saturday morning. They were J.K. Yates, former detective under Commissioner Jamison but assigned to South Side mounted service under Commissioner Parsley and Patrolmen J.A. Boyle, R.J. Poe and N.M. Pressley, all new men.

The bonds and commissions of the four men were cancelled at once on the request of Commissioner Parsley. W.P. Royston has been appointed to succeed Yates in the mounted service. Positions of the other men have been filled from extra ranks.

Poe refused the appointment because he obtained a better position with the Northern Texas Traction Company, his petition said. The others did not assign reasons for their resignations, but it is understood they were disappointed with their appointments.

The Yates household had fallen on hard times since Kid had resigned his post with the police department. He had taken to going to work as a special officer at the train yard drunk. No one there dared utter protest or suggest discipline.

His daughters Bessie and Selma sometimes went days without speaking, even to each other. Their best option for safety was silence and trying to remain invisible. There was no safety or kindness to be offered them from anyone in the adult world.

Yates and a brakeman named Ish Corn had taken to passing their shift in some empty train car drinking and plotting their revenge on what they mutually perceived was an unjust world. After a week or two of such commiserating, Ish, in a whiskey stupor, volunteered to help rid Yates of one mouth to feed by offering to marry Bessie. The proposal was made not out of love for the young woman or even out of friendship for Yates; it was a business arrangement. Bessie, already ruined in the eyes of society, would be put to work as a soiled dove in Corn's lean-to in the bottoms.

When Bessie was informed of her upcoming nuptials, a deep night ritual of sorts developed in the Yates home. Kid would drink to black out at the kitchen table.

Selma slept fitfully.

Bessie would silently enter the kitchen an hour or two after Kid blacked out. She would walk to the kitchen counter, open the knife drawer, and slowly withdraw the butcher knife.

She would turn and almost glide to within inches of the back of her father's chair. There she would stand, sometimes for hours. Waiting for the courage to thrust the blade into his spine. The courage never came.

Crickets chirped and the night breeze barely moved the curtains in the kitchen window. Bessie and Kid Yates passed the night locked in their individual nightmares.

* * *

The day was brisk and clean. Texans are conditioned that when the sky is clear and blue and the sun big and yellow, it usually means you can fry eggs on your forehead. But this was one of the few fall days where the sun caressed and the breeze renewed the citizens of Fort Worth. It felt like a reward for surviving another blistering Texas August.

Yates had been sober as a judge for over two weeks. As the rest of Fort Worth reveled in the day, Yates walked up Main Street almost completely unaware of his surroundings. While no one nodded in his direction or acknowledged him with a tip of their hat, no one seemed to avoid him. It was a good fall day.

Yates had not consciously decided to walk to the courthouse on this day. He had, in fact, made his decision the same day he sobered up, but he had circled no particular day on his calendar.

In his mind, today simply was the day.

His wife had died years ago. His oldest offspring was dead to him, and he had never formed a paternal bond with his youngest. He had no use for the world in which he found himself, and more importantly, the world had no use for him. He was more than a stranger in a strange land. He had come unstuck to the world. He belonged to no one. No one belonged to him. He was lighter than air and completely untethered.

J. K. Yates strode up Main Street calmly. He was heavily armed yet light in his step.

September 29, 1917
Dallas Morning News

Double Killing Takes Place at Fort Worth
Police Commissioner Parsley Slain by Former Detective Yates in His Office
Yates Shot by Police
Slayer of Commissioner First Tried to See Mayor Davis in His Office at City Hall.

C. Edward Parsley, Commissioner of Fire and Police of the city of Fort Worth, was shot and killed instantly by J.K. Yates, former member of the city detective force, while seated at his desk at his office in the City Hall at 2:45 o'clock this afternoon. One bullet penetrated the head just in front of the left ear and another entered the left side just under the arm and penetrated the heart. From indications, the Commissioner fell from his chair to the floor, dying instantly. His head was lying in a pool of blood near the front entrance to the office when members of the police department forced the door.

When the shots were heard by members of the police department they rushed to the door of the Commissioner's office to find it barricaded. A hole was broken in the blind glass in the door by Policeman Grisso, who stated that when he gained a view of the room Yates was seen crouching behind Commissioner Parsley's desk in the office. Mr. Grisso immediately fired and he was greeted by a fusillade of bullets from within, one of which grazed the right side of his face, inflicting a slight powder burn.

There was a short intermission, during which time members of the police department, headed by Chief of Police O.R. Montgomery and Assistant Chief Rufe Porter, secured the riot guns, which are held in reserve in the police headquarters. An entrance to the room was forced amid a fusillade of shots, and Yates was found dead on the floor in a pool of blood. One shot had entered his head between the eyes, another had torn away the top of his head and another had broken his right arm.

Asks to See Mayor.

Just prior to entering the office of Commissioner Parsley, Yates had entered the office of the secretary to the Mayor and called for the Mayor, it is understood. He was told by W.T. Coleman, weights and measures inspector of the city, that the Mayor was not in his office, when he departed for the office of Commissioner Parsley, next door, and the shooting immediately followed.

It developed after the shooting that Yates was armed with three pistols. Reports are that he had threatened the lives of Mayor W.D. Davis, Police Commissioner Parsley and Bill Little, former desk sergeant at headquarters and now a member of the detective department.

When the new administration assumed control of the city's affairs, Yates was a member of the detective department. He was switched by Commissioner Parsley to the South Side station and it is reported that at that time he left the City Hall in a rage and threatened the life of the Commissioner. On the same afternoon Mayor Davis visited him to discuss the matter and was assured by Yates that he was angry at that time and that nothing would come of the threat. About two weeks thereafter Yates resigned his place at the South Side station and had not been seen about the City Hall until this afternoon.

Assistant Chief of Police Porter this afternoon said that when he reached the scene he fired directly at Yates, and it is believed that this was probably the fatal shot. However, there is no way of determining, since almost a dozen men were engaged in this battle, using pistols and riot guns.

Commissioner Parsley was elected to his position last April. He won the Democratic nomination for the office over Hugh Jamieson by a substantial majority and was serving his first term. Some years ago he served as Assistant Chief of Police under the Polk administration. He was one of the best-known peace officers in this section and was making a remarkable success in the administration of police affairs. He was unarmed at the time of the tragedy this afternoon. It is believed that he received the shot in the heart when he threw up his left arm in an endeavor to ward off the assault of his antagonist.

Charged with Other Killings

Yates had served throughout the former administration and was regarded as a capable officer. Some months ago he shot and killed Tex Wallace in a local resort. This willing [killing?] occurred while he was in the discharge of his official duties. On March 28, 1911, he killed Claude Styers in Dallas, the trouble occurring, it is alleged, over private matters. His wife is dead and he is survived by two daughters.

The death of Commissioner Parsley will necessitate the calling of a special election in the city to fill the vacancy. Much regret at untimely death was expressed by city officials this afternoon, but no formal statements were issued.

W.T. Coleman, inspector of weights and measures, was being warmly congratulated this afternoon upon his presence of mind in causing Yates to leave the Mayor's office. At the time he was there, the Mayor was in his private office, but Mr. Coleman had a presentiment that it would not be proper to admit the former policeman and denied him admittance. It is believed that this act alone saved the Mayor's life.

Commissioner Parsley is survived by a wife, a daughter, Alma, and a son, Howard. The body is held by the L.P. Robertson Undertaking Company, pending funeral arrangements.

Mr. Yates is survived by two daughters, Mrs. Bessie Corn and Miss Selma Yates, both of this city. The body is held by the Fort Worth Undertaking Company pending funeral arrangements.

The officers stood about the carnage with looks of sickness and disbelief. It was as if each man, hardened as they were by their jobs, was trying to unsee what they were seeing but had nowhere to turn their eyes to trick the mind.

Assistant Chief Rufe Porter said, to no one in particular, "Go get Pastor Norris." Policeman Grissom immediately turned and left to fulfill Porter's order.

No one really moved. There was no policy to cover what had just occurred. The bodies had been covered. The medical examiner had been called. But now, no one had a clue what should be done next.

So they stood, slowly exhaling and inhaling the putrid smell of blood, gunpowder, and fear.

Quickly and quietly, others came. Others who had not been involved in the blood bath. One by one they led the men away from the scene. It was all anyone knew to do.

September 29, 1917
Fort Worth Star-Telegram

Ruse Kept Slayer From Mayor's Office, Davis There All Time

As J.K. Yates sat in a chair in the reception room at Mayor Davis' office Friday afternoon before killing Police Commissioner Parsley, the mayor, whom he sought, was in his private office talking to a friend. That Yates did not overhear the mayor, recognize his voice and insist on seeing him is considered a miracle by city officials.

All of the city officials give much credit to W.T. Coleman, city weights and measures inspector, for his presence of mind in preventing Yates reaching Davis.

"I knew Yates very well," said Coleman Saturday. "I recognized him the moment he entered the office and asked to see the mayor. Of course, none supposed he was bent on killing someone, for he was quiet and calm. But knowing he was vexed because of not getting the position he wanted and knowing his past record, I decided to keep him from the mayor if possible, and avoid trouble.

Takes Seat at Door.

"I told him the mayor was away and would be gone for an hour, so he sat down in a chair right by the mayor's door and waited two or three minutes, saying, 'Well, I guess I'll stick around a while.' He did not seem at all nervous, said little and spoke pleasantly to W.F. Lowry who sat only a few feet from him.

"Two minutes after he left this office and entered Parsley's, we heard two loud shots, and I was certain immediately that Parsley or someone had been killed by Yates. I hurried into Davis's office. 'Are you armed?' I asked the mayor. 'No,' he replied, 'what is the matter?' 'Yates has just killed someone, likely Parsley,' I said.

"I advised the mayor to stay right where he was and locked both doors leading to his private office. I was afraid that Yates would come into my office through the side door which opens into Parsley's office, but he never came. I was unarmed myself and going into the hall found a number of officers there, including Chief Montgomery.

Officer Doubly Armed.

"One officer carried two six-shooters. 'You can't handle two guns, let me have one,' I suggested, but the officer kept them both. In another minute or two the fusillade of shots began and then all was quiet."

The shot that killed Yates, probably fired by Assistant Chief Porter, is considered one of the most remarkable on record. Porter was standing in the door of Chief Montgomery's office, sixteen feet from Parsley's door, the glass in which had been broken by Yates' bullets. Through the jagged hole providing an opening of only four or five inches, Porter aimed his riot gun and calmly waited. Once Patrolman George Gresham yelled at Yates he was coming in. Porter yelled to Gresham to desist and ordered him aside.

"Wait just a minute, boys," said Porter. "Keep back!" The officers in great suspense stepped back a foot or two and Porter, his eye even with the barrel of his gun, finally saw the peak of a felt hat rise slowly above the top of Parsley's desk.

A half inch, one inch, two inches—Porter still waited. Then the green glasses Yates wore came into view. Still the man behind the gun waited and waited. Fractions of a second seemed hours to the onlookers. When Yates' nose appeared above the desk Porter then knew the supreme moment had come. He knew the man hiding there, expert shot and reputed killer, was armed and ready to fire. It was a question of who could fire first and it was the chief's slashed first.

Porter Shoots Twice

Porter fired twice, once at the man's body concealed by the desk, and again at his head.

The door had been partly kicked open by officers by this time and they would have rushed the barricaded slayer had not Chief Montgomery held them back.

"It would have been suicide for them to have entered the trap," said the chief, "so I made them get back and had the riot guns brought up while we covered the door with our pistols."

After the fusillade the officers called to Yates but there was no answer.

"Oh, let's go in and get him! We can't wait any longer!" exclaimed an officer, and led by Montgomery, the men pushed the door wide back and crowded into the office, firing six or seven times at Yates who lay on the floor behind the desk. A hurried examination of his body showed he was dead. Parsley, who lay twelve feet from Yates behind the office door, had been killed instantly, and in the opinion of Montgomery and Porter and other officers, was shot in the back first and in the head next.

Believe No Words Spoken

If any words passed between Yates and Parsley no one knows what they were, and it is not believed at the city hall that Yates said anything to his victim, firing after he had closed the door.

It was established definitely Saturday that Yates entered Parsley's office first and then called to the commissioner who was standing on the steps of the city hall entrance, talking to Corporal H.D. Woods of the military police. Parsley started for his office, saying: "I'll be back in a minute, men." They were the last words anyone heard him speak. Woods went into Montgomery's office then, and it is supposed that Yates closed the commissioner's door, fired on him as he was on his way to his desk, and as he turned fired another bullet into the back of his head.

When Gresham, Motorcycle Officer Salsburg and Sergeant Little hurried to the door Yates could see their shadows through the window and he fired several shots at the men. One of these bullets touched Little's left cheek. Bullet holes could be seen on both sides of the door after the shooting. The office of Parsley, following the shooting had the appearance of being the scene of a pitched battle.

Room Shot to Pieces

The wall behind the spot where Yates had stood had a score of holes in it and a large section of the plaster had been shot away. The floor was powdered with plaster. Parsley's desk had innu-

merable bullet holes and even papers on his desk looked like
sieves.

Salsberg saw Yates as he came to the city hall, stopped him a
moment and told him some relatives had been inquiring regarding him.

"I thank you 'Sal,' for that; I sure do appreciate it," said
Yates. He then passed on up the steps where the commissioner
was talking to the military police. Yates recognized his former
employer by mumbling a word of greeting and Parsley exclaimed
"Howdy Yates."

Porter had been talking with Parsley shortly before the
shooting and Montgomery was seated at his desk in his own office
when Yates first fired. Two of Yates' bullets pierced the entrance of
Montgomery's office, passed close to where he sat and penetrated
the south wall, close to where Parsley's picture hangs.

Riot Guns Used First Time

Montgomery was unarmed and when other officers wanted to
go right in to get Yates he ordered them first to bring up the riot
guns, kept loaded in a case in the sergeant's office. It was the first
time they had been used. Those who took part in the attack on
Yates besides Montgomery and Porter were H.O. Gossett, city
labor agent, W.J. Clark, saloon owner, Sergeant Little, Detectives
Mulkey and Ladd, Patrolmen Dysart, Gressham, Grissom and
Langdon and Motorcycle Officer Salsberg.

Yates had been on the police force in several capacities the
last several years. During the former administration he served
as inspector of police and then as detective and when Parsley
assumed office last April Yates was appointed as mounted officer
at the South Side station, a job he disliked, and he declined to buy
a horse and in three weeks he handed in his resignation to the city
commission.

Tried to Calm Him

During the last three months he was known to have threatened
several times to come to the city hall and make a general "cleanup'
by killing Mayor Davis, Commissioner Parsley, Chief Montgomery

and Detective Chief Connelley. Both Porter and Montgomery had been warned of this threat of Yates and efforts had been made to calm him down and Yates himself not long ago declared nothing would come of his threats. Mayor Davis was one of those who talked with Yates in an effort to placate him.

Six weeks ago Yates went to Mineral Wells to have his eyes treated and has been back in Fort Worth three weeks.

Parsley was in the best of spirits Friday and joked with friends at the city hall and went about his business with much spirit. He was 52 years old and several years ago served one term as assistant police chief. He formerly operated a transfer service here. Parsley was not only exceedingly popular among all of the officials at the city hall, but was held in high esteem by every member of the police and fire departments. He was instrumental in getting the men of both departments increases in salaries. He took great pride in the fact that affairs of his office ran smoothly and often declared he never hired a man simply because he voted for him, but chose men for their efficiency as officers. This was proven by his selection of many men who opposed him in his last campaign.

Three revolvers of large caliber were found on Yates' body and in addition he had many extra cartridges in his pockets.

After the shooting Montgomery County Attorney Spoonts and others were discussing the tragedy in the chief's office. "Well, boys," said the chief, "he came ready for all of us as he said he would," and he jerked open the drawer of his desk, displaying the three wicked pistols that Yates had carried. Tears appeared in the eyes of the chief as he spoke.

Throngs of men still crowded around the office of Parsley Saturday morning examining bullet holes and discussing the killing.

Resolutions on Parsley

Resolutions on the death of Police Commissioner Parsley were adopted at the meeting of the park board Saturday. The meeting adjourned without transacting any business.

September 29, 1917
Fort Worth Star-Telegram

Claude Styers Slain By Yates Mar. 27, 1911.

Claude Styers, an accountant, was killed by J.K. Yates, at that time
a patrolman on the Fort Worth police force, March 27, 1911. The
shooting took place at Styers' office, Main and Poylras streets. Yates
used two automatic pistols and riddled Styres' body with bullets.
There were no witnesses to the killing. Yates pleaded self-defense
and the unwritten law.

In the preliminary hearing, Yates was released on $1,000 after
he had declared that Styers had written letters to his daughter,
Miss Bessie Yates. Yates declared he had come to Dallas for the
purpose of killing the accountant.

After the killing Yates said that while night Marshal at
Lancaster he had killed a man named Dick Whitworth. He was
acquitted in both the Whitworth and Styers cases.

Police Commissioner Parsley was an intimate friend of Police
Commissioner R.L. Winfrey of Dallas.

"I had known Commissioner Parsley for years," Winfrey said.
"He was building his department up and was making a splen-
did record. Commissioner Parsley and myself had established a
complete co-operation between the Dallas and Fort Worth police
departments which was resulting successfully."

October 1, 1917
Dallas Morning News

Over 3,000 Persons Attend Funeral of C. Edward Parsley

More than 3,000 people this afternoon attended the funeral of
Police and Fire Commissioner C. Edward Parsley, who was shot
and killed in his office in the city hall Friday afternoon. Services
were held at the residence, 1606 May street, conducted by Dr.
H.A. Boaz, president of Texas Woman's College, assisted by the
Rev. C.R. Wright, pastor of the Central Methodist Church. The
cortege which followed the body to Greenwood Cemetery was one
of the longest ever seen in Fort Worth. Policemen, soldiers and city

officials headed the precession. As it passed down Throckmorton
street by the city hall the bell in the Central Fire Station was softly
tolled. At the city hall the police and soldiers spread, forming a
double line, through which the procession passed.

Funeral services for J.K. Yates were held this morning at the
chapel of the Fort Worth Undertaking Company, after which the
body was sent to Lancaster for interment.

After Parsley's funeral about a half dozen officers went back to County
Attorney Spoonts's house. They sat and stood in Spoonts's backyard,
smoking cigars and drinking beer and whiskey. No one spoke much
other than exchanging general pleasantries and niceties about the service.
Cicadas sang in the trees, and scores of dragonflies skittered about the
yard catching their fill of mosquitos.

"He knew there would be more killing from Yates. He said as much
to me," said Officer Middleton.

"Aye," said Detective Mulkey. "Me too."

"He said it to all of us, I imagine," said Detective Ladd.

"What is to become of the girls?" inquired Mulkey.

Spoonts answered, "Yates had the foresight to purchase an insurance
policy, and the department took up another collection, so they have
money. I heard tell they were moving somewhere in Kansas; the mother
has family there. They own some sort of mercantile, so Bessie will have a
job and both girls will have family."

"Still, that is a hard thing to live down," said Middleton. "Even if
don't no one know."

"Old ways do not die easy," said Spoonts.

Mrs. Spoonts came out the back door carrying a basket of freshly
fried chicken. She was followed by two other wives carrying potato salad
and beans.

1903-1920

SON OF HAM

1903

December 29, 1903
Dallas Morning News

Have A Possum Dinner
Janitor Jeff Daggett Entertains His Friend
in Federal Building

Every year Jeff Daggett, janitor of the federal building, gives a 'possum dinner to the superintendent and clerks of the railway mail service and the clerical force of the federal court. So long has he continued the custom, that the fortunate guests look forward to the feast with a great deal of pleasure. A few days before the time fixed for the dinner Jeff makes all arrangements. He catches the 'possums himself, and under his personal direction they are prepared. He is expert in cooking 'possums.

Yesterday he served the dinner and the large number who enjoyed the affair were loud in their praise of the holiday treat afforded them. They say Jeff improves every year, and that he cooks 'possum better every time the dinner is served.

✳ ✳ ✳

Gooseneck McDonald, one of the richest men in Fort Worth and the richest black man in town, hired Jeff as a special policeman for Douglas Park. It was certainly a step up from being a janitor. Special policemen were hired by private parties as security for bars, hotels, or banks and were commissioned by the chief, city council, or mayor as a pro forma for the establishment hiring the officer. Still, as a black man with no formal training and little experience in anything other than gambling and fighting, Jeff was happy and proud to have the commission and work. He felt it was the kind of job more in line with his abilities and might even lead to a spot on the Fort Worth police force.

Dusk was falling in Douglas Park. Families packed up their picnic supplies, called in their children, and began heading home. Young couples headed to nooks and crannies, away from prying eyes, to do what young couples do.

Jeff Daggett walked the perimeter of Douglas Park like a banty rooster. It had been a quiet afternoon. Nothing to break the monotony of the beat but suggesting eateries or guiding a few out-of-towners back to their hotels, and a few frantic moments dealing with the mother of a lost child who was summarily found. Still, Jeff was whistling a tune and walking fairly jauntily when he came upon two white men that appeared to be drunk, stumbling along the path.

"You men appear to be lost," said Jeff.

W. A. Chambliss worked as a "splitter" at the Swift packing plant, and his friend, Bob White, also a Swift employee, was a "knocker." A knocker belted the penned cattle in the forehead, hopefully killing it but usually just stunning the beast enough to be sent down the line to a slow, piecemeal death. A splitter used a large, razor-sharp blade to split the cow down the spine so it could be parsed and sent to more delicate butchers. The two men spent twelve hours a day dispensing death and walking on sheets of blood. They had been drinking and whoring in the Acre and were on their way to a private gambling house when they decided to shave off a block by cutting through Douglas Park.

"We ain't lost, nigger," said Chambliss.

Jeff stood a little taller, "Well, you ain't going any farther," he said.

White, who was a little more inebriated than Chambliss, almost immediately began to turn around. Chambliss reached and stopped White by grabbing his shoulder. "Hold on, Bob. That ain't a real badge and uniform." He then turned and directly addressed Jeff. "It's just an uppity nigger."

Jeff snapped, but before he could pull his billy club Chambliss kicked him in the groin. Bent over and helpless, Jeff cried out in pain. Chambliss then hit him in the back of the head with his balled-up fist. Jeff, barely able to keep his feet, stumbled about, numb and dazed. Chambliss stepped back and White stepped up. His forearm and fist, thick with muscle built up from knocking cows twelve hours a day, leveled the knockout blow to Jeff's back. As all the breath left his lungs, Jeff collapsed to the ground.

He was out for several minutes. Just as he began to stir, Chambliss and White returned with two policemen. It wasn't enough to beat Jeff senseless. They wanted him arrested for accosting two white men. He must be taught a lesson and made to pay.

"There is the uppity nigger," Chambliss pointed to Jeff as he spoke. The two officers quickly approached Jeff before he could fully regain his senses and his feet. One officer grabbed the badge pinned to Jeff's chest and ripped it off, tearing a swath from his shirt.

"Niggers with badges make me sick to my stomach," he said.

The second quickly pinned Jeff's arms behind his back. "You are under arrest," he said. "Take his gun, Goad." The first officer disarmed Jeff and gave up his handcuffs to the second officer.

Before Jeff could even remember where he was or what had happened, he was hauled off to city jail.

Chambliss and White decided to skip the gambling and returned the way they came to brag about beating a nigger cop and drink to blackout.

After losing his commission from McDonald because of the ballyhoo in Douglas Park, Jeff had taken a stab at politics. While he was elected as a delegate to the Democratic Black convention in Austin, he again found his quick temper and inability to compromise threw up roadblocks to advancement. McDonald felt bad about the beating and arrest, so he called in a favor and got Jeff a job working security at a dive saloon on the edge of the Acre. His no-nonsense approach and ability to deal with gamblers and card sharks mostly served him well.

June 6, 1915
Fort Worth Star-Telegram

First Prize Pigeons Are Announced
Eighty Awards Made by Judge Charles W. Wern Saturday.
Home Breeders Lead.
Show Free Today
Public Will Be Admitted Until 6 P.M. Officials
Pleased With Results

The first day of a two-day exhibit by the Fort Worth Pigeon Club
at 1012 Houston street was concluded Saturday night with the
awarding of prizes. Charles W. Wern of Galveston was the judge.

Practically all of the entrants were awarded premiums of some
kind. Eighty first prizes were given. Fort Worth exhibitors won a
majority of the prizes.

The morning was devoted entirely to judging and the exhibit was
thrown open to the public in the afternoon and night. The public will
be admitted free all day today. The exhibit will close at 6 p.m.

President Ben LeGett and Secretary Cary Rall expressed satisfaction with the results of the first exhibit.

The following is a partial list of the first premium winners,
classes and owners, as compiled Saturday night:

Best fancy bird, Lee Laswell; best utility bird, M.C. Martin;
best 1915 flying homer, W.H. Coffey; best 1915 show homer,
W.H. Coffey; best 1915 show homer C.E. Rall; best 1915 red
carneaux J. Ben LeGett; best 1915 yellow carneaux, J. Ben LeGett;
best 1915 white king, J. Ben LeGett.

LeGett had switched sides in the law field and went to work for the Fort
Worth Police Department. He quickly made the rank of detective. The
pay wasn't great but it was steady, and he quickly gained a reputation as a
hard-nosed officer. He also curried favor with the old guard.

"Ben, I need you to go down to McDonald's place on Fourth Street
tonight, ask for a man named Stege," said Mayor W. D. Davis.

LeGett had been in County Attorney Marshall Spoonts's office for about
an hour discussing various upcoming trials. Different city prosecutors had
come and gone during the time but for the past twenty minutes Spoonts

and LeGett had simply been discussing pigeons. Spoonts had been interested in buying some birds for a nephew and was seeking LeGett's advice. Mayor Davis had stepped in specifically looking for LeGett.

"Of course, sir. Any particular time I should arrive?" asked LeGett.

"You know coons," replied Mayor Davis. "He'll likely be there from dinner Friday till church on Sunday." All three men laughed, and the mayor bid his farewells and left.

LeGett neither asked nor cared what he was supposed to say or do when he met this man Stege. If there were something to deliver or information to relay, he would have been told. It was not his business to ask questions. He ran errands for various wealthy business owners through the mayor, often in the Acre and other parts of town where they could not be seen without raised eyebrows and wagging tongues. These men did business in every corner of Fort Worth with all sorts of people and sometimes needed surrogates. It did not hurt that an envelope containing cash usually accompanied these chores.

❊ ❊ ❊

Saturday night LeGett strolled in the front door of the Grackle saloon on the edge of Irish Town. To say he looked out of place was an understatement. It took Jeff about three seconds to spot LeGett and make his way over to him.

"State your business," demanded Jeff.

LeGett paid no heed and brushed past Jeff without even looking him in the eye.

Enraged at LeGett's dismissal, Jeff raised his voice and bellowed, "I said . . . " Jeff was not allowed to finish his sentence when LeGett wheeled on his heels and let loose a close-quarter punch that stunned but did not fell him. A quick body blow and knee to the head left Jeff in a passed-out heap.

The Grackle went stone silent. LeGett turned and proceeded to the rear of the saloon in search of Stege. No one moved to help Jeff, and certainly no one moved towards LeGett. Everyone in the room knew who he was and likely knew who sent him.

By the time Jeff came around, LeGett was long gone. He was in two more fights that night, as men saw him as wounded and weak and thought they could take advantage. Jeff had the ability to black out pain and took both men down quickly. He loudly boasted to one and all he would kill that bastard LeGett next time he saw him. Jeff threatened LeGett mostly to show those in the crowd that were thinking of taking him on that he was not to be trifled with and was still a bad man.

❊ ❊ ❊

There wasn't really much cartilage left in Jeff's nose before LeGett smashed it sideways. It had been broken and flattened way too many times over the years. Still, it was swollen and caked with dried blood when Jeff got home early Sunday morning. His breath was shallow and rapid, as the body blow had cracked a rib and made regular breathing painful and tear-inducing. There were still cobwebs in his brain and a knot on the back of his head. Hester cleaned him up as best she could. Every time Jeff took a beating he developed a new limp, hitch, or ache. He refused to go to a doctor or Saint Joseph's Infirmary, the only hospital in Fort Worth with a Negro ward.

"You got punched up pretty good," said Hester.

Jeff sat and seethed. He winced when she felt for the bump on the back his head. "I've a mind to kill that bastard."

"You do not need another trip to Huntsville, Jeff. Let it blow over."

"I will not," said Jeff. "He sucker-punched me in my own place. If I let it stand, folks will try and take advantage. I'll be brawlin' every night and lose my job, sure as hell."

"Surely there is another way. That's all I'm sayin'." Hester stood back and looked at her husband, sitting in a kitchen chair, tired, beaten and bruised. She shook her head in wonder that he had managed to live as long as he had. "Ain't much I can do and that's it," she said.

"Maybe you right," Jeff said. His mind began to turn. "No reason for that bastard to be there lessin' he was sent. Only reason I stopped him was to find out who he was looking for and he just bow up, right off." The ointment Hester had rubbed over Jeff's ribs and back had eased the muscles and lessened the pain, allowing him to breathe slightly better. "Maybe I should take a trip downtown. Show them I've changed. I ain't such a hothead. Prove I know what's what and can be trusted and that LeGett bastard is the hothead. Stirring shit ain't got to be stirred." Jeff sat in his chair and ruminated. "Maybe I can get another commission."

"That is the thinking man I know," said Hester.

* * *

Jeff rose early and dressed in his best suit. Jeff was one of only a handful of black men in Fort Worth who owned a "best suit." He had several. Hester had made him a hearty breakfast, and Jeff was out the house by eight.

He walked to the barbershop on Fourth Street, got a trim and straight razor shave. He then sat on the bench and had his boots shined to a high gloss. He wanted to make the best impression possible at the courthouse.

For the first time in a long time he felt hopeful about his life. He felt as if a weight had been lifted. Jeff had spent most of his life angry. Angry at his family, white and black. Angry at the world he lived in. Angry at himself.

He felt different now. He felt he was ready to make his own place in Fort Worth, on his own merits. He felt worthy and willing to do the work required. Jeff Daggett Smith strode the street head held high.

* * *

In another part of town Ben LeGett was getting his own shave and shine. Sitting in the shoeshine chair at the Congress, LeGett read the paper while Little Joe polished his Justin boots. Little Joe had been working the shine chair vacated by Tom Lee four years ago.

"Scuse me for interuptin', Mr. LeGett," said Little Joe.

LeGett lowered the paper and looked down at Little Joe. Little Joe did not raise his eyes to meet his gaze. "I thought you might want to know I heard mention of your name las' night."

"In what manner?" replied LeGett.

"An acquaintance said he was at the Black Grackle las' night and Jeff Daggett was loud talkin' 'bout killin' you. I heard tell you roughed him up a might and he was fightin' mad and big talkin'."

"He threatened me," LeGett said. He looked incredulous and a slight smile crossed his lips. "Jeff Daggett threatened me."

"Yessuh. That's what I was told."

"I do declare." LeGett folded his paper and laid it in the chair next to him. "How much longer on these boots, boy?"

"Lessin' a minute, Mr. LeGett. Almost done." From the look on LeGett's face Little Joe was certain his news would warrant a larger tip.

He was mistaken.

* * *

Daggett spent the better part of the day finding and talking to witnesses to his confrontation with LeGett. He had spoken to five men present at the Black Grackle who promised to testify that LeGett had attacked Jeff unprovoked and with excessive brutality.

Truth told it wouldn't have been hard to find twenty men or more willing to say anything that would get LeGett in trouble or kicked off the force. In his short time as a detective, LeGett had garnered a fierce reputation as a rough cop, especially if you were black or brown. LeGett's days in New Mexico had not softened him towards Mexicans in the community.

When Jeff arrived at the courthouse around four in the afternoon, he walked right by the front steps and circled around to the basement entrance on the north side of the building. Son of a founding Fort Worth family or no, Jeff had to use the back entrance like all people of color.

Once inside, he eschewed the elevator and marched up to the second floor, headed straight to County Attorney Marshall Spoonts's office. Jeff was calm and found himself with a newfound confidence in the knowledge he was doing the right thing. He was acting in a manner that would have made his grandfather proud. He would show Spoonts and the others in power he had matured enough to be trusted with real power and responsibility.

Spoonts was not to be found in his office or anywhere on the floor. While it was obvious Jeff was looking for Spoonts, or anyone in authority, the whites walking past ignored him completely.

After several minutes Jeff again took the stairs down to the first floor. As he entered the main hall he saw Commissioners Rufe Snow and O. W. Gibbons walking his way.

"Mr. Snow," said Jeff. "I've been looking for Mr. Spoonts. Have either of you gentlemen seen him? I was just in his office and he was not there."

"Can't say I have, Jeff. What call do you have with him?" said Snow.

"I'm here to file complaint on Detective LeGett," Jeff replied. "He attacked me with no cause last night."

"No cause, you say. That don't seem like LeGett. Surely you riled him in some manner," Snow rejoined.

"Yes, sir. No cause at all, and it ain't right."

"Well, Jeff, I suppose you've a right to file a complaint, but I can see no good come of it." Snow was anxious to brush Jeff off and get on with his business.

"None at all, Jeff," Gibbons added.

"A man has no right to strike another without cause. I have witnesses." Jeff reached into his suit jacket and withdrew the long list of the names of witnesses he had collected. "Plenty of people will swear to my story. I'm here doing right and demand that right be done to me." Jeff's voice began to rise. After a lifetime of being ignored and brushed off, he knew when he was being dismissed.

"Now hold on a minute, Jeff. I'm not sure you have reason to demand anything, especially from a Fort Worth detective, likely acting in the line of duty? Where did this attack take place?" Snow did not like Jeff raising his voice to him. He considered it a severe breach of manners from the black man.

"The Black Grackle," Jeff answered.

"So, a bunch of drunk negroes say a police detective assaulted another drunk negro. I don't think that quite holds water, Jeff."

"I was not drunk, sir." Jeff's dander began to rise. He did not like where this conversation was surely headed. "If I do not receive justice here, I will deliver justice myself." With that, Jeff stormed off down the hall.

Snow and Gibbons stood and stared as Jeff stormed away. "That is one mad nigger," said Snow, half amused.

"I'd say dangerous," replied Gibbons.

"Maybe so," said Snow. "Maybe so."

Snow and Gibbons decided that Spoonts needed to know an angry negro was in the building, and knew if Spoonts wasn't in his office they could likely find him with the mayor.

They were correct. As they headed towards the mayor's office, Spoonts was just coming out the door.

"Marshall, we may have a situation," declared Snow. He quickly filled him in on Jeff's mission to complain about LeGett.

"I know just where to find Ben," said Spoonts. "I thank you gentlemen for averting any trouble." He left Snow and Gibbons to go about their business and hurried to find LeGett.

Spoonts found LeGett in the tax assessor's office. "Ben, I have some troubling news," Spoonts began. "Jeff Daggett is looking for you and he seems to be grinding an axe."

"Lordy," said LeGett. "You are the second to make me aware of that nigger's intentions."

"I'm sure nothing will come of it." said Spoonts, "but Daggett's got a hot temper, and I thought you should know he is in the courthouse looking for you."

"I will make sure nothing comes of it, Marshall." LeGett tipped his hat to Spoonts and walked swiftly away. The hunted had become the hunter.

After searching the first floor in vain for Spoonts, Jeff decided to return to Spoonts's office and simply wait for him to arrive. He headed back to the main hall and entered the elevator.

"Afternoon, Jim," Jeff greeted elevator operator Jim Shivers. Jeff knew Jim from when he had worked at the courthouse himself. Jim was an old-timer and had spent over twenty-five years working in the courthouse.

"Same to you, Jeff. Where you headed?" Jim inquired.

"Second floor. I have business with Attorney Spoonts." Jeff entered the elevator still holding the piece of paper with the names of the witnesses. The paper represented his desire to handle the matter the right way. He was disappointed in his emotional eruption with Snow and Gibbons and was determined not to let it happen in his meeting with Spoonts.

LeGett spied Jeff in the elevator and began to approach. Jim, about to close the door, spied LeGett heading their way and held the elevator, thinking he also needed to ride upstairs.

As LeGett was one step outside the elevator, he halted. At that moment Jeff's eyes rose from the paper and met LeGett's gaze. LeGett drew his revolver and calmly fired three shots, hitting Jeff in the throat, shoulder, and right breast.

Jeff had no time for a reaction. He died as he hit the floor. Jim jumped at the sound of the gunfire.

The bustle of the courthouse came to an abrupt halt. Some folks ran, some folks hit the floor, most jumped, then realized the shooting was over as fast as it started. Slowly people began to gather behind LeGett, who calmly turned and faced them.

Spoonts came running when he heard the shots. When LeGett saw his fast approach he walked to meet him. The crowd parted to let him through. LeGett flipped the revolver in his hand so that he held it by the barrel.

"Marshall," LeGett calmly said, "I am turning myself in. I defended myself against Jeff Daggett. He appears to be dead."

Spoonts took the butt of LeGett's gun and turned to a group of approaching officers who also had come running to the sound of gunfire. Pointing to LeGett he said, "Take this man to my office."

Jim Shivers had stepped over Jeff and was standing two steps outside the elevator with his head in his hands. Two bystanders entered the elevator and examined Jeff. "He is dead all right," one of them said.

Justice of the Peace Hugh Small had entered in the hall just as the shots were fired. "Officers!" he shouted to the two men leading LeGett away. "Bring Ben back here, Marshall, come with me." Small entered the elevator and turned to face the crowd of men. "Marshall, get in, let's all go down to my office."

None knew quite what to do, so they followed Small's commands. "You men stay as well, we'll need help with the body." Marshall Spoonts, JP Small, the two bystanders and the two officers escorting LeGett all crowded inside the elevator, gingerly stepping around Jeff's bloody corpse. "Jim!" Small shouted to elevator man Jim Shivers. "God dammit, man, run us down to the basement!"

Jim just stood with his eyes covered and wept. "Tarnation, I'll do it myself."

With that, Small closed the elevator door and pressed the button sending the loaded elevator down.

When the elevator reached the basement, Small opened the door and marched out and headed duly towards his courtroom, just a few paces down the hall. Spoonts exited next, followed by LeGett and the two officers. The two commandeered bystanders exited last, dragging Jeff behind them by the arms.

As Small entered his JP court he bellowed, "Court is now in session!" He walked behind his desk, picked up his gavel, and rapped it three times. "I assume you have charges to file, Attorney Spoonts?" he said as he took his seat.

Shooting from the hip, Spoonts gathered himself in lawyer mode and said, almost by rote, "It is hereby charged that Ben LeGett did unlawfully with malice aforethought, kill and murder one Jeff Daggett by shooting him with a pistol, from the effects of which said shooting, the said Jeff Daggett did then and there die."

LeGett stood in front of JP Small, hands on hips. Even though he was being charged with murder, no one thought he should be handcuffed. He listened calmly to the charges brought before him.

"I claim self-defense," he said.

"The plea is so entered," said Small. "Defendant is free to go." He rapped his gavel three more times and stood from his bench.

Spoonts interjected, "Bond, Your Honor?"

"Of course." Smalls thought for a moment and spoke almost as a question, "One thousand dollars." LeGett nodded. Smalls picked up the gavel and rapped it again, just for good measure.

The two bystanders finally made their way into the courtroom dragging Jeff. "Lay him in the corner," said Small. "Someone have a negro fetch the undertaker." Spoonts looked at one of the officers and motioned for him to do the deed. The officer headed toward the door.

As an afterthought, Spoonts said, "And have them notify the family."

"Yes, sir, will do," said the officer as he exited.

Spoonts then turned and addressed the remaining officers and the two bystanders, "Thank you, gents. I reckon y'all can go about your business." The three men left the courtroom. Spoonts, Smalls, and LeGett stood in front of Jeff's lifeless body.

"Was he armed?" asked Small. LeGett bent down and rifled through Jeff's pockets. He produced a wallet, eleven cents in change, a house key, four shotgun shells, and a pocketknife.

"Looks that way," he said. "You don't carry buckshot unless you intend to get a shotgun." Spoonts cocked his head at LeGett's logic but said nothing.

"Think we ought to tell Bud?" inquired Small.

"I reckon he'll hear, if he hasn't already," replied Spoonts.

October 24, 1917
Dallas Morning News

Negro Is Killed By County Detective
Shot To Death While In Elevator At Courthouse
Negro, Jeff Daggett, Is Said To Have Threatened Life Of
Detective J. Ben Le Gett

Special to The News

Fort Worth, Texas, Oct. 23.—Jeff Daggett, a negro who resides on Chambers avenue, was shot three times in the courthouse elevator and instantly killed late this afternoon.

County Detective L. Ben Le Gett was charged by complaint in Justice Small's court with the killing and was released on a bond of $1,000.

After the negro was shot his body was lowered in the elevator to the half story basement, where Justice Small's office is located, and was then placed on the floor in a corner of the Justice's courtroom, where it remained until it was removed by the undertaker.

The shooting occurred while the elevator was standing at the first floor landing about to ascend. The negro had entered to go to the second floor and Jim Shivers, the elevator man, had his hand on the lever and was about to close the cage door when he saw Detective Le Gett approaching. Shivers told Justice Small at the inquest that he thought Le Gett wanted to enter and go to the next floor above, where his office is located, and waited for him. Le Gett walked to open the door and fired into the elevator, which at the time contained no one but Shivers and the negro. Justice Hugh Small and others were standing only a few feet away.

Three Bullets Pierce Body

The negro was pierced by three bullets from an automatic pistol. One struck him in the neck, one in the shoulder and the other in the right breast. He was killed instantly.

Causes for the shooting as given by County Attorney Marshall Spoonts were that the negro had threatened to kill Detective Le Gett, who has been unusually vigilant in hunting down negro lawbreakers, as well as other lawbreakers, since he has been in office.

County Attorney Spoonts said:

"The negro Daggett was at the courthouse and met County Commissioners Gibbons and Snow and told them that he intended killing Le Gett. They told me of the threats and I informed Le Gett without loss of time."

The negro was not armed, but four shotgun shells and a pocket knife were found in his pockets after he was killed.

This is said to be the first killing that ever occurred in the

Tarrant County courthouse, although there have been numerous encounters therein from time to time and on one occasion former District Judge Jim Swayne had a narrow escape from being shot while he was sitting on the bench holding court.

1918

February 6, 1918
Dallas Morning News

Aged Negro Is Killed and Money and Chickens Stolen

Special to The News

Fort Worth, Texas, Feb 5 – William Hawkins, a negro, said to be 99 years of age, was found this morning at 10 o'clock in his cabin, a mile north of Stop [Unreadable] on the Fort Worth-Dallas interurban, with his body bearing unmistakable evidence that he had been murdered.

A blood-stained ax was found by his side, his pockets had been rifled and it is supposed that he had been robbed of a small sum of money which he had saved.

The old negro had a flock of about 150 chickens, from which he realized considerable money. Of these, only about twenty-five were left in his yard by his assailant, who had apparently carried off the others.

County Detective LeGett investigated the case and stated that it appeared to him the old negro had been killed and robbed of his savings and chickens.

It took more than a year to bring Ben LeGett to trial for the murder of Jeff Daggett. It wasn't that the defense was toiling away building an alibi or that the prosecution was burning midnight oil building a case. Actually, most everyone had forgotten about the charge, and LeGett was still doing his duty as a detective on the Fort Worth police force. It hadn't been but a few years since the riot over Tom Lee, and truth is no one rightly wanted to stir up racial anger on either side. Fort Worth was walking an uneasy peace, and those making such decisions had opted to leave better off alone.

Eventually, however, it was decided to get the trial over with. It was really a foregone conclusion, but it had come time to close the books. Marshall Spoonts was prosecutor and a defense witness. No one thought that the least bit odd. If the jury had left coffee in the box it would not have turned cold before they returned with a not guilty vote, and Ben LeGett was declared a scot-free man.

1920

November 20, 1920
Fort Worth Star-Telegram

Negress Breaks City Jail With Spoon; Goes to County

That Emma Wilson, a negress, charged with assault to rob, picked the lock of the city holdover with a spoon handle, walked out of city hall past policemen and that she was not missed until she had waived examination in Justice Maben's court and had been released on bond, was told at the courthouse Wednesday.

"I wanted them to transfer me to jail," she said, "and they paid no attention to me, so I got a spoon and picked the lock. I walked out into the hall and spoke to one of the officers, but no one paid any attention to me. When I reached home, I telephoned my attorney, Ben LeGett, and went before Justice Maben. I just wanted to show them that if they wouldn't transfer me, I'd do it myself."

LeGett continued lawyering, but he seemed to lose favor with those in power after the trial. While clearly Daggett had crossed the line attempting to file charges on a white man, still, there were those that thought gunning down anyone, even a black man, in midafternoon in the county courthouse, was past the limits of modern society. The days of gunfights in the streets, let alone a government building, where supposed to be in Fort Worth's past. While black men were not considered real men on level with whites, there was a new decorum, a new way to conduct yourself in modern society, and blasting away into an elevator was not in keeping with the times.

LeGett left Fort Worth, this time taking his wife with him, and moved to Clackamas County, Oregon. Under the name Jim LeGett, he took up chicken farming and lived the rest of his life undisturbed with his birds, wife, children, and grandchildren.

ABOUT THE AUTHOR

Mark A. Nobles is a sixth-generation Texan. Born on Fort Worth's infamous Jacksboro Highway, Mark proudly claims blood and kinship with Thunder Road's gamblers, outlaws, and wastrels. He is a Pushcart nominee, and his work has appeared in various publications and anthologies. He is the author of *Fort Worth's Rock and Roll Roots* and has produced three feature documentaries. Mark lives in Fort Worth but hopes to die in the desert. He loves his two dogs, two daughters, and Texas, but not necessarily in that order.